TRUE BLUE MYSTERIES • BOOK TWO

Ice Cold BLUE

AWARD-WINNING AUTHOR
SUSAN PAGE DAVIS

Scrivenings
PRESS
Quench your thirst for story.
www.ScriveningsPress.com

©2021 Susan Page Davis

Published by Scrivenings Press LLC
15 Lucky Lane
Morrilton, Arkansas 72110
https://ScriveningsPress.com

Printed in the United States of America

Paperback ISBN 978-1-64917-153-5

eBook ISBN 978-1-64917-154-2

Library of Congress Control Number: 2021945605

Editors: Erin R. Howard and Linda Fulkerson

Cover by Linda Fulkerson, www.bookmarketinggraphics.com.

1

Murray, Kentucky
Late June

Xina Harrison wasn't used to having doors slammed in her face.

She stared at the paneled oak door and tried to make sense of what had just happened. After nearly twelve hours on the road, her mind might be a bit frazzled, but this wasn't right. Nothing lined up the way it should, so she raised her fist and pounded again.

"Aunt Katherine, please! It's me, Xina. I just want to talk to you."

"Go away." The old woman's voice came faint but distinct through the thick door.

"I drove all this way," Xina shouted. "Please let me in."

The door opened a crack and her aunt peered out at her. "I told you, I don't want any visitors tonight."

"But I drove all day, Auntie. It's almost your birthday, and I brought you a present."

"Don't want any presents."

Tears sprang into Xina's eyes, and her throat ached. "Please! I don't have to stay here. I can get a hotel. Just let me step in for a minute and say hello. It's been so long."

Finally her aunt opened the door a grudging foot. Xina took that as a sign of acceptance and stepped forward, pushing the door open just enough to let her in. She shut it quickly behind her, so there was no doubt she was staying for at least a short time.

She blinked, waiting for her eyes to adjust in the gloomy house. The living room drapes were closed. Just one lamp gleamed, and no lights shone in the kitchen beyond. The air was nearly as warm as the muggy evening outside, and she wished the air conditioning could be bumped down a couple of degrees, but she said nothing. Instead, she summoned up a big smile and held out the gift bag she'd brought.

"I hope you like this."

Katherine gazed at the bag for a moment then took it and almost robotically transferred it to a side table by the door. Without a word, she turned and walked across the living room to a stuffed recliner and sat. Xina gulped and followed her.

She took a seat on the sofa, noticing that the throw pillow Aunt Katherine's long-haired cat favored wasn't in evidence. "Where's Sasha?"

Katherine gazed at her for a long moment. "Gone."

"Oh. I'm so sorry." Xina swallowed hard and wished she'd thought before speaking. The last time she'd visited her aunt, the cheerful housekeeper had showed her in and gossiped about the neighborhood while she fixed Xina and Aunt Katherine a cup of tea. After the monosyllabic implication about the cat, Xina didn't dare ask about Mrs. Conley.

"So." She tried for another smile but it felt like a near miss. "How are you?"

"Why are you here?"

"To see you. I wanted to come at Christmas, but you said you weren't feeling well." And the time before that, Aunt Katherine had put her off by claiming to be on a pressing deadline for her publisher. "You know, it's been a very long time since I've seen you. Are you well now?"

"I'm fine."

"Good, I'm glad." Xina wanted to get closer to her aunt and have a good view of her. She looked pale in the low lamplight, and very thin. Xina glanced around. The room looked the same, mostly. Her gaze paused at the mantelpiece. The framed painting above was different, and ... "Oh, where's the photo of Grandpa and Grandmother?"

Katherine paused for a moment before answering. "I put it up in my room."

Xina nodded, but something felt off. That framed family photo had sat on the mantel shelf for as long as she could recall, beneath the painting Grandfather had splurged on long before Xina's birth, and maybe before Katherine's. She tried to remember what else had been on display when she'd last visited, and beyond that, back to her teen years.

"I suppose you expected to stay here," Katherine said in flat tones.

"Oh, well, I wouldn't want to inconvenience you."

"Good. I'm really very busy, and tomorrow is Rita's day off."

"Rita?"

Katherine brushed a hand through the air. "My current housekeeper."

"Ah, so Mrs. Conley's gone, then."

"I had to let her go."

"Oh." Xina frowned. "I'm sorry. I really liked her."

"She passed her usefulness."

Xina swallowed hard. Surely Mrs. Conley wasn't any older than her aunt. In fact, in Xina's mind, she was several years younger.

She'd wanted to say, "Don't worry, I can make up my own bed, and I don't need a big breakfast." But Aunt Katherine's manner told her the suggestion would not be welcome. She noted that, as far as the poor lighting revealed, the place looked clean, so she didn't doubt that there was actually a new housekeeper.

"Well, I'll take a hotel room in town," she said. "It's no problem."

Katherine gave a brisk nod. "All right then." She shifted forward in her chair as though about to rise.

"Uh, will you go out to have dinner with me?" Xina asked.

"I've eaten."

"Oh." It was a little late, but Xina was disappointed. In the old days, her aunt would have scraped up a light supper for her or come along with her just for the company.

"There are some restaurants on Twelfth Street and a couple on Chestnut."

"I remember." Xina stood uncertainly. "May I come back in the morning?"

"I'm very busy."

"Working on your next book?" Xina tried to keep her tone light.

"Always," Katherine said.

Xina wanted to ask a score of questions, but Katherine was edging her toward the entry.

"Well, it was nice to see you."

Kathrine opened the door and stood with her hand on the knob. Xina leaned in to kiss her on the cheek. Her aunt's skin felt papery and cool. *She's aged since I've seen her.*

"Maybe we can catch up a bit tomorrow."

"Perhaps," her aunt said.

That didn't sound promising. Xina stepped out onto the porch. She turned back, but the door was already closing. She heard the deadbolt slide into place.

KEITH FULLER COULDN'T HELP OVERHEARING the conversation when he went out to the front desk to check the overnight log.

A striking woman of about forty stood talking to Patrol Officer Denise Mills, who had desk duty this morning.

"She was just so cold," the woman said. "She's never treated me that way before. Ever. And I'd driven all day to see her."

"When was the last time you saw her?" Officer Mills asked.

"Five years ago, but I was living in California at the time and flew back here on my vacation, mostly to see Aunt Katherine. I spent a week with her and had a lovely time."

"And you stayed at her house?"

"Yes. I moved to Asheville about two years ago, and I've tried to get over and see her twice since then, but she put me off both times. This time, I figured I'd just come and surprise her. She couldn't ignore me, right? But that's practically what she did last night. And this morning I knocked and knocked, but she didn't come to the door."

"Well, ma'am," Mills said carefully, "we can't do anything if a relative simply doesn't want to see you."

"Of course," the woman said quickly. "It's just ... well, she is getting older. I wondered if she's all right. And I didn't see anything beyond the living room, but there appeared to be some things missing that had always been there before. An old family picture, for instance. I admit, I'm worried."

"What sort of worries?" Mills asked.

Keith stood still, his back to the two women, listening for the answer.

"I wondered if she's in financial straits. Or whether someone else has been taking things. She's changed housekeepers—got rid of one she had for decades. I'm afraid something's going on, and she needs help but won't admit it."

Keith turned and walked over with a smile. "I'm sorry, I couldn't help hearing what you said." He nodded to Mills to let her know his intention was not to undermine her. "I'm Detective Keith Fuller. It might be possible for the police department to do a wellness check."

The woman nodded, a flicker of relief in her eyes. "That might be helpful. What would it entail?"

"We'd go to the house and tell her we were checking to make sure she was all right. We'd ask some general questions."

"Bascd on what you've told us, we can't get too specific unless she offers more information or seems in distress," Mills put in.

"Of course. Well, yes, that sounds good to me. If she says everything's okay and still doesn't want to see me, I guess I'll go home to North Carolina."

Keith looked at the form Mills had begun to fill out and said, "Why don't you give Officer Mills your contact information, and I'll line up another female officer to go with me. We'll come and let you know how it goes afterward."

"All right. I'm staying at the Marriott."

"Oh, Detective," Mills said, "I think I'm the only female on duty this morning."

Keith wasn't surprised. They only had two women in uniform. Murray was a small college town, and right now they didn't have any female detectives, though he knew Mills hoped to take the test soon.

"Can you get someone else to take over desk duty?" he asked.

"Yes, I think so."

"Okay. I'll go get ready, and I'll meet you in the parking lot in five minutes."

A TIMID KNOCK sounded on the office door, and Campbell McBride looked toward it and set down the coffee carafe.

"Come right in," her father, Bill, called from where he was seated at his desk. The True Blue Investigations office consisted of one large room and a tiny bathroom, so the staff was of necessity very informal.

Campbell walked toward the door, which opened and revealed a smartly dressed woman with a decidedly nervous air.

"Hi. I'm Campbell, and this is the boss and my father, Bill McBride. Won't you come in."

"Thank you. My name is Xina Harrison."

Bill stood and nodded. "How can we help you, Ms. Harrison?"

"Well, I went to the police with a small matter this morning, and a very kind detective recommended I hire a discreet private investigator. He gave me directions here."

"That was very good of him," Bill said. "Detective Fuller, right?"

Campbell smiled. Keith Fuller was a friend of her dad's, and he'd become a special friend to her when her father went missing a few weeks earlier and she attempted to find him.

"Yes, it was Detective Fuller. He and Officer Mills were very nice to me."

Bill indicated a chair in front of his desk, and while Ms. Harrison settled herself, Campbell wheeled over the desk chair she'd been using while Bill's employee, Nick Emerson, was out on medical leave.

"May I get you some coffee?" Campbell asked.

"No, thank you, I'm fine."

Bill studied the woman for a moment. "What's going on, Ms. Harrison?"

"It's my aunt." Out poured the tale of how she'd traveled from North Carolina to see the older woman and been rebuffed. "I've never known Aunt Katherine to be so rude before. It was as though she threw ice water in my face." She shivered. "And the police didn't even get into the entry. Detective Fuller said she instructed them to tell her snoopy niece to go home and leave her alone. They couldn't do much. She wouldn't even take his business card."

"What did you do after she turned you out last night?" Bill asked.

"I got a hotel room and decided to sleep on it. This morning she wouldn't pick up the phone. I drove to her house and knocked repeatedly, but she didn't come to the door. That's when I went to the police station. I was afraid something was wrong in that house. I couldn't leave Kentucky without finding out."

"Of course not," Campbell said.

Bill opened one of the small reporter's notebooks he used on the job. "How old is your aunt?"

"Late sixties. Sixty-eight, maybe?"

"Hmm. That's not that old."

"I know, but I hadn't seen her in five years, and she's definitely aged. She looked all right physically, but I didn't know if—" She broke off and took a shaky breath.

"You're afraid she might have early dementia?" Campbell asked gently.

Ms. Harrison shrugged. "Maybe. I just don't know. She definitely *looks* older. Her hair's much grayer, and ... and she wouldn't talk to me. This is so unlike her. If something's not right medically, I want to make sure she gets the care she needs."

"Of course." Bill guided her through the tale of her move to California and her return to the East two years previously, as well as her prior attempts to visit her aunt. Campbell reached for a tablet and jotted some notes of her own.

"She said last night she was working on her next book, but I don't know."

"What do you mean?" Bill asked.

"Well, when I tried to see her last year, she said she was on a deadline, but she hasn't published a new book for about three years now."

"Your aunt's an author?"

"Yes. Romantic suspense. She was putting out a couple of books a year for ... I don't know, decades. I've got an entire bookcase full of her stories."

"What's her name?" Campbell asked.

"Katherine Tyler."

"No! And she lives here in Murray?" Campbell looked at her father. "How could I not know this?"

"What? I don't know ..." Bill swallowed his words.

"Obviously my dad doesn't read romantic suspense," Campbell said with a chuckle.

"And you do?" Xina asked.

"Yes, I've read several of her books. It's a great escape, and she writes with such fascinating detail."

"My daughter was an English professor," Bill said drily. "I had no idea she was into romance."

"Oh, Dad." Campbell scowled at him. "Ms. Tyler's books aren't trash. They're wonderful. The dramatic tension is first class. I'm amazed she could produce them so frequently."

"She used to have someone help her with the research. I'm not sure she's still doing that. The house was empty except for her when I was there yesterday."

"And that's not normal?" Bill asked.

"She used to have a lovely full-time housekeeper, Mrs. Conley, but Aunt Katherine said she had to let her go. Now she apparently has someone who comes in a couple days a week to clean." Ms. Harrison shook her head. "It just doesn't make sense to me. Unless she's having money problems, but I find that hard to believe. She's always been frugal, and I know she invested some of the earnings from her earlier books."

"The recession impacted the publishing industry," Campbell mused. "And if she's not able to write as quickly as she used to, she may have a much smaller income now."

"I'm afraid maybe someone was—well, you know—taking advantage of her." Ms. Harrison folded her hands in her lap and hesitated as if her next revelation pained her. "You see, not only hasn't she launched a new book lately, but some things I remember from her living room were gone. Things that had been there since I was a child."

"What sort of things?" Bill asked.

"You understand I only had a quick look around the front

parlor—her living room, but ever since I can remember, she'd had a framed landscape hanging over the fireplace, a Milne Ramsey oil. But it's gone now. There's a Winslow Homer print hanging in its place—the sort you could buy in a department store. I could tell at a glance it was a cheap reproduction."

"You think she sold the genuine painting?"

"Maybe. I don't know." Xina spread her hands in helplessness. "She wouldn't talk to me, so we never got around to that. When I asked a few questions, trying to make sure she was all right, she got angry and told me she was fine and that I should leave, so I did. But there were other things—little things. The furniture and carpets were the same. A framed picture of her parents had always been on display on the mantelpiece, and it's gone now."

"Did you mention these things?"

"I asked about the photo of my grandparents, and she said she'd put it in her room. But there was an old match holder with long fireplace matches, and it was missing too. I remember it well because I took a picture of it about ten years ago when I was visiting. It was an advertising piece for an old coal oil company, and I loved it."

Campbell wrote it down.

"If I had time and could think about it more systematically, perhaps I could tell you about other things in the house. But I know some things are changed." Xina shrank down in her chair.

"Still, people do change their decorations over time," Bill said.

"Yes, you're right. I guess it struck me as odd, since Aunt Katherine never did. At least, in my memory she hadn't. I couldn't help wondering if she had to sell some of her things, either for medical expenses or home repairs—or if someone else is draining her funds and getting her to give them money. Or maybe someone's pilfering valuables from her."

"We'll see what we can find out without upsetting her," Bill said.

"You can do that?"

"I'm very good at poking around without alerting the person I'm observing."

"That's a relief."

"And this painting that seems to be missing would be quite valuable?" Campbell asked.

"I think it might have been. Some of the older artists like Milne Ramsey sell well these days."

"What time period was he from?" Bill asked.

"Early Twentieth Century, I think, or late Nineteenth."

Bill looked at Campbell, and she wrote it down. The artist's name was vaguely familiar.

"We'll look into it," he said.

"Thank you. Of course, she may have just moved it to a different room. I'll feel ever so much better knowing someone's doing a little investigating while I go back to work in North Carolina."

"And what do you do there?" Bill asked.

"I'm human resources director for Simon-Dryer. Their headquarters is in Sacramento, where I worked previously, but I was more than happy to move back to their Asheville division." She picked up her purse. "I'd like to give you a check before I go."

"That would be terrific, Ms. Harrison." Bill told her his usual retainer, and she seemed to think it reasonable. "That will give us a couple of days to see if we can get to the heart of things," he said.

"Please call me Xina. What else do you need to know?" She took her checkbook from her purse and quickly wrote out the check.

"Could you tell us a little more about Ms. Tyler?" Campbell asked.

"Well, as you know, she's a successful novelist. I guess you might say she's a little eccentric. I wouldn't have said she was reclusive, but now I'm not so sure. She's changed so." Xina blew out a breath. "Oh, she has an agent, but I don't remember his name. I met him once at a banquet, where Aunt Katherine was receiving an award, but that was at least fifteen years ago."

"Where did this take place?" Bill asked.

"In Chicago. I was still in Louisville, my hometown, at the time, and Katherine flew me up for the event. It was very exciting." Xina frowned. "But I seem to recall that he died. A heart attack, I think. I never met her new agent, but she has someone."

Bill nodded. "And who is her publisher?"

"I'm not sure."

"We can get that information from her last book," Campbell said. "Do you know if she has a website?"

"I don't think so, but I could be wrong."

"Social media?"

Xina shook her head. "Maybe she's been more of a recluse than I realized. But she liked her privacy, you know. I suggested that she get online more several years ago, but she resisted the idea."

"We understand," Campbell said. "Her books are so popular, I'm sure the publisher does most of the publicity for her."

"Yes, but she did do speaking engagements last I knew, and she was keynote speaker at a couple of writers' conferences every year back when I was in college. I'm not sure if she's still doing that. But she wasn't a hermit. She used to go to church almost every Sunday. I went with her a few times when I was younger and stayed with her for a few weeks in the summer." She gave them the name of Katherine's church.

"What about friends?" Bill asked.

"Hmm, a lot of her friends were other writers. There was one woman who lived in this area. A teacher. Aunt Katherine took me to her house once for lunch. But she'd be retired now. Her name was Pam. I'm sorry, I'm not sure I can recall her last name." She frowned for a moment. "Rogers, I think. Yes, Pam Rogers."

Campbell wrote it on her notepad.

"And who does she have for living family, other than you?" Bill asked.

Xina blinked rapidly. "My mother was her sister, but she passed away. There were no other siblings. My grandparents are both gone. I can't think of any cousins on Mom's side. I suppose there are some more distant relatives, but if there are, I don't know them. My father's alive, but of course, he's not related to Katherine by blood. He retired to Arizona last year."

After a few more questions, Xina rose and shook hands with both of them. "Thank you again," she said. "This is a big load off my mind."

"We'll get right into it, and we'll call you tomorrow night to let you know what progress we've made," Bill said as he led her to the door.

2

A s soon as she was gone, Bill turned to his daughter. "I'm going to set up the file for this. It has some urgency, so why don't you jump right into research? Nail down the publisher and agent if you can. I'll find out how long Ms. Tyler has owned her house and try to find out if she has any large outstanding debt."

"How can you do that?" Campbell asked. Her father's eyebrows shot up and she smiled. "Remember, I'm a newbie. You need to teach me all your investigative secrets."

"I guess I do. It's nothing underhanded, just a little sneaky. Most people don't realize how public some of their records are, especially if they're not careful to conceal them. But judging from what Xina told us, Ms. Tyler may be one of the ones who makes sure everything's buried in several layers."

Campbell observed carefully as he prepared the manila file folder and opened a new computer file with the name Xina Harrison as its title.

"I like multiple backups," he said. "Sometimes paper is better than digital, and I'll copy this computer file to an external drive too."

Campbell nodded. She'd lost electronic files more times than she liked.

"And remember, every single word she told us is confidential," Bill said. "In fact, we don't want to reveal to anyone that Xina is our client, or that we're investigating her aunt."

"Right," Campbell said. "Of course, Keith already knows."

"Yeah. So if we need a police consult, he's the man we contact."

"Absolutely. And I thought we might try to contact the old housekeeper, Mrs. Conley."

"Excellent," her father said. "If she's still living in Murray, she could be a gold mine."

Campbell took her chair back to Nick's desk and woke up her laptop. This was the first case she'd worked on for the firm, other than a few boring bits for a law firm that frequently hired True Blue to find details they needed for a legal case. Her dad had walked her through those to familiarize her with some of the online resources he often used.

But this was a real case. An interesting case. And it concerned one of Campbell's favorite authors. Well, besides Jane Austen and Thomas Hardy. One of her favorite contemporary authors. She set to work.

Trying to find Mrs. Conley turned out to be a frustrating exercise, as so many people by that name were listed in the local phone book. And many folks didn't have landlines these days and weren't listed at all.

After half a dozen dead ends, Campbell decided to look for Katherine's friend Pam Rogers instead. To her relief, she located the woman's phone number quickly, and Pam answered on the third ring.

"Katherine?" Mrs. Rogers said. "Oh, dear, I haven't seen her for some time. It's true we used to do a lot of things together, but not for a while now."

"How long is a while?" Campbell asked.

"Years. We used to go to the same church, downtown, but Katherine quit coming. I think she started attending somewhere else. And she dropped out of a women's club we were both in. I phoned her several times, but she seemed to be very busy. We just ... never caught up."

"That's a shame."

"It is," Pam said. "But what is your interest in our friendship?"

"I'm actually inquiring for a family member." Guilt stabbed Campbell. Had she just broken her dad's rule by revealing the client? She glanced over at him, but he was concentrating on his computer file.

"Her niece, I suppose," Mrs. Rogers said. "I remember Xina."

"Well, she went to see her aunt last night, but Katherine wasn't very welcoming."

"Oh, dear, I know the feeling. It was quite hurtful at first, but after a few months of rejection, I moved on. I thought it was just me, though. Is she all right?"

"That's what we're trying to determine."

"Now I feel bad for giving up on her."

"No, you mustn't feel bad," Campbell said quickly. "Xina just wants to make sure she's in good health."

"Maybe I should try to call Katherine again," Pam said.

"Well, we're trying to do this quietly, so if you do contact her, please don't mention Xina or me. We don't want to upset her."

"I see. Maybe I'll hold off a while. I could call her next week."

"That might be good. Give her time to get past whatever made her uneasy last night. She did speak to Xina for a few minutes, but she didn't invite her to stay and visit."

"That doesn't sound like her." Pam sighed. "We're getting older, but Katherine was always on the ball. Still, she's lived alone for so long. And I haven't seen her in years, as I said."

"Well, don't blame yourself." Campbell ended the conversation as quickly and gracefully as she could.

She delved into Katherine's publishing history for the next hour, turning up bits and pieces online.

"Ready for lunch, Soup?" her father called across the room.

Soup was a nickname her dad had bestowed on Campbell when she was a toddler. He'd started tossing it out there again over the last couple of weeks, while she pampered him through a recovery from a physical ordeal and then eased into working at the office with him.

"What? You want soup for lunch?" she asked with a grin.

"Nah, I'm thinking roast beef. How does Cracker Barrel sound?"

"Great." She closed her computer files but grabbed her notebook so they could discuss business over lunch. Her father's routine of eating out on workdays had seemed extravagant at first, but he told her he earned enough to justify it. In the past week he'd scheduled two lunch meetings with clients. Between the business aspect and the need to shop less, his system worked out to be somewhat efficient—and he hated to cook.

Once they'd settled in at the restaurant and given their orders, Bill pulled out his pocket notebook. "Okay, I've wrapped up everything that was urgent as far as the legal case went, and I don't need to start the insurance fraud one until Monday. I learned that Ms. Tyler inherited that house from her parents forty years ago. Thought we might cruise by there when we're done eating and take a look."

"Good." Campbell flipped to her latest notes. "Most of her books were published by Random House, but not the last one."

Bill's eyebrows arched in interest.

"She sold it to a smaller publishing house—one she'd never worked with before," Campbell went on.

"I wonder what that was about."

"Me too. And there was a two-year gap between the release of that one and the last one with Random House."

"Okay," Bill said. "I wonder if we could get a handle on sales figures. How long since that latest book launched?"

"Almost three years. I haven't been able to find anything new since."

"Very interesting."

"I got a name for her agent." Campbell looked up and smiled at him across the table, proud of herself for her resourcefulness. "It was in the dedication of one of her old books."

"How old?"

"Ten years or so. Xina did say Katherine switched agents a while back, though. It may do no good to call this one."

"Only one way to find out," Bill said. "And may I suggest you check the acknowledgements in all of her books from that point forward. Pick up any names of people she thanks or seems to have worked with closely."

Campbell nodded. "Editors, professional consultants, publicists, whatever. Xina did mention a researcher."

"Good point. Find out if Katherine's stopped using him or her."

Their meals arrived, distracting them for several minutes. Campbell loved Cracker Barrel. Their pot roast tasted just like her mother's. She was sure it affected her dad the same way, but she didn't mention it because she didn't want to tear up.

When he'd finished his main course and asked for more coffee, Bill sat back and surveyed her. "How about the housekeeper?"

Campbell shook her head with regret. "I haven't reached her yet, but there are several Conleys listed in the area—Connellys too. I'll keep sorting through them this afternoon."

"Okay. At this point, I haven't found that Ms. Tyler has any large debts, but I can say with confidence she hasn't bought a new car in more than ten years, and she always pays her utilities and taxes on time. Doesn't seem to use credit cards much, though she has a couple. Tends to pay them off as soon as she gets the bill, on the rare occasion that she uses them." He wiggled his eyebrows at her. "There's one other thing I learned that should interest you."

"What?" Campbell picked up her glass of iced tea.

"That painting Xina talked about."

"Oh, yeah, the Ramsey. What did you find?"

"An auction house in Atlanta sold it last fall."

"You're kidding me." She set down her glass with a thump. "Do you think Xina's right about her aunt's financial situation?"

"It's the first thing we've found that seems to support that she needed money. But the auctioneer wouldn't reveal the seller's name."

Campbell frowned. "So ... somebody else could have sold it?"

"It's a possibility, either on Ms. Tyler's behalf or on their own."

She thought about that. "If the painting was stolen, wouldn't Keith know?"

"You'd think so."

"And if a thief tried to sell it, wouldn't the auctioneer demand proof of ownership?"

"They should."

She supposed Ms. Tyler could have commissioned someone to sell it for her. She might even have sold it locally, and then the new owner put it in the auction. "How much did the painting sell for?"

"Thirty-two grand," her father said. "With Ms. Tyler's modest lifestyle, I figure that would keep her going at least a year—if she was the one who got the money."

"What about her investments?" Campbell asked.

"That's harder to evaluate, and really hard to get at without bending some laws. She strikes me as the type of person who would let them sit and grow until she needed them. She is past full retirement age, but she still has a paid housekeeper." He shook his head. "She must have residual income from her older books. I don't think she's hurting too badly."

"And yet she sold a valuable painting."

Bill shrugged. "Maybe she didn't like it."

"And left it hanging over her mantel for forty years?"

"Yeah. Well, what can I say? I'll send you a link so you can see a photo of it, courtesy of the auction house. It didn't grab me, but there's no accounting for other people's taste, right?" He took out his phone and pushed a few buttons.

Campbell opened the link and studied the picture. The painting showed a wooded path, with light filtering through the foliage.

"It's okay," she said.

"Yeah. Thirty-two grand. The auctioneer seemed pleased. He said it was one of the best Ramseys he'd ever seen, and the bidding went higher than he'd expected."

She smiled. "I think if you were going to spend that much money on art, you'd pick something more exciting."

"Probably. I'm not much for landscapes. But anyway, who knows what the grandfather paid for it in 1950? That's when the auctioneer's blurb said the family bought it."

"And did Katherine's bank account reflect a deposit from the auction house?"

"I don't know." Bill scratched his chin. "It should have, but I don't expect we'll find out."

"So what now?" Campbell asked.

"So far, we have no indication that Ms. Tyler's physical or mental health has declined, and we've found no reason for her to be upset with her niece. I say we take a look at the house, and then we keep doing what we're doing."

"Dad, do you think Xina was honest with us about their relationship?"

"I thought so. She seemed open and genuinely concerned, but that is something to keep in mind. We have only her word for the things she says happened."

They turned down dessert, and he paid the check. A few minutes later, he drove slowly down a residential street and Campbell watched the house numbers.

"There it is."

He pulled in at the curb. "Nice old house."

"Yeah." She stared at the two-and-a-half-story wood-frame structure. It blended in with the others of the neighborhood. Probably they had all stood there several decades, hunkered silently on the shady street. Anything that old and large would require frequent maintenance. Why would a single woman choose to live there so long? Drapes or blinds were drawn at every window. "She doesn't like sunlight, does she?"

"Or nosy neighbors is more like it."

The lawn had been mowed recently, but there was no evidence of gardening. While a few low evergreens lined the walk, no one had added flowerbeds or ornamental plants.

"Hmm. A car in the driveway." Bill pulled out his cell phone.

Campbell hadn't thought about it, but now she studied the blue compact. "That's not Xina's car."

"No, she's halfway back to Asheville by now." He leaned past Campbell and snapped a couple of photos.

"Can you trace the license plate?" she asked.

"Yeah, hold on." He worked on his phone for a minute then looked up at her. "Caleb Henry. How do you feel about ringing the doorbell?"

"I thought we were going to be discreet."

"We are. If Katherine Tyler answers, you can be a fan who just learned she lived here."

"I would have brought along a book for her to sign."

"Okay. Well, anyhow, I figure someone else will open the door."

"Who?"

"Her new housekeeper."

"Riiight. Didn't Xina say today was Rita's day off?"

Her dad shrugged. "Well, somebody's in there."

Campbell pulled in a deep breath and walked slowly up the driveway, watching the windows. No one looked out at her. She took the flagstone walk to the porch. No doorbell. She looked back at her father's car and gulped before knocking. She waited a few seconds. Should she knock again?

The door opened, and a woman of about thirty, wearing stretchy pants and a T-shirt, gazed out at her. "Hello."

"Hi," Campbell said. "Are you Mrs. Conley?"

"No, I'm Rita Henry."

"Oh. Well, I'm trying to find a Mrs. Conley."

The young woman said softly, "She doesn't work here anymore."

"Oh. Sorry. Do you happen to know where she is now?"

"Uh ..." Rita glanced over her shoulder and then said, "She worked here before I came, but I think she lives down in Hazel."

"Okay. Was there a problem when she left?"

"I don't know, but ..."

"Well, maybe it's best if you don't tell your employer I was here."

"Right." She started to shut the door.

Campbell said quickly, "May I ask how you got this job?"

Rita frowned but said, "There was a newspaper ad in the *Ledger & Times*."

"Thanks." Campbell couldn't see much past her, but the inside of the house looked dim and gloomy. All she could see in the entry besides a narrow side table was an umbrella stand with a black cane and a furled umbrella sticking out of it. The cane's handle was a brass duck's head. She smiled at Rita. "I'm out of your hair now." She turned and walked quickly back to the car.

"Well?" her father asked, throwing the transmission into gear.

"You were right, it's the new housekeeper. She says she thinks Mrs. Conley lives in Hazel now. Where's that?"

"Just down 641, between here and the Tennessee border. It's not far."

"I'll get online again and see if I can locate some Conleys down there, then. Rita was a little nervous talking to me about it."

"You look for Mrs. Conley, and I'll keep working on Ms. Tyler's financials."

Back at the office, Campbell was surprised to see a Jeep sitting in their small parking lot.

"Nick's here."

"Ah, that kid." Bill parked, and they both went to the door. It was unlocked, and they walked in to find Nick Emerson sitting at his desk looking at Campbell's laptop. His left arm was still in a cast, but he'd graduated from the bandage on his head, and the hair shaved by the hospital staff was growing in around the scar on the left side.

"Hey, Nick!" Bill strode over to shake his hand. "You're supposed to stay home and rest until Monday, man."

"He just came in into snoop on my computer," Campbell said in a snarky but not-too-upset voice. She tugged the laptop away and snapped it shut.

"Hey," Nick cried in mock offense. "You just wrecked my solitaire game. Where y'all been?"

"Just getting some lunch," Bill said. "But seriously, the doctor says with that head injury you shouldn't try to do much for a few more days. Did you drive over here?"

"Yeah, I did. I'm telling you, I'm fine now. Really. No double vision, and the headache is gone so long as I keep on top of the Tylenol schedule."

"Got your short-term memory back?" Campbell asked. It was a sore spot with Nick, and he hadn't accepted the possibility that it might not come back.

"I remember everything," he said firmly. "Well, everything except the exact moment when that jerk whacked me over the head."

"That may be a blessing," Bill said.

Nick grimaced. "Yeah, I'm not sure I want to remember the impact in great detail. That guy's staying in jail, right?"

"You bet." Bill moseyed to his own desk and sat down. "Tell you what, Nick. We've got a new case, and there are lots of things to check out by closing time tomorrow. How about if we give you a few of them, and you can go home and putter away when you feel like it? That way, if your mother calls here to see if you sneaked in to work, I can honestly tell her you're not here."

Campbell tucked her laptop under one arm and reached out gingerly with the other hand and picked up an open bag of barbecue chips from the desktop with her fingertips. "What's this? I've never seen you eat these before."

Nick gave her a smile that may have been an attempt at omniscience or seduction but failed either way. "There's a lot you don't know about me, Professor."

"Ew." She dropped the bag, and orange potato chips sprinkled across the desk.

"Hey," Nick cried, snatching the bag. "I've just been craving those lately."

That sounded crazy, but maybe his head injury had something to do with it.

Nick scowled at her. "You gotta get you a desk of your own."

She could see the wisdom of that, especially if Nick was coming back to work soon.

"What do you think, Dad?" she asked.

Bill had begun checking his phone messages, and he said absently, "It'd be pretty crowded."

Campbell frowned. Was he saying he didn't want the three of them working together in here? She looked around. It would be a little snug, but if they moved the file cabinets a foot to the right ...

Her dad was punching in a phone number. Obviously this wasn't the time to discuss the office floor plan.

"Oh, by the way," Nick said as he picked the chips one by one off the desk and popped them into his mouth, "some guy named Steve wants to know if you want him to ship your boxes, or if he can drive down next weekend with them."

"He called the office?" She blinked at Nick in confusion. She hadn't given this phone number out to any of her friends in the Iowa college town where she'd lived for the last two years.

"No, he sent you an email."

Her jaw dropped. The glare she tried to pin him with had no visible effect. "You read my email?" It was nearly a scream, and her father jerked his head up and waved frantically for her to quiet down.

"Yes, Ryan," he said smoothly into the phone. "Sorry about that. Just a little office skirmish. I think we can work that out."

Campbell's cheeks felt as if Nick had taken a blowtorch to them. She leaned over his desk and hissed, "How could you?"

"Easy. You hadn't—"

"I don't mean technically, you troglodyte. I mean morally." She straightened, trying to excise her mind of the non sequitur she'd just uttered. "Oh, excuse me. I forgot—you don't have morals."

"Is that fair? I ask you."

They locked gazes for a long moment. Campbell sensed she wasn't going to win. If his arm wasn't in a cast ...

3

C ampbell was embarrassed, not just for being noisy while her father was on the phone, but because she didn't usually behave like a juvenile. Nick had always rubbed her the wrong way, but they'd managed to get along and even do some productive work together while her father was missing. And to be honest, he was right. She *wasn't* being fair. Why was she furious with him now? And letting it show? She looked down at her laptop.

"Don't you ever touch my computer again. Ever."

"I thought I was doing you a favor."

"Surc." Shc turned away and walked to the counter where the coffeemaker stood. With a little juggling, she managed to find enough space to set down the laptop. She didn't really want coffee, but she needed to do something credible that would excuse her from looking at Nicholas Emerson.

What did I expect? That Nick would never come back, and I'd work here happily ever after alone with Dad?

She measured coffee into the filter basket, feeling guiltier by the second. Was she jealous of this guy? The son her father never had? As a child, she'd sometimes daydreamed of having a big brother. But not a little brother. Everyone knew they were nothing but a pain. And something about Nick brought out the worst in her.

Maybe she shouldn't have turned down that job offer of teaching freshman comp classes this fall at Murray State. Her father's business had run smoothly before she came. She didn't want to ruin that.

Bill hung up his phone. "Coffee ready?"

"Not yet," Campbell replied. "I just started a new pot." She turned toward him, but her father was looking at Nick.

"So, Nick, that was Ryan Crawford, the lawyer. He needs us to do a diligent search for an heir. Could you handle that at home while you finish your convalescence?"

Nick snorted, perhaps to indicate the question was a no-brainer, or perhaps at Bill's use of a four-syllable word. "Of course I could. Can't I just do it here? I'm not in quarantine."

"No, but your mother is serious about making sure you follow the doctor's orders. I don't want to be responsible for her flying up here from Florida to ride herd on you."

Nick's eyebrows drew together, but he didn't contradict Bill. He obviously hated being treated like a kid, but he and Campbell both knew his mother was perfectly capable of booking a flight to Paducah if she thought he was overdoing it.

"I guess."

Bill smiled and glanced at his daughter. "Good. And in the meantime, Campbell and I will discuss the furniture situation here. You two each need your own workspace, that's obvious. I can't spend my time refereeing your squabbles."

"Sorry, Dad," Campbell said.

"Don't tell me. Tell Nick."

She looked over at the offender, but she just couldn't get the words out.

"I'm the one who should apologize," Nick said. "Campbell, I'm sorry I cracked into your computer. I shouldn't have done that. I was just bored."

Her jaw felt tight, but she managed to speak. "You read my emails."

"It was a challenge, since I had to do everything one-handed."

"We won't have any more of that, will we, Nick?" Bill said.

The smirk faded from Nick's lips. "No, sir."

Campbell could barely believe Nick's humble attitude. Was he putting it on for her dad?

"Glad to hear it." Bill gave him a perfunctory smile. "Where's your own computer?"

"At my place," Nick muttered.

"Well, I'm going to send you the details on this search. You'll have them when you get home. Mr. Crawford would like to see some results by Monday if possible, so he can carry on with distributing the estate."

"There's a missing heir?" Campbell couldn't help asking. The idea of tracking down people who had a nice legacy coming their way appealed to her.

"Yes, a grandson who left home ten years ago and hasn't been heard from since. Nick is very good at tracing." Bill tapped away at his keyboard while he spoke. "Okay, I've sent you my notes and attached a copy of the file Crawford sent me. I'll leave that with you, Nick. If you have any problems, let me know later. Otherwise, it's your case."

"Thanks." Nick didn't sound truly grateful, but he stood and picked up his potato chip bag and phone. "Guess I'm out of here."

"Hey," Bill said, "it's not that I don't want you back at work. I just want you to be good and rested when you start putting in eight hours a day. So don't work too hard on this, you understand me? I can chip away at it this weekend if it turns out to be more difficult than I think it will."

"Okay." Nick looked over at Campbell. "I guess this means you're going to be a permanent part of True Blue, so welcome. And I truly am sorry. I was out of line."

She nodded. "Get some rest, Nick. And when we're done with the Harrison case, I'd like to learn to do the kind of search you're tackling. Maybe you can help me." She let out a breath as the door closed behind him. "I'm sorry, Dad. The last thing I want to do is squeeze Nick out."

Bill held up a hand in protest. "You won't. But he may be wondering. Now, I've still got that insurance fraud case. Nick can work on that one next week and free me up for the Harrison case. Are you going to get working on finding Katherine Tyler's old housekeeper, or do you want to shop for a desk first?"

The sound of the Jeep's engine starting outside prompted another objection. How could Nick even drive with that cast?

Her father's sober expression warned her not to voice it.

She swallowed hard. "Let's work, Dad."

CAMPBELL LOOKED ONLINE for the minister of the church where Xina had told them Katherine Tyler attended.

"Should I call the pastor?" she asked her father.

"I'd go in person. Ministers are cautious about giving out information on their congregation, as they should be."

"Right." She spent some more time working on tracking down Mrs. Conley. Her father gave her a few tips, and by two o'clock she was confident she'd located the right person.

"I'm pretty sure her first name is Doris," she said. "Should I call first?"

"I usually get better results if I show up unannounced," Bill said.

"That seems to be a pattern."

"It is. Want me to go with you?"

"Well, I was going to go by the minister's house first and then see if I could find Doris Conley."

Bill nodded. "You go ahead. I'll stay here and keep working on this end. Call me if you run into problems."

Campbell hesitated. "Okay, but is that legal? I don't have my license yet, and I'm supposed to assist you. Is it all right for me to go off and question people on my own?"

"I don't think it's a problem." Bill sifted through the papers on his desk and opened the folder with *Harrison* on the tab. "The regs don't get that specific. I'm supposed to instruct and train you. So let's talk about what kind of questions you should ask Doris Conley, and also the ones you don't want to ask."

A few minutes later, she set out for the parsonage near the church Ms. Tyler had attended. The minister's wife answered the door and showed Campbell into her husband's study.

He greeted her cheerfully, but when she asked about Katherine Tyler, he frowned and opened a computer file on his desktop model.

"I've only been here a couple of years, and I don't believe I've ever met Ms. Tyler. Her name seems to be on our membership roll." He sat back in his chair and stared at the far wall for a moment. "I wonder if one of the older ladies in our church might be able to help you." He reached for his phone. "I don't like to give our members' contact information to outsiders, but I can give this woman a call."

"That's very kind of you," Campbell said.

He punched in a number and then waited. He smiled when he got a response. "Hello, Brenda. I'm fine. How are you? I wanted to ask you about another one of our members. Do you know if Katherine Tyler has attended any of our services lately? No ... I see. Well, thank you very much."

Replacing the receiver, he looked across the desk at Campbell. "She says that Ms. Tyler hasn't been to a service here in several years, to her knowledge."

Campbell nodded soberly. "Well, thank you very much."

"I should probably pay a call on her," the pastor said. "You said you're looking into her background on behalf of a family member?"

"Yes," Campbell said. "I understand she's become quite

reclusive. This person was concerned. But if you do contact Ms. Tyler, please don't say anything about it to her. I don't want to upset her."

He frowned. "All right."

"I assure you, we have only Ms. Tyler's best interests at heart."

She rose and shook his hand then went to her car. It was a short trip south to Hazel, a small, picturesque town heavy on antique shops. Campbell hadn't spent much time exploring this part of Kentucky, and so far, she liked it. Teaching at a university five hundred miles away had allowed her only brief visits to her father's adopted home.

Following the GPS directions, she turned onto Doris Conley's street, where she pulled the car over to the shoulder. The afternoon sun had brought a shimmering heat. A bottle of water, unopened, sat in the cup holder, and she twisted off the cap and took a deep swallow. For a moment she sat still, breathing slowly and preparing herself for the interview.

She walked up to the front door of the compact brick ranch, where she rang the bell. A middle-aged woman opened the door.

"May I help you?" Her gray eyes peered at Campbell through bifocals.

"Hi, I'm looking for Doris Conley."

The woman's eyes narrowed. "Your name?"

"Campbell McBride."

"I'm Doris. Come on in."

Campbell entered a small, tiled foyer. Beyond it, she could see a cozy living room.

"How may I help you, Miss McBride?"

"I understand you used to work for Katherine Tyler."

"Yes." Mrs. Conley said cautiously.

"How long were you employed by Ms. Tyler?"

"Why do you want to know?"

"I'm an investigator." Campbell remembered her father's counsel to give as little information she could.

Doris frowned. "What sort of investigator?"

"The private kind."

"Has something happened to Miss Tyler?"

"I don't think so. Her family is concerned about her, and we're looking into her activities and her general wellbeing."

"Her family? You must mean her niece," Doris said. "That's all the family she has left."

"Have you met her niece?" Campbell asked.

"Several times. I first met Xina when she was about twelve. But she's got an MBA now. Works someplace out in California, I think."

That meshed with everything Xina had told them, and Campbell was relieved. "Why did you leave Miss Tyler's employ?"

Doris stepped back. "Why don't you come through and sit down?"

Campbell followed her down a short hallway, through the well-appointed kitchen, and out onto the shady back patio. They both settled in lawn chairs.

"Now, what is this for, exactly?" Doris asked.

Campbell ran down Bill's list of "rules" and tried to think of the least revealing answer she could give. "I'm with True Blue Investigations. I'm not allowed to discuss the arrangements of the case with you, but I assure you, we have Miss Tyler's best interests at heart."

Doris studied her face for a few seconds. "Well, all right. The truth is, she fired me."

"Did she say why?"

"No. One Monday morning, I was getting ready to go over and clean her house, and she phoned me. Said my services weren't needed any longer, and she would mail me a check for my last week of work."

"That sounds rather abrupt."

"It was. Especially when you've worked for someone twenty-eight years, and they never complained once. She didn't give me any warning at all." Doris shook her head. "I wasn't sure I could get another job. I called a few times, to ask if she would give me a reference, but she wouldn't answer."

"Did that upset you?"

"Well, sure. Wouldn't you be upset? I still have no clue what I did wrong."

"Have you found another position?"

"Yeah, three days a week, and I pick up another lady for a fourth day—just light cleaning for her. It isn't too bad. But I liked working for Miss Tyler."

"Did you talk to her much while you were there?"

"Some. She might keep to her bedroom some days, or the little room she had fitted up for an office. If she was working on a new book, she barely spoke to me. But most days we'd chat a few minutes, or even have a cup of tea together. I got to know her over the years, and I thought we got along fine."

"And then she let you go without warning," Campbell said. "Can you tell me when that was?"

"Uh ... well, it's nearly five years now. I think it was July, five years ago. Somewhere near then."

Campbell nodded. "Thank you. Is there anything you remember that was odd the last few times you went to the house?"

"No, I don't think so."

"Our client mentioned that a few items of Miss Tyler's seemed to be missing."

Doris's face blanched. "Is she accusing me of stealing something? She never said anything like that to me."

"No, no," Campbell said quickly. It's just that a couple of items that used to be in the house aren't there now. A Ramsey painting, for instance, in the front parlor."

"That landscape, you mean? Over the fireplace?"

"That's right."

Doris frowned. "It was there when I was last in the house."

Campbell jotted it down in her small notebook. She glanced

at the list of questions her father had told her to ask. "What about a family photo from the mantel, or an antique match holder?"

She squinted her eyes for a moment. "I remember those, but I have no idea what's become of them."

"Do you remember anyone else that Miss Tyler had contact with? Maybe people in the area that she did business with?"

"Hmm. I did most of her shopping. If something broke down, she would have a repairman come. Sometimes I set that up for her. She paid somebody to mow the lawn, and one of the neighbors would do a chore for her once in a while."

"Do you remember any names?"

"Just the furnace guy. I'd done business with him once before." Doris gave Campbell the repairman's name.

"What about the neighbor?"

"Hmm, Ben something. He lived right next door, if that helps."

"What about her doctor and dentist?"

"I'm sorry. I can't recall any names."

"Did Miss Tyler drive herself if she had an appointment?"

"Sometimes she'd take a taxi."

Campbell noted the fact. "She didn't have a car?"

"She did, but she didn't drive it much by the last of my time with her. It was still in the garage, though. She'd take it out now and again, but not long distances. The last conference she spoke at, she paid me to drive her to the airport in Nashville."

Campbell hurried to keep up. "And do you recall who her agent is?"

Doris shook her head. "I never talked about the publishing business with her."

"All right, thank you. If you think of anything pertinent, would you call me?" Campbell wished she had new business cards with the office number on them. She took out one of her old ones and wrote the office number on the back.

Doris took it. "You live in Iowa?"

"Not anymore. I came home recently to work in my father's agency."

To Campbell's relief, Doris didn't probe about that. She seemed more worried about Katherine Tyler's current activities.

"She's not saying I took that painting, is she?"

"No, not at all. You can rest easy on that. So far as I know, Miss Tyler hasn't said a word against you. I just wondered if you knew anything about its history. Thanks for your time."

Doris walked through to the front door with her, and Campbell went to her car. Had the painting been switched out for the Winslow Homer print last fall, just before it was sold in Atlanta? Maybe the new housekeeper would know, if they decided it was important enough to ask. She punched in the office phone number.

"True Blue Investigations," her father said briskly.

"Hi, Dad. It's Campbell. Listen, I need some business cards. Don't know why I didn't think of it before. Do you have a place that you order from?"

"Yeah, I use a job printer downtown. What do you want on them?"

Campbell scrunched up her face as she thought about it. "Maybe model them on yours, with the logo, but put my name? And the office address and number on there, the way it is on yours."

"Sounds good. I'll place the order. Did you talk to Doris Conley?"

"I did. I'm on my way back, but I thought I'd go to Ms. Tyler's neighborhood and interview some of her neighbors."

"Okay. Be discreet. Park where your car can't be seen from her house."

"Got it." The last thing she wanted was for Katherine Tyler to look out a window and see her making the rounds of her neighbors' doors. "How's it going there?"

"Busy. I've had a call from another prospective client. He's coming in tomorrow morning to talk."

"Wow. The whole time you were missing, all we got were routine insurance and legal cases."

"Well, the publicity from the Beresford and Shepherd cases drew a lot of attention to us. Not to mention the missing exchange student case you solved."

"*We* solved. I guess so." Campbell could hear the pride in his voice, and it felt good, but she hoped she could live up to his expectations.

"We can't wait until one case is closed before we agree to take another," her dad said.

"Right."

Campbell drove to Ms. Tyler's street and rolled by the house, trying not to stare at it. She parked farther down the block, out of sight, and walked back toward the white house. Two doors before Katherine's, she approached a charming Princess Anne and rang the bell. No one was home, either there or at the house directly across from Katherine's.

Back in her car, Campbell drove around the back of the block. She parked at the other end of the street and ambled to the neighbor's on the other side of Katherine's. After scouting to make sure no one was looking out from Katherine's, she hurried up onto the porch.

This time, a man answered her summons.

"Hello," Campbell said with a smile.

He peered at her through black-rimmed glasses. His graying hair looked a little greasy, and his brown eyes were set back into his puffy face.

"Who are you?"

"I'm Campbell McBride. I wondered if you're acquainted with Miss Tyler, next door."

His eyes narrowed. "Are you a cop?"

"No."

"Then I don't have to talk to you." He started to shut the door.

Campbell put out her hand. "Please wait."

He hesitated with the door open about three inches.

Campbell said quickly, "I'd just like to know if you have any contact with Miss Tyler. Do you ever talk to her?"

His hard eyes shocked her. Did her dad get this reaction often? She didn't like the tightness in her chest as he glared at her.

"You get out of here, or I'll call the cops." He shut the door in her face, and the deadbolt clicked.

4

W hen Campbell walked into the office, Detective Keith
Fuller was sprawled in a chair facing Bill across his desk.
He stood and smiled at her.

"So, Campbell, your father tells me you've been tracking
down old housekeepers and helpful neighbors in Ms. Harrison's
case."

Keith's easy manner and cheerfulness lifted her spirits, not to
mention the mere sight of him. She liked him very much but
hadn't seen much of him for the past couple of weeks.

"Sort of," she said. "I did find Doris Conley, Katherine Tyler's
former housekeeper. She was quite helpful."

"Do you think she stole the Ramsey painting?" Bill asked.

"No. Doris seemed like a nice person. I believe what she told
me—that Ms. Tyler fired her without warning, and that the
painting was still there when she left."

"Okay. But she might be lying. She still could have taken it.
Especially if Ms. Tyler got tired of it a while ago and put it in the
attic. Mrs. Conley could have taken it from there without Ms.
Tyler ever knowing. And she could have taken other things from
the house over the years, and her employer found out."

Campbell smiled wearily. "I suppose. Or she could have some

39

resentment against Katherine, but she didn't seem that way. Just baffled as to why Katherine let her go so suddenly. The neighbors weren't nearly as forthcoming as Doris." She sat down behind Nick's desk, and Keith resumed his seat. "I was threatened this afternoon."

Keith's shoulders tightened. "What was that about?"

"The guy living in the house just to the left of Katherine's was the only neighbor I found at home. As soon as I asked if he knew her, he told me to leave or he'd call the police."

"Overprotective?" Bill asked.

"Maybe," Campbell said. "But I hadn't even told him I was a P.I. And after I got in my car and was making some notes, he was watching me out his window with binoculars."

"Maybe *he* stole the painting," Bill said.

Campbell shrugged. "If he had, why would he threaten to call the police? He'd want to avoid them, I'd think."

"Good point," Bill said, "but that was probably an empty threat to get rid of you."

"Why?"

"Because you were snooping around."

Campbell pursed her lips. "Well, if he didn't have any contact with Katherine, he probably wouldn't have reacted that way, would he? I'd expect everyone to want to talk about the reclusive neighbor lady."

Keith nodded. "I agree. But he may have thought you were a reporter, wanting some nuggets about the famous author."

"Yeah, he may have had some bad experiences in the past with the press." Leaning back in his chair, Bill surveyed them. "So, he doesn't want to talk to strangers about her, but that doesn't mean he has no contact with her."

"Maybe she asked him not to talk to people about her." Campbell grimaced at her dad.

"Or maybe they've had disputes in the past. Neighborly feuds can get out of hand easily."

She sighed. "So how can we find out who the neighbor is?"

"A couple of ways. We could look at the property maps at city hall, but lots of times you can find a person by searching his address online."

"Of course." Campbell brought up a search engine and typed in the address. In less than a minute she was reasonably sure that Katherine Tyler's neighbor's name was Benjamin Tatton. Close enough to the name Doris Conley had given as a helpful neighbor. "Now what?"

"I'll see if I can find any background on him," Bill said. "I'm thinking that if we go back when the other neighbors are home—say, early evening—we might learn a lot from them about Mr. Tatton. He sounds like quite a character. And other people nearby will know if he's the one who did odd jobs for her."

"Do you think we should keep following the art lead?" Campbell asked.

"I can look through the police database and see if there have been any art thefts reported lately," Keith said.

"Great. Make that within the last five years. If you don't turn up any connections, we'll assume for now that she sold it herself." Bill looked toward the coffeemaker. "Anybody for a cuppa?"

Campbell accepted a mug of coffee that he brought her and took a sip. "This is good, Dad. I'll let you make the coffee all the time."

He laughed. "It's a fancy flavor a client gave me." He arched his eyebrows at Keith. "How about you?"

"No, I'd better get going." He looked wistfully toward Campbell. "Good to see you both. I'll let you get back to work."

"Bye, Keith." As she watched him amble out the door, Campbell wished they weren't quite so busy. She and Keith had attempted a couple of dinner dates in the past, but it seemed they always got interrupted with business.

"So, what do you want to do about this potential new client, Jacob Gray?" Bill asked.

Campbell shrugged. "Do you think we should both be here when he comes in tomorrow?"

"You don't have to be. I'd like to keep you on the Harrison case. When Nick's here, I try to have him sit in, and then we decide who is best suited to the case." Bill ran a hand through his hair. "I hope he's good to work on Monday. We could really use him right now."

"He seemed eager."

"Yeah, but I'm going to insist he takes care of himself. That head wound ... I don't know."

"He seemed fine," Campbell said. "Acted like his old self."

"It was hard to tell." Bill made a face. "I didn't expect you two to pull off the gloves like that."

"I'm sorry, Dad. I overreacted when I found out he'd been snooping in my email."

"No, you didn't. I could fire him for that. On the other hand, part of the reason he's useful to this office is his talent for cyber sleuthing. How about you put a password on that laptop of yours and another one on your email account?"

She moaned. "That would be such a pain. And Nick could crack that too."

"Yeah, but it would remind him that we've set some boundaries."

"I'll consider it."

"That's all I ask."

She eyed him keenly for a moment. "Dad, be honest with me. Can this business support three people?"

"I think so, especially with this trend of new private clients. If Nick can wrap up the missing heir trace this weekend, he'll have earned a week's wages right there."

Campbell nodded slowly. "But we won't get any publicity out of Xina Harrison's case, right? Whatever we find out about her aunt will stay hush-hush."

"In theory, yes, but we might get some word-of-mouth clients when Ms. Harrison recommends us to other people. Hey, only half an hour until quitting time."

They both settled down with short lists of items to check online and phone calls to make. Campbell delved into Katherine's publishing history and found it fascinating. Here and there she found snippets of information, usually in book reviews or short news briefs published when one of Katherine's new books released.

"Dad, remember how Xina told us that Katherine's latest book came out three years ago?"

"Yeah. Is she due for another one soon?"

"I don't know. I found an online publication called *Publisher's World*. It has all the news and gossip about the publishing industry. There isn't any buzz on her. But prior to that, she came out with about a book or two a year for twenty years."

"Wow. Maybe she's sick. That could explain a lot."

Campbell flipped through her small notebook. "Xina didn't think she looked ill, but she only saw her for a couple of minutes. She did say she'd aged. Maybe she has some illness like cancer or M.S., and she doesn't want anyone to know. I mean, she never did a lot of interviews or photo ops. Maybe she hates having anyone talk about her."

"Yeah, Xina said she was always a private person, but more social in the past than she apparently is now." Bill leaned back in his chair and sighed. "Maybe she did have to sell some things lately to supplement her income. Before you came back, Keith told me the police haven't had any reports connected to Katherine Tyler. Seems she's not only shy, she's an upstanding citizen."

"So, it's not likely the painting was stolen or they'd have a report. Xina was afraid someone was pressuring Katherine or manipulating her—draining her funds somehow."

"We can't know without seeing her bank records."

"And you can't access them."

"No, but I did see a couple of credit reports." Bill sat for a moment deep in thought, his expression glum.

Campbell checked the time. "Maybe we should break here for tonight and talk to more neighbors tomorrow." She stretched her arms.

"Okay, where do you want to eat?"

"What's wrong with home?"

Bill shrugged. "Nothin', I guess."

"Dad, restaurant meals for two cost a lot more than restaurant meals for one. We should try to save your money, or else I'm paying my own way."

"You feel like cooking?"

She closed her laptop and stood. "Yeah, come on. How do tacos sound?"

That evening, she sat in the living room with her father. While he answered the mail and paid a few household bills, Campbell shot off an email to Steve. *Send the boxes. We're really busy, so I couldn't entertain you if you drove down. Funds on the way. Let me know if it's not enough. Thanks.* Then she went to PayPal and sent him an amount of money she thought would cover the cost of shipping.

She had a few notifications through her Facebook account, and she clicked on one that said her friend Lisa Turnbull had tagged her. Lisa was an associate professor in Feldman's sociology department, and they'd been casual friends while Campbell worked there.

Someone swiped the Steiger medal! Old Smithy's having fits.

Mildly shocked, Campbell clicked to read more.

According to Lisa, a prestigious award the college presented each year at graduation had gone missing. It had been awarded just weeks ago to Dr. Daniel Griffin, head of the math department, much to the dismay of at least half Feldman's faculty. Between the ceremony and her departure for Kentucky, Campbell had heard at least a dozen people complain that

Griffin didn't deserve the award. Dr. Smith, "Old Smithy," had been one of the protestors.

Lisa provided a link to a news story, and Campbell clicked on it. The police in the college town were investigating an apparent break-in at Dr. Griffin's home and the theft of the Steiger Medal. Nothing else appeared to be missing.

"That's kind of weird."

"What?" her father asked.

"Oh, it's a medal the college awarded at graduation to an outstanding faculty member. It's prestigious, supposedly, but I'm sure it wouldn't impress anyone outside Feldman circles. Anyway, it's been stolen from the professor who won it this year. And the thief didn't take anything else, just that medal."

"He obviously got what he was after," Bill said.

"Right." He or she, Campbell thought. One name she'd frequently heard as most deserving, leading up to the presentation and afterward, was Dr. Ilsa Kepler, head of the foreign languages department. But a dignified fifty-year-old woman like Dr. Kepler wouldn't break into someone's house and steal a trinket, would she?

Campbell closed the browser. "It's probably a prank. There was a lot of controversy when the award was made last month. Well, I'm not going to worry about it. I've got more important things to think about."

ON FRIDAY MORNING, Bill left for the office at his usual time, but Campbell took her own car and headed for the library.

She looked around to orient herself. At least a dozen patrons browsed or sat at reading tables. A couple of the four computers along the back wall were in use. A mother came in with two toddlers and herded them toward the children's section. The thought that this many people still wanted to read books encouraged Campbell. Love of literature was something she would never shake.

She ambled into the fiction section. It didn't take her long to find fifteen of Katherine Tyler's books on the shelves. She was a little surprised there weren't more, and a little disappointed that the newest one wasn't among them. After collecting the most recent three they had, she made her way to the circulation desk.

"Find what you wanted?" the librarian asked with a smile.

"Partly." Campbell slid the Tyler books across the counter. "I was hoping to find Ms. Tyler's newest book. I suppose I could get it as an eBook."

"Oh, we have it in hardcover," the librarian assured her. "Maybe someone's checked it out." She turned to her computer for a moment. "Yes, the regular copy is out, but we also have it in large print. Do you want me to see if that's on the shelf?"

"That would be great," Campbell said. "I never thought to look there."

The woman left the desk and was back in a minute with a mylar-covered copy of the book she'd requested. Campbell told her she'd just moved to Murray and didn't have a card yet, so the librarian quickly issued one for her. She swiped each book and handed over the stack.

"I guess her books are pretty popular," Campbell said.

"Yes, especially here. She's a big-name local author. I wish she'd come out with another book."

Campbell was glad she'd found print copies of the author's most recent books. She could have downloaded them onto her digital reader, but she wanted to hold each volume, heft its weight, and study the covers and the front and back matter. It might not do any good so far as the case was concerned, but she was certain it would help her understand Katherine better.

When she got back to True Blue and entered the office, a man of about forty was seated across from her father. Campbell tiptoed to Nick's desk and sat down, she hoped unobtrusively. If business continued to flourish, maybe

46

someday her father could have a private office with a receptionist out front.

"All right, you bring that by this afternoon, and we'll get right on it," Bill said. The two men rose and walked toward the door. When they came even with Campbell, he said, "Oh, and this is my daughter, Campbell. She's a crackerjack investigator. Honey, this is Mr. Gray."

Campbell looked up and gave a restrained smile. "Nice to meet you, Mr. Gray." She didn't want to act too happy or enthusiastic. Most people who hired an investigator had troubles and weren't in the most cheerful state of mind.

When he was gone, her father came and sat on the corner of her desk. "He wants us to find his daughter. She ran off about two years ago, and they haven't heard a word from her since."

"How sad."

"Yeah." He reached out and patted her head awkwardly. "Makes me glad you're here."

"So, will you be working on that?"

"I thought I'd put Nick on the initial computer stuff. But not until we get some documentation and photographs from Mr. Gray."

"Documentation?"

Bill nodded soberly. "As I explained to him, nothing against this guy, but we need to be a hundred percent sure she's really his daughter before we start looking."

"Oh."

"There have been cases where someone asked a P.I. to find a relative of theirs, and it turned out that person wasn't really related to them. Or they were, but the person they were looking for didn't want to be found."

"Like, someone running away from an abusive relationship?"

"That would be one example."

Campbell thought for a moment. "What if she really was his daughter, but she had reasons not to want her family to know where she was?"

"That will be the first thing I ask her when we find her, before I give Mr. Gray any information on her whereabouts."

"But ..."

"I know, I know," Bill said. "He's the client, not her. But I'm not going to enable an abuser to get his victim back or help a criminal by blowing a protected witness's cover. Nothing like that."

"So, what now?"

"He says he'll bring us a copy of her birth certificate and her vaccination record and a few photos. She didn't have a driver's license when she left." He shook his head. "She was barely sixteen. I'll have Nick check out the story with people who knew the girl before she left. If everything looks okay, we'll start the search. But she's over eighteen now, so if she's still alive she has some rights to her privacy, if that's what she wants."

"It's like an obstacle course, isn't it?" Campbell asked.

"In some ways." Bill smiled. "You just never know with this job. A couple years ago, a lawyer had me trace a missing heir. When I found him in Texas, he said he didn't want the bequest his father left him, and he wouldn't claim it. His share went to his siblings. Sometimes that's how it is. But not usually." As he spoke, he fingered the pile of library books. "Catching up on your reading, are you?"

"Yes. I'm trying to do what you said and glean information from her books." She opened the latest book, *Ice Cold Blue,* to the publication information. "This last one was published by Krata Press. I've never heard of it. Have you?"

"No, but that's not really in my wheelhouse. Why don't you look them up online?"

"I intend to. I wondered if maybe she self-published it, and that's her own imprint. A lot of authors are doing that now, starting their own micro presses. But I can't see an author that popular needing to do it."

"Or that old?"

Campbell chuckled. "She's not that old, Dad."

"But why did she leave the other publisher? That's something we need to find out. She must have made them some nice profits in years past."

A quick search on her laptop told Campbell that Krata Press was a small house and had been in business only fifteen years. They did have about twenty authors listed, but Campbell didn't recognize any of the other names. That seemed like quite a comedown for an author like Katherine Tyler. Campbell checked the other books and stopped at the front material in one released about seven years earlier.

"Hey, guess what," she said fifteen minutes later.

"What?" Bill asked.

"I think I found out who Katherine's agent is. She had listed some people on the Acknowledgements page of one of her books, and I tried to look them all up. One of them is Bruce Waverly, and he's a literary agent. I'm pretty sure he's not the one Xina met. This book was published seven years ago."

"Good work!"

She basked in her dad's smile for a moment. This was the rewarding part of the job—or a small fraction of it. Fitting the pieces together felt almost as good as seeing her literature students get fired up over William Blake and Alexander Pope.

"One thing I found was a little depressing, though."

"What was that?" Bill asked.

"Apparently she doesn't do dedications. You know how in the front of a lot of books, it will say 'To my dear husband,' or 'To my best friend Rudy'?"

"Yeah. Katherine doesn't do that, huh?"

"Not in any of the books I've checked out."

"I guess we knew she's not sentimental."

"It's sad, don't you think? She doesn't have any friends. No family members to dedicate her books to."

"I wonder if she ever did any dedications," Bill said. "Maybe when she was younger and more of her family was alive."

"I'll try to check. Xina might know." Campbell reached for

SUSAN PAGE DAVIS

her purse. "Meanwhile, I should probably go bother some more of her neighbors."

Bill stood. "I can go with you."

"What about Mr. Gray's case?"

"I've got the file set up, but I can't do much until he brings me that documentation. I can give the Harrison case a couple of hours." He pocketed his phone and pulled out his key ring. "Let's take my car. Anyone who saw yours yesterday afternoon might recognize it."

5

Campbell let her father do most of the talking to the residents on Katherine's street. She listened to his tone and the way he phrased his questions to get maximum response from people without alarming them. They'd already agreed not to be pushy or visit too many people on the same day, as word might get back to Katherine.

"I've lived here three years, and I don't think I've ever seen her," the woman diagonally across the street said. "There's lights on at her house in the evening, but she hardly ever goes out."

Her husband said, "Aw, you've seen her. You told me a few months ago that she called a cab."

"That's right," the woman said. "And she came out and got in the taxi, but I didn't see her face. It was in February or March, and she wore a heavy coat and some kind of hat. A knitted one, I suppose. But she was really covered up. I didn't see much."

The next woman they talked to, Vera Hill, was more helpful. She had lived in her home more than twenty years, longer than Benjamin Tatton, whose house was just across from hers.

"Now he's a strange one, that Ben Tatton," Mrs. Hill said.

"How do you mean, strange?" Bill asked.

"He can be nice when he wants to. In fact, he'll go around

and do things for people. This spring he brought over some tomato seedlings and said he had too many. He gave me half a dozen."

"Does he sometimes do chores for Miss Tyler?" Bill asked.

"Yes, I think he does, now and then. There's a young fellow who's hired to mow the lawn for her, but I've seen Ben over there a few times. Once he was fixing something. A broken windowpane, maybe. And I've seen him gathering fallen branches after a windstorm for her."

"When was the last time you spoke to Miss Tyler?" Bill asked.

"Oh, it's been a while. She's all right, isn't she?"

"Yes, I'm sure she is," Bill said.

"Good. She has someone go in and keep house and cook. I see that gal come and go." Vera waved a hand in dismissal. "I rarely see Katherine, although she does do that charity luncheon every year for the literacy volunteers."

Bill's pen skittered over the page of his notebook. "What do you mean, she does the luncheon? Does she speak?"

"No, no. But she donates to the cause, and she usually attends the event. I think she went this year. I was visiting my daughter in New Hampshire, so I missed it this time, but she usually goes. I can only remember one time she didn't."

"When was that?" Campbell said quickly.

"It was a few years back. I figure she was sick or something. A lot of people were disappointed. She's famous, you know, but she doesn't make many public appearances. I don't think she even goes to church."

Bill smiled and stepped back. "Thank you, Mrs. Hill. You've been very helpful."

They walked toward his car.

"Why didn't you give her your business card?" Campbell asked.

"It's a bit awkward. If we say we're trying to make sure Ms. Tyler is all right, they'll wonder why we don't knock on her door and ask her. And Mrs. Hill might be one who would mention our visit if she did happen to see Ms. Tyler."

Campbell nodded. It was a delicate situation all right. "Maybe we should let it rest for today."

"Yeah, I think so. Come on, let's get lunch and then go back to the office."

In the car, they talked over the information they had gained and planned what they would do next.

"Why don't I reach out to the old publisher," Bill said. "They probably won't talk to me, but you never know. And I'd like you to find out more about this literacy volunteer thing." He scratched his chin. "Maybe a little genealogy research is in order too."

Campbell blinked. "Why? Xina told us she's all Katherine has left for family."

"Let's make sure."

They had a quick meal downtown and plunged back into their research. Bill made a few phone calls, and she tuned him out while she worked. A call to the head of the literacy volunteers told her that Katherine hadn't attended their annual luncheon for at least three years. So much for Mrs. Hill's memory.

"I didn't get much out of the old publisher," her father called across the room an hour later, "but Waverly was Katherine's agent when she was publishing with them, at least for the last three books. Apparently she signed on with him when her former agent died, as Xina told us. We need to find out if Waverly's still working with her."

Campbell looked up from her screen, where she'd been immersed in family group sheets and descendant charts. "Sounds like it. And, Dad, apparently Xina was straight with us about the family. Katherine never married. Her sister, Xina's mother, has been dead several years. Both Katherine's parents are deceased, and there are no first cousins living. Xina is an only child, and what she said about her dad living in Arizona checks out."

Bill pursed his lips and nodded. "So it's entirely reasonable that Xina is Katherine's only living relative. Within a few removals, of course."

"Is that important?"

"It could be. Listen, why don't you try to contact the agent, and I'll—" He broke off as the door opened and Jacob Gray looked in.

"Mr. McBride, I've got the records you asked for on my daughter."

"Great," Bill said. "Come on in." He shot Campbell a keen glance, and she nodded. If she interpreted that correctly, he wanted her to get on with tracking down Waverly.

The agent's website was easy to locate, and she studied his picture. He was a distinguished-looking man, perhaps in his early fifties—but then, she didn't know how recently the photo had been taken. She clicked on CONTACT BRUCE WAVERLY. An email form popped up, and below it was a telephone number. She hesitated, wondering if she should make the call with Jacob Gray in the room.

Bill opened the manila envelope the client had given him and spread out a few papers and photographs on his desk.

"That one's the latest picture we have of her," Gray said, pointing.

"Okay, I'll get right on this." Bill saw him to the door.

"Sounds like you'll be busy," Campbell said when the client was gone.

"Yeah. But it's okay, we can handle it." He gathered up the pictures and documents. "In fact, I think I'll give this to Nick now. You and I can focus on the Harrison case. I'd kind of like to take the weekend off, though."

"Oh?" She waited, not sure what to expect.

"I thought we could drive over to Bowling Green Saturday and visit your mother's grave. Mart says he'll barbecue, and we can have lunch with his family."

"I'd like that." Campbell hadn't been to the cemetery where

her mother was buried since before Bill had moved to Murray. His friend Mart, however, lived near the graveyard. He'd also been a big help when Bill disappeared, and he'd spent a week in Murray afterward, helping them catch up on the agency's work while Bill got back up to speed and Nick recovered from his injuries.

"Tell him we'll be there," she said. "But that means I've got to get to work now. I'm going to call Katherine's agent."

Before she could do it, the office phone rang. Bill picked up the receiver on his desk.

"Hi, Keith. What've you got?" He listened intently for several seconds. "You're kidding me. When?"

Campbell's heart began to pound. She could tell from her father's tone and expression that something was wrong.

"Okay," Bill said. "Can we go over? All right, let me know." A moment later, he hung up.

"What is it?" Campbell asked.

"Benjamin Tatton, the rude neighbor."

"Yeah?"

"Someone smashed him over the head. They're taking him to Murray-Calloway County, but he might not make it."

6

Campbell stared at her father. "We were just over there."

"I know. Sounds like the call came in right after we left the neighborhood."

"Quite a coincidence," Campbell said.

"Yeah."

"What happened? You said—"

"They don't know, but Keith says it looks like someone came at him in his kitchen. No weapon on the scene, though. A UPS driver found him. He thought it was odd Tatton didn't come right to the door, since he usually does. Apparently he orders a lot of stuff online. The driver looked in the window and saw him lying on the floor."

She shivered. "I'm glad I told Keith about my encounter with Mr. Tatton yesterday."

"Tell me about that again."

She thought for a moment. "Well, when he came to the door, he told me he didn't have to talk to me, and that if I didn't leave, he'd call the cops. So I left."

"And you didn't go inside."

"No, he slammed the door in my face."

"And what time was that again?"

"After I came back up from seeing Mrs. Conley in Hazel. I checked a couple other houses on Katherine's street, but the people weren't home. Tatton's was the last stop I made before I came here."

Bill checked something on his computer. "Must have been after three o'clock."

She nodded. "I didn't get back here until almost four."

"Okay, good. Keith will want to reconstruct Tatton's day."

"Should I tell him about the time?"

"Send him a text," Bill said.

"Right." Keith was a busy man, especially in the middle of a homicide case. She'd had his private number almost since she'd met him—over another dead body. Campbell quickly sent him a message giving the approximate time she'd talked to Tatton on Thursday.

Her father made several phone calls, one of which she could tell was to Nick. She only half listened as her dad patiently explained what he wanted Nick to do as a start on Jacob Gray's file. Campbell turned her attention back to Waverly's website and picked up the desk phone. Might as well give it a try.

"Hello?" said a male voice.

"Mr. Waverly?"

"That's right."

She swallowed hard and tried to sound cheerful but businesslike. "Hi. My name is Campbell McBride, and I'm a private investigator. I wondered if I could talk to you about Katherine Tyler. You represent her, don't you?"

"Well, yes, but I can't talk to you about my clients."

"Oh, I just wanted to get a little general information," Campbell said. "You've worked with Ms. Tyler for a long time now—ten years or more?"

"That's right," he said. "Look, I can't verify your identity over the phone, and I'm not comfortable with this."

"I'm sorry. Your business email is on your website. I can send you a link to True Blue Investigations. My father, Bill McBride, is the owner, and I work with him."

"Uh, okay, but that doesn't mean I can discuss a client."

"I understand. But I wondered why she left her former publishing house and went to Krata Press."

"That's not something I can tell you. Have you tried contacting Ms. Tyler directly? If she wants you to know that stuff, she'll tell you."

Campbell winced.

"Look, I'm very busy," he said before she could speak again. "Goodbye."

She stared at the receiver. "He hung up on me. Dad, he hung up on me!"

Bill looked over and raised his eyebrows. "You win some, you lose some."

She got the feeling he'd been on the receiving end of a lot of rudeness in this job. "So what do I do now?"

"Nothing. Did you get anything out of him?"

"She's still his client of at least ten years. Period."

"Okay, give it a rest. If something important turns up, you can try him again."

"Maybe I should have told him her next-door neighbor was attacked."

"No, I don't think so. But the folks at Krata Press may be more willing to talk to us than Random House was. They're small and eager, and Katherine is probably their new star."

"Yeah," Campbell said. "We could ask them if she has something new coming out this year."

"You call them," Bill said. "You can pose as a blogger. Katherine must have a lot of fans out there, and you want to be able to tell them she's not done writing. Something like that."

"Okay," Campbell said, but she didn't feel confident with misrepresenting herself. Before she could ask him a question, her cell phone pinged. She picked it up and found a new text from Keith. "Dad—"

"Yeah?"

"Keith says Tatton was DOA. He died on the way to the hospital." She gazed at him bleakly.

The office phone rang. Her father scowled at the interruption but quickly squelched the expression as he reached for the receiver.

"Bill McBride. Oh, hello, Ms. Harrison." He gave Campbell a meaningful look.

She sat back and listened to him give his report on their work so far. He filled her in on Campbell's visit to Doris Conley and the minister, and their limited success with the neighbors.

"There's one other thing I should tell you," he said. "Ms. Tyler's next-door neighbor Benjamin Tatton has been killed." After a pause, he said, "We're not sure. Sometime between three o'clock yesterday, when my daughter talked to him, and noon today. The police are handling it."

He listened for several minutes, making reassuring comments, and finally said, "All right, we will. But after close of business today, we won't be back in the office again until Monday. I'll call you if anything urgent comes up. Okay." He hung up and swiveled toward Campbell. "She wants us to keep working on it, at least for another day. And she's more worried than ever about her aunt, in light of Tatton's death."

"I can't blame her," Campbell said. "An older woman living alone, and her nearest neighbor's been murdered."

"She's hoping we can check on Katherine personally to be sure she's okay, or get the police to do it. I'll call Keith and ask if they've contacted her."

Campbell wished she'd thought of it. If one of her relatives was in a situation like that, she'd want to know too.

A few minutes later, Bill hung up the phone and turned his chair toward her. "Keith says canvassing the neighbors was one of the first things they did. He personally saw both Rita Henry and Ms. Tyler this afternoon. He said Katherine looked pale but otherwise okay."

"That's a relief."

Bill nodded. "Ms. Henry will stay with her longer than she normally does on a Friday, just to keep her company while the neighborhood is full of cops. Ms. Tyler doesn't want to have to answer the door, so she's paying Ms. Henry extra to stay into the evening."

"That sounds like something she'd do," Campbell said. "Although, I'm a little surprised she'd pay extra if money's tight."

"We're not sure that it is," Bill reminded her. "Keith said they'll keep a patrol car in the neighborhood tonight. And, Campbell, they think Tatton may have been attacked last night."

"He lay there all night, bleeding?"

"Apparently so. It's a good thing Nick's back on the job. It sounds like the two of us will be busy on this."

"What about that missing heir he was looking for?"

"Oh, he found the guy already, out in Texas." Bill grinned. "I'm telling you, Nick's sharp. He's got that one all wrapped up except for turning in the report. As soon as I get it from him, I'll pass it on to the lawyer and send a bill."

Campbell couldn't help being impressed. When she first met Nick, she may have thought she was smarter than him. Now she knew they were smart in different ways.

Without high expectations, she called Krata Press. The switchboard operator put her through to a woman named Celeste Dunford. When Campbell explained she was seeking background information on Katherine Tyler, Ms. Dunford went into a positive spiel about how glad the company was to have the famous author on board. Her tone sounded a bit wary, however.

"Can we expect a new release from Ms. Tyler soon?" Campbell asked.

"I'm told she's hard at work on her next book, but I don't see a publishing date on the schedule yet."

"Is that unusual?"

After a telling pause, Ms. Dunford said, "Not really. With

someone as established as Ms. Tyler, we work with her on things like the delivery date."

"I see. Krata has only published one book by Ms. Tyler so far. Is that correct?"

"Uh, yes."

Campbell frowned. "Would it be possible for me to speak to the editor who worked with her on that project?"

"One moment."

After a pause of at least twenty seconds, a woman said, "Hello, Inez Jasper."

Campbell scribbled the name on a memo sheet. "Hi. I'm calling about Katherine Tyler. I understand you worked with her on *Ice Cold Blue*."

"That's right."

"Could I get a little information on Ms. Tyler and her latest project?"

"I'm afraid not right now."

"Oh," Campbell said. "Should I call back at a more convenient time?"

"No, I'm not able to give out any information on that right now. It's still in the very early stages."

"I see. But Krata Press has issued her a contract for her next book?"

"I believe we have first refusal on her next project."

"Oh. Is there anything you can tell me about it?"

"No, nothing."

"How did you like working with Ms. Tyler?"

"I'm sorry, but I'm extremely busy right now. I'm afraid I need to get back to work."

"Okay. Well, thank—" Campbell realized she was talking to empty air and hung up. She looked over at her father. "Well, that was productive. Not."

Bill smiled and paused his typing. "Did you get anything at all?"

Campbell replayed Ms. Jasper's words carefully in her head.

"She said they have first refusal on Katherine's next project. I think that means Krata hasn't actually contracted it. Not yet, anyway."

Bill's eyebrows lowered. "Why not?"

"They want to see the manuscript before committing. But I imagine in her last contract, the one for *Ice Cold Blue*, they had some kind of clause that locked them in as publishers of her next book, provided they like it."

"So they could turn it down."

"Right. And it's been three years since the last one came out. Longer than that since she handed it over to them."

Bill gave a low whistle. "Sounds like Ms. Tyler has writer's block."

KEITH FULLER RETURNED to the police station Saturday morning after a meeting with the medical examiner. He didn't like what he'd heard, and he wasn't sure how to proceed. This was supposed to be a day off for him, but he didn't want to lay aside the investigation.

"What have you got?" he asked as officer Mel Ferris approached his desk. Ferris was considered one of the more expert computer techs in the department. Their budget didn't run to an officer who concentrated on the tech end of things, but maybe they should change that, with the rapid growth of online scams and other cybercrimes.

"Tatton had a lot of information on his computer about Ms. Tyler, but I'm not sure that's relevant."

"What kind of information?" Keith asked.

Ferris shrugged. "He'd bookmarked articles about her, going back several years, and some interviews and information about her book releases and so on. But he may have just been fascinated by the fact that he lived next door to a celebrity, you know?"

"Mmm. Maybe. He did do some chores for her occasionally."

"Yeah, the team found notes of times she paid him to do stuff."

"Oh? I thought he was just doing it out of neighborliness."

"Maybe for small things, but she paid him now and then for particular jobs. He was very meticulous in his record keeping. Last winter, she gave him small checks for snow removal, and once he took down a tree in her back yard."

"I'm surprised she didn't call professionals for that," Keith said.

"It must not have been a very big tree."

"Or maybe she just doesn't like people she doesn't know coming around her property," Keith said.

Ferris shot him a dark look. "She'll have to get someone else now."

REAGAN BRADY OPENED the door to Mart's house in Bowling Green and grinned at Campbell. The twenty-year-old had short, dark hair and brown eyes, and she wore shorts, a red WKU T-shirt, and flipflops.

"Campbell!" she squealed and launched herself into Campbell's arms.

"Hey. Long time no see."

"You're not just a-kidding!" Reagan disentangled herself. "Uncle Bill, how ya doing?"

Bill gave her a hug. "I'm good, kiddo. Where's your dad?"

"He's out back starting the grill. Come on in. Jas and Tony are here too."

"Oh, good," Campbell said as they walked through the house to the patio door. "That means I get to hug Marcus too."

"If you can catch him," Reagan said. "He's in the wriggly stage."

They emerged into the bright sunlight of the back yard and

greeted Mart Brady and Jasmine, his middle daughter, along with her husband, Tony Caxton, and their toddler. Campbell scooped Marcus up into her arms, but he immediately fussed and squirmed so much she set him down again.

"Yep, he's wriggly all right."

Reagan laughed. "Told you."

The three young women caught up on what was happening in their lives while they prepared the salad and side dishes for lunch and set the picnic table.

"So you've stopped looking for a job?" Reagan asked.

Campbell shrugged. "For now. Dad wants me to stay on with him."

"Do you like it?" Jas asked, catching Marcus's hand before he could snatch the mustard bottle from the edge of the table.

"So far, it's fascinating. But we'll see. Once the novelty wears off, I may decide it's not what I want to do for the rest of my life."

"You want to go back to teaching?"

"No. Not yet, anyway. Teaching is a good thing, but ... I don't know how to explain it, but I feel like this may be a better fit for me."

"You saved your dad's life," Reagan said.

"Well, I had a lot of help. But we also solved a couple of murders. That makes me feel good."

Jas nodded. "You brought those families some closure."

"Yeah. And now I realize how important that is." The memory of the days when she nearly despaired of ever knowing her father's fate hit her like an icy wind. "Still, solving murders on my first try may have been a fluke."

"You'll get to work on a lot of interesting cases, I'm sure." Jasmine put a stuffed toy in Marcus's pudgy hand, and he threw it on the floor.

"So how's that cute investigator, Nick Emerson, doing?" Reagan asked.

Campbell laughed. Trust Reagan to bring her out of the doldrums. "You knew he was injured?"

"Yeah, Dad told me all about it when he came home from Murray."

"Well, Nick's doing fine now," Campbell said. "He's still on medical leave, but Dad gave him some homework for this weekend on two missing persons cases. He's already solved one. The plan is for him to come back full time on Monday."

"Great." Reagan's bright smile made Campbell wonder if her interest in Nick went beyond his health.

"Burgers are ready," Mart called from the grill.

His son-in-law carried a platter of meat over to the table. Bill and Mart joined them, and they sat down to continue the lively chatter as they ate. A large patio umbrella shaded the table, but the sun's rays grew hotter by the minute. After they finished eating, they moved inside where it was cooler.

"Your life sounds very exciting, Uncle Bill," Reagan said. "Dad complains that he doesn't have enough to do since he retired. Maybe he should come work with you over there."

Mart laughed ruefully. "I can only take so much fishing and puttering around the house."

"Do you regret retiring?" Campbell asked.

"Not really, but some days I wish I had something to dig into."

"You should start your own agency," Bill said.

"Oh, I don't know. You moved away from this burg because there wasn't enough business."

"There were two other private investigators in town then. There weren't any in Murray at the time."

"And now you've hired on an assistant."

"Two," Bill corrected him. "Campbell's full time now."

"I thought you loved teaching," Tony said.

"I did." Campbell gave a little shrug, "But I got downsized, and now I'm finding out I love investigating even more."

Bill looked over at Mart. "Didn't you tell me Bob Prentiss is out of the business now, Mart? I bet there's enough work for another P.I. here."

"Maybe."

"Well, it took me three years solo to get up enough trade to hire Nick," Bill noted. "We're doing pretty well now. This summer, things are booming."

"I think it was all the publicity we got from finding you and solving Darrin Beresford's murder," Campbell told him.

Mart nodded. "I think you're right."

"A year ago, half my clients were insurance companies and another forty percent were lawyers," Bill said. "But we've had three new private clients since Campbell came home."

She smiled at her father. That sounded good. And the little house in Murray felt like home now too.

Soon Campbell and Bill said reluctant goodbyes to their friends and drove to a florist's shop and then to the cemetery. Bill parked in the grassy lane nearest the family plot, and they carried their bouquets to where the McBride headstone stood.

Precisely etched lettering on the rosy pink granite declared her mother's name, birth and death dates. A painful lump formed in Campbell's throat. She couldn't ignore the empty space that would one day bear her father's name. She'd come so close to losing him a few weeks ago. Now she knew she could survive if her father died. Faith and people like the Brady family would help her through it. But she didn't want to have to face that for a long, long time.

Bill stooped and laid his bouquet of roses on the grass at the foot of the stone. With tears in her eyes, Campbell added her daffodils and ferns and reached for her dad's hand. They stood for a long moment together. He squeezed her hand, and a tear rolled down his cheek.

"I miss her every day," Campbell whispered.

He made a small sound in his throat and nodded. She put her arm around him, and they turned toward the car.

7

The choir was just finishing a rousing hymn when Keith's phone vibrated in his pocket. He eased it out and glanced at it, holding it below the back of the pew in front of him. The dispatcher was sending him an urgent summons.

With a sigh, he picked up his Bible and slipped into the aisle and out the door of the church. He was supposed to have most Sundays off, but sometimes every officer was needed. He'd also left instructions to be contacted if anything new came in on one of his active cases.

Several yards from the building, he called in.

"There's a 10-50 out in the county," the dispatcher told him. "The sheriff's office responded, but you may want to communicate with them. The vehicle is registered to a person you had contact with recently."

Keith strode toward his SUV while getting as many details about the crash as he could. Sitting in his vehicle, he called Deputy Morton, the chief investigator of the accident.

"They're putting her in the ambulance now," Morton reported, sounding a bit overwhelmed. "Look, the tow truck's just getting here, and I've got to go give them instructions. You can come out here if you want, but there won't be much to see by the time you get here."

"Did the car go through the guardrail on the bridge?" Keith asked.

"No, it seems like the driver missed it on the approach and went down the embankment pretty fast. Must have been distracted."

"Any witnesses?"

"No, which makes me think it may have happened in the dark. Poor night vision added to a distraction—maybe a deer ran across the road or something."

"Okay," Keith said. "I'll call you later. Thanks."

Not good. Not good at all.

AFTER CHURCH, Campbell and Bill went home to eat the beef stew she'd put in the slow cooker the night before. As they finished up their lunch and discussed their plans for work the next day, Bill's cell phone rang.

"Xina," he said in an upbeat voice as he answered it. "What's up? No, that's okay. Campbell's here with me. May I put you on speaker so she can hear too?"

He pressed the button, and Xina's voice came into the room, higher pitched than normal.

"I wasn't sure, with the time zone change. Anyway, I know you're not working today, but I wanted to tell you that I'll be over there tomorrow. I plan to leave here first thing in the morning, and I should reach Murray by suppertime."

"Has something happened?" Bill asked.

"Yes. The police just called me. It appears Aunt Katherine's had an accident. She's in the hospital."

Bill met Campbell's startled gaze. "What kind of accident?" Campbell asked.

"A car wreck. She'd gone out this morning, and apparently

she lost control on her way home. After the police called I spoke with the hospital staff. As her next of kin, I need to be there, so I've arranged for the week off."

"Is she in the hospital at Murray?" Bill asked.

"Yes, at least for now. They said she might be transferred to Nashville, but they're not sure yet. I plan to call them again in the morning, before I set out. I don't want to drive all the way over there and then find that she's in Nashville and I have to backtrack two hours."

"Right," Bill said. "What can we do for you, Xina?"

"I've got some loose ends to tie up here today, or I'd be on the road now. I guess maybe talk to Detective Fuller and see if you can get more details?"

"Sure," Bill said. "We'll call you if we get anything you should know."

"Thank you, Bill. If they keep her in Murray, I hope I'll be able to stay at her house, but that's not certain at this point. I'm going to try to reach her attorney, just to be clear, but I may not be able to get in touch with him until tomorrow. I plan to go straight to the hospital unless something else comes up, and I'll call you when I arrive."

Bill closed the call and sat looking at Campbell for a moment.

"Wow," Campbell said.

"Yeah."

"Don't you think it's odd that she had a massive car crash two days after her next-door neighbor was killed?"

Bill reached for his coffee cup. "I don't know. Maybe she had the wreck *because* of it. She might have been upset by the news, and it distracted her."

"I suppose. Maybe we should try to talk to Rita Henry and see what she knows."

"It's Sunday. She may not know anything yet." He sipped his coffee.

"Well, we should definitely talk to Keith."

"You call him. Find out exactly where the accident was and who the responding officers were. See if he knows any more about Katherine's condition or where she went in the car. Didn't the neighbors tell you she didn't drive often?"

"They did. So, what are you going to do?" Campbell rose and collected their dirty dishes.

"I'm going to go see Nick and try to help him with the work I gave him on the Gray case. We may need him on this tomorrow."

After starting the dishwasher, Campbell called Keith. He answered right away, and she asked him about Katherine's accident, writing down the details he gave her.

"Xina Harrison will be back over here by tomorrow evening," she told him.

"That's good, I guess. Campbell, there's something else about Tatton. I know you and Bill are taking it easy this weekend, and I didn't want to bother you, but you should probably know about this."

A lump of dread settled in her chest. "What is it?"

"He wasn't just hit over the head. We haven't told the press, but he was stabbed too."

"What? That's crazy!"

"Not really," Keith said. "The examiner thinks he was probably brained first, but that didn't kill him. Then he was stabbed with a big knife."

"How big? Like a butcher knife?"

"Maybe. Or a large hunting knife. We'll know more after the autopsy, but that's the gist of the preliminary report."

She shuddered. "Somebody really wanted to make sure he was dead."

"I'd say so."

"Thanks for telling me." She almost wished he hadn't, but they needed to get as many facts as they could. When they'd ended the call, she stood there for a long moment, thinking. She didn't envy Xina, staying next door to the murder victim's house.

THE MCBRIDES HAD BARELY UNLOCKED the office door Monday morning when a call came in from Xina. Bill put her on speaker.

"I contacted Katherine's attorney this morning," Xina said. "I had his number on my copy of the medical document my aunt made a decade ago. He confirmed that I'm still her medical power of attorney."

"Okay, good." Bill wrote down the name of the local law firm.

"I didn't tell him about how she acted last week when I went to her house," Xina said.

"Probably a good idea."

"I thought so. He saw no reason why I shouldn't use the house while I'm in town. I set out a couple of hours ago, and I just stopped for gas. I'll be there by five if all goes well."

"One of us will go talk to the housekeeper." Bill gave her the limited information they'd gotten from Keith that morning on Katherine's condition. "Basically, nothing's changed. She hasn't regained consciousness, and they did surgery to remove her spleen and close up the cuts. For now, she's still in Murray. If we hear anything major, we'll call you. Drive safely, and we'll see you later."

When Bill had hung up, Campbell said, "How likely is it she'll stay in the local hospital? They took Nick to Paducah first thing."

"I don't know. Serious cases usually go up there or over to Nashville. Maybe they just don't want to move her because of her injuries. I got the impression there was a good surgeon in the hospital when she arrived. Maybe that influenced the decision to operate there."

They hashed over their assignments for the morning. As a result, Campbell was sitting in her car in Katherine's driveway at nine, when Rita Henry showed up for work. No patrol car graced the Tatton driveway next door, but yellow crime scene tape was fixed across the front steps.

Campbell walked over as the housekeeper got out of her car.

"You're the private investigator," Rita said with a frown.

"Yes. Campbell McBride." She extended her hand, and Rita took it. "Did you know that Ms. Tyler was in a car accident this weekend?"

"The police called me. They wanted to know if I knew where she'd gone, and what time. I hadn't been here since Friday evening, and I couldn't help them. But they said I should come here as usual today, since her next of kin would be arriving this evening."

"They're talking about her niece, Xina Harrison," Campbell said.

"I've never met her, but I understand she was here last week."

"She's very nice."

Rita's features clouded. "She's the one who hired you to come to the house and ask about Katherine?"

"Because she was concerned about her aunt." Campbell watched her face as she went on. "Ms. Harrison has been in touch with Ms. Tyler's attorney, and we believe, as next of kin, she has every right to stay here in order to be near her aunt while she's in the hospital."

"Katherine told me Thursday not to let her in if she came back here."

Campbell swallowed hard. "I'm sorry to hear that. Xina often stayed with her in the past. The lawyer told Xina yesterday that she has a right to be here, and she could get keys to the house from you."

"I'm ... I'm not sure I should." Rita's brown eyes surveyed her gravely.

Campbell pushed down her frustration. "I understand, and you're right to want to know everything's the way it should be." She held out a slip of paper. "This is Ms. Tyler's attorney's number. Xina Harrison has copies of the documents Ms. Tyler filed with him several years ago, giving her authority in this situation. You can call him and double check if you want."

Gingerly, Rita took the square of paper.

"Since Ms. Tyler is unconscious, it's impossible to know exactly what she wants right now, but she did leave official instructions," Campbell went on. "As I said, Xina Harrison has her medical power of attorney. The lawyer can confirm that for you if you want. Legally, it's up to Xina to make sure her aunt gets the best care."

Rita nodded slowly. "I thought this past week that Katherine was acting a little funny."

"How do you mean?"

"She left the door to her office open, and I saw her pacing in there. That would be Monday, a week ago today. I usually come Monday, Wednesday, and Friday. But last week she asked if I could do a few hours on Thursday."

Campbell frowned. "The day I came here was Thursday."

"Yes. Normally, I wouldn't have been here. She said people had been coming to the door and she wanted me to tend to it if anyone came. She didn't want to be bothered."

"The police came here Thursday morning on a wellness check."

"I knew there was something." Rita shook her head. "That must be when she called me to see if I could come over—after the police had come. I wasn't here when her niece came. When I got here Thursday, I asked Katherine if everything was all right. She said she was fine, but that her niece had for some strange reason asked the local constabulary to check on her."

"Did she tell you Xina had been here the night before?" Campbell asked as they walked up onto the porch.

Rita fitted her key into the front door lock. "Not then, no. But Friday afternoon the police were back, and they said Ben Tatton was injured. They'd called an ambulance, and they asked me to stay with Katherine until they were done investigating at his house, so I did. That's when I learned the niece had been here Wednesday night. The detective mentioned it."

She swung the door open and led Campbell inside and to the kitchen. Campbell noted the gloomy interior and the outdated furnishings.

"How late did you stay Friday?"

"Hmm, let's see, the cops left, all but one, around eight. They'd said they would leave a patrolman at the scene all night, so there was a car in Ben's driveway. Katherine told me to go home, and that she was perfectly safe with a cop outside, within earshot if she decided to scream. She laughed about it, but I didn't think it was funny. I admit I looked over my shoulder when I went out to my car."

"Someone told me she didn't like to drive much anymore."

"That's right," Rita said. "Now and again she'd go shopping. Mostly she had me do it, though. I'd go to the post office for her too."

"I see. How was her general attitude last week?"

"She's been a little snippy lately."

"What do you mean?" Campbell asked.

Rita winced. "Hard to explain. A little more brisk, and she didn't want to talk Friday. Pretty much avoided me the whole time I was here. She sat in the parlor, watching out the window after the police told us about Ben Tatton. When I served her supper, the police were still at Ben's house, but we hadn't heard any more. She was quiet. Sometimes she's like that—very uncommunicative, which is kind of strange for a writer."

Campbell looked over at the sink, but it was spotless, with no dishes waiting for attention. She remembered the fingerprints the police had lifted from a coffee mug when her father was missing. "Does she do her own dishes on the weekend?"

"She loads the dishwasher."

"Is there anything else out of place?"

Rita's eyes narrowed. "Let me look around."

She walked slowly through the downstairs rooms, scanning

the floors and other surfaces. "I don't notice anything," she reported.

"What about the trash? When did you last empty it?"

"I always do it Wednesday. They pick up Thursday morning. Sometimes she brings the can back to the house, but usually I do it first thing Friday. Only I was here last Thursday afternoon, so I brought it in then, after the garbage truck was here. It's in the garage now."

"Okay." Campbell made a mental note to mention this to her dad, in case he thought it was worth pursuing. Probably not.

"I was pretty distracted Friday," Rita said. "I was thinking about Ben Tatton being killed, and the police coming here, and wondering why the niece had sent them the day before to check on Katherine. And, to be honest, why Katherine hadn't let her stay here. As far as I know, she'd always gotten along with this niece."

"That's our understanding too." Campbell pressed her lips together. They had only Xina's word for that. What if Katherine had something against her niece, something Xina hadn't told them?

"I wish I was here when she came Wednesday evening," Rita said.

Campbell's cell phone rang, and she looked at it. "It's my dad. He may have more information. Excuse me."

"Sure, go ahead." Rita opened the dishwasher and started taking clean dishes out and placing them in the cupboards.

"Hi, Dad, I'm with Rita Henry at Ms. Tyler's house. What's up?"

A moment later, she was able to tell Rita in a cheerful tone, "So, Ms. Harrison is on her way. She left home early, and she expects to be here by five o'clock. We wondered if you'd stay until she gets here and make sure she gets settled in?"

Rita shrugged. "I guess so. I'm usually here until five on Mondays, and I fix supper for Katherine. After I get her room ready, I could make a meal for Ms. Harrison and stay an extra hour."

"That should do it."

Rita glanced toward a door at the end of the countertop. "I guess her car's not out there now, huh?"

"Oh, is that the garage door?"

"Yeah." Rita trudged over to it and opened the door. "Yup, car's gone."

"May I?"

Rita stepped back, and Campbell looked into the one-car garage. She flipped the light switch near the door. The parking space was empty. Tools hung neatly along the far wall.

"That old car ran real good," Rita told her. "Like I said, she hardly ever took it out—never in bad weather. But it just purred."

"Does anything look out of place, other than the car being gone?" Campbell asked.

"Not that I can think of."

Campbell noted the position of the trash can, near the small man door that led outside. She turned off the light, stepped back, and closed the door.

Rita threw the deadbolt and turned to face her. "Do you know where the car is now?"

"The police no doubt had it towed after the accident."

"I suppose." Rita's face was pale, and she leaned against the counter. "This is all so bizarre. Do you know how she's doing? I called the hospital right after I heard, but they wouldn't tell me anything."

"My father just told me Ms. Tyler is still unconscious, but they've upgraded her condition to serious."

"That's good, right?"

"Yes, it is," Campbell said. "Last night she was in the critical category. I don't have details, though. I'm sorry. Maybe Ms. Harrison will be able to get a more complete update when she gets here."

"I just keep praying she'll get better."

"That's all we can do right now." Campbell gave her one of her new business cards. "This is the agency phone number, and I've written my cell phone on the back. You can reach me or my father, Bill McBride, anytime. Call us if you need help, or if anything happens to upset you."

"Like what?" Rita blinked at her.

"I don't know, but you've said yourself that some odd things have happened around here over the past few days. If you feel uneasy, don't hesitate to call the police or True Blue Investigations. I mean it. We're there for you if you need help or just want some reassurance."

"Okay."

"Thank you so much for your help, Rita." Campbell headed for the front door. On the way, she glanced into the living room and noted the Winslow Homer seascape hanging over the fireplace. She wouldn't have thought the print out of place if Xina hadn't told them about the substitution.

She turned back and looked at Rita, who stood in the kitchen doorway.

"Was that print over the fireplace here when you started working here?"

Rita walked toward her, frowning. "No, there was another picture. Something woodsy. She brought that home last fall and asked me to hang it for her."

"Do you know where the other one is now?"

"No. I haven't seen it since, and she hasn't said anything."

Campbell gave her a perfunctory smile. "Okay, thanks."

She turned toward the door and stopped short to stare at the umbrella stand.

"Uh, Ms. Henry?"

"It's Rita. What is it?"

"When I talked to you the other day, I saw a cane in that stand. One with a duck's head on it."

Rita came closer and peered at the stand, frowning. Today it held only a dark blue umbrella.

"That's odd."

"Would Ms. Tyler have taken it with her? Did she use it when she went out?"

"Oh, no. It was a family keepsake. It's been sitting there since I started working for her, and I dust it every week when I vacuum the hall."

Campbell met her gaze. "I'm pretty sure it was there Thursday. It caught my eye when we talked in the doorway."

Rita nodded. "I don't know what to say."

"Would you call me if it turns up?"

"All right."

Campbell hurried out to her car, thinking about the heirlooms and old furnishings Katherine had inherited with the house. She hoped Xina would stay long enough to do some sorting. Katherine had sold a painting. Had she sold other antiques? Where was that cane?

8

K eith strolled up the walk of the house directly across from Benjamin Tatton's, the fourth one he'd visited on the street that morning.

"Hi," he said when a gray-haired woman opened the door. "I'm Detective Fuller, with the Murray police. I wondered if I could talk to you for a few minutes about your neighbors."

"I heard Katherine Tyler's in the hospital," the woman said.

Keith always marveled at the speed of the neighborhood grapevine. "That's right, she is."

The woman swung the door wide. "You may as well come in. I'm Vera Hill. Coffee? I just made a fresh pot."

"That'd be great. Thank you."

She led him into her living room and waved toward the couch as she continued on to the kitchen. She returned a minute later with two steaming mugs and sat down in a velveteen-covered recliner.

"I wondered," she said. "I saw Katherine's car come out of her garage Saturday night around eight, but I never heard it come back."

"Were you watching for her?" Keith sipped his coffee. It was flavored—hazelnut, he guessed. Not his usual, but it was good.

"Not really," Mrs. Hill said. "But I did stay up until eleven. I was watching a movie. Our street's real quiet at night, and I think I'd have noticed, but I'm not sure."

"And you had no idea where she'd gone?"

She shook her head. "I thought maybe, if she was away overnight, she'd gone to one of those writers' conferences or something. She used to speak at them, but I hadn't heard anything like that lately. Or she might even have gone to visit that niece of hers that used to come round in the summer and on holidays. I'm not sure where she lives now, but I think I heard she'd moved back east from California."

"I know our people talked to you Saturday about Mr. Tatton's death," Keith said. "I wondered if you've remembered anything else that might help us."

"I don't think so. Ben was just ... Ben. He could be cantankerous, but he could be friendly too, when it suited him. Not my favorite person, but still, I can't imagine anyone killing him."

"Okay." It was a long shot. Keith took a big gulp of coffee.

Mrs. Hill waved a hand through the air. "He had a big dustup last fall with the folks who border him along his back fence."

"Oh?"

"Yeah. I think they were having a dispute over where the fence should be. No, that's not right." Her forehead furrowed. "A tree, that was it. Something about him taking down a tree. It hit the fence, I think. They wanted him to fix it."

Keith frowned. "I heard he took down a tree for Ms. Tyler."

She snapped her fingers. "That's it. Not his place, hers."

"Did he pay to fix the fence?"

"Somebody did." She eyed him darkly.

"You mean Ms. Tyler paid?"

"I don't know for sure, but it got done. How *is* Katherine? Have you heard anything this morning?"

"As far as I know, her condition hasn't changed. Still unconscious."

Mrs. Hill shook her head. "So tragic. I love her stories. Have you read any?"

"No."

"I used to buy every one of them and take them over and get her to autograph them for me. There hasn't been a new one for a while, though."

Keith wound things up and left as soon as he could. He drove around the block and calculated which house shared the fence with Katherine Tyler's back yard. When he rang the bell, a woman of about fifty opened the door.

Keith introduced himself and acknowledged Mrs. Barber's response. When he asked about the tree incident, she snorted.

"I told her to call a tree surgeon next time. Ben Tatton isn't —" She stopped and gulped. "Sorry. I heard yesterday he's dead."

"That's right, he is. I don't suppose you noticed any activity around his place Thursday night or Friday?"

"No." She looked down at the ground. "We hardly ever talk to him."

"And how long ago was the tree incident?"

"Oh, it was September last year, I think. Came right down on the fence and into our yard fifteen or twenty feet. Someone could have been killed." She looked up at him eagerly. "You want to see where it fell? It nearly hit our chair swing."

Keith followed her around the house into her back yard. He could see clearly where the new section of fence fitted with the old.

"Did Mr. Tatton pay for the repairs?" he asked.

"Ben? Oh, no! Miss Tyler paid. It was her tree, after all." Mrs. Barber set her lips in a grim line. "I told her. Get a tree surgeon. You get what you pay for, and that's the truth."

Keith gave her a card and his usual instructions to call if she thought of anything else pertinent. He walked back to his vehicle mulling the relationship between Katherine Tyler and her neighbors. They interacted, as neighbors usually did, though

Katherine seemed less outgoing and communicative than most people.

His canvassing wasn't turning up anything helpful in the Tatton murder case, and he'd found nothing that hinted at a connection between it and Katherine's accident.

He stopped by the station and sat at his desk for a few minutes, reviewing for the third time the medical examiner's preliminary report on Benjamin Tatton. Hit hard on the temple with a blunt instrument, breaking the skull. Why? Keith ran a hand through his hair. The Barbers' fence had been fixed, at no cost to them. That seemed to be the worst dispute Tatton had been involved in.

At this point, he had no suspects in the murder. Other than a few spats with neighbors over the years, his life seemed to hold little drama. Tatton had taken early retirement from a long career in insurance, and Keith had found nothing there.

The victim's family consisted of a sister and a couple of cousins locally. The sister had seemed sad but not overly shocked when told of Benjamin's death. The cousins had admitted he had a fractious disposition, but both claimed they hadn't seen him in weeks and had no personal quarrels with him. Nothing to go on.

Tatton also had an older brother in St. Louis, who had come across as angry when Keith phoned him. He blamed the police somehow for his brother's death and implied that the department's detectives weren't smart enough to find out who killed him. Keith had checked up on his activities and found there was no way he could have traveled to Murray at the right time to do in his brother.

Officer Ferris walked past Keith's workstation.

"Mel," he called.

Ferris stopped and leaned on the divider. "What's up?"

"Any word on Tatton's phone yet?"

"Nope."

The police hadn't gotten into the victim's password-protected phone. Some telephone companies were cagey about that, even in a murder case. Tatton's server had agreed to turn over their records if the family gave permission.

His sister had complied and signed a form, but so far the records hadn't come through. When asked, she said she didn't know Benjamin's password. His brother had acted offended when the question was put to him. Why on earth should he know the password for Benjamin's phone?

Would the brother come down from St. Louis for the funeral? That event promised to be a real joy, but it wouldn't happen until the coroner released the body. Keith let out a big sigh. At least they would have access to the phone and past phone records soon.

Could he squeeze out time to stop off at True Blue before lunch? He'd like to get Bill's perspective, and Campbell's too, when it came to that. Bill might have some insight, and Campbell was quite intuitive.

Just the thought of seeing her again made him smile. He couldn't remember when he'd felt so in tune with a woman. Keith gathered his notebook and keys and headed out the door. Losing her job in Iowa may have been a bad blow for Campbell, but he couldn't feel too sorry about it.

CAMPBELL WALKED into the office to find both Nick and her father kneeling on the floor with pieces of wood and tools spread out around them, in full furniture assembly mode.

"Oh, wow! My desk came."

"No, pieces of your desk came." Nick brandished a pack of screws in her direction. With his left arm still in a cast, he held a side piece of the desk in place through the pressure of leaning on it while Bill screwed it in place.

"We'll have this together in no time," Bill said.

Nick frowned at the Kroger bag she set on his desk. "What's that?"

"It's a peace offering. Barbecue chips. Consider yourself thanked for putting my desk together."

"What did you bring me?" her father asked.

"Lots of love and assurance that Xina will be welcome tonight. Rita will have her room and her supper ready."

"Good job," Bill said.

The door opened and Keith Fuller walked in.

"Hi." Campbell tried not to let her face show just how glad she was to see him, for fear Nick would tease her about it later.

"Well, it looks like I'm just in time to join the construction crew." Keith nodded at Nick. "Glad to see you back at work. How you doing?"

"All right, but I'll be better once we get this desk put together so Campbell has her own space."

Keith laughed. "Want me to take over?"

"Sure." Nick handed him the screws and stood.

"Almost done," Bill said. "So, what's up, Keith?"

"I'd like to hear your take on the Tatton murder."

Bill finished installing the runners for the desk's drawers and looked up at him. "Let's tip this up, eh?"

They righted the desk, and Keith reached for one of the drawers.

"I'm not sure what's going on," Bill said.

"Well, I don't think it was a random intruder." Keith squinted as he fitted the drawer into place. "No sign of forced entry, and the weapons were removed."

Bill grunted. "Any updates on Ms. Tyler's condition?"

"The doctors don't know if she'll survive." Keith's shoulders sagged.

"I thought she was stable," Campbell said.

Keith shook his head. "A call came in just as I was leaving the station. Turn for the worse, and her blood pressure's up. I wish she could answer some questions for us."

"I hope Xina doesn't get here and find out she's passed away." Campbell looked to her dad for assurance.

"It's in God's hands," Bill said.

She shot up a silent prayer for Katherine, and for a safe journey on Xina's behalf.

"There!" Her father lumbered to his feet. "How about we park this thing between my desk and Nick's, at an angle?"

"We might have to move mine over a little." Nick walked around his desk and shoved it a foot across the wood floor with his hip.

Bill gritted his teeth. "Easy on the finish, kid. You've got people here to help you lift stuff like that."

He and Keith positioned Campbell's new desk, and Bill brought over the chair they used for visitors. She sat down and opened her laptop on the desk. "Thanks, guys. This feels official."

Bill laughed and started picking up his tools. "We'll have to get you a good chair."

"I ordered one already." She gave him a guilty smile. "I asked them to assemble it before we pick it up too."

"Good. One more thing off my list," Bill said.

"You want coffee, Keith?" Nick asked.

"Sure." Keith went to the coffee station with him, and the two poured out their brew.

Doctoring his mug one-handed, Nick told him about the case he was working on for the insurance company. "And when we finish that, we've got to find a guy's missing daughter."

Keith raised his eyebrows. "Wow, you folks are busy."

"We are," Bill said. "I think it's going to work out, though. Especially if people like you keep sending us clients."

The office seemed a little small with the extra desk and four people in it. Campbell opened her browser and brought up her package tracker.

"Oh, Dad, it looks like the boxes Steve shipped me have been delivered."

"Not that Steve guy." Nick rolled his eyes and took a gulp of his coffee.

"Cut it out," Campbell said.

Her father jumped to her defense. "Yeah, Steve is just a friend."

"Sure, sure." Nick turned away with a sneaky smile.

Campbell shook her head in exasperation. Nick said things all the time just to get her riled. She was getting tired of it, especially when Keith was within earshot.

The detective was watching her, his brown eyes full of speculation—which was what Nick was aiming at, she was sure.

She sighed and glared at Nick. "I left a couple boxes of books with him when I came home, and now he's shipped them to me. That's all."

"Whatever you say, Campbell."

Nick's knowing smile infuriated her.

"That was fast," Bill said.

"Yeah, it was." Campbell was grateful to her dad for turning her attention away from Nick. "I'd better run home and take them inside."

"Why don't you and Keith go take care of it?" Bill said, ambling to the coffeemaker. "Stop on your way back for some burgers for the four of us."

"It's too early for lunch," Campbell said, throwing Keith a wary glance.

"Thanks, but I need to get back to the station," he said. "If you need help, though, I could swing by your house first."

"I can handle two cartons of books," she said, though she remembered regretting she'd packed them so full when she'd taken the heavy boxes to Steve's apartment.

"I don't mind."

Campbell shrugged, hoping she didn't look too eager—not that she minded Keith knowing she wanted to spend more time with him, but with Nick standing right there, she was in for a lot of future ribbing, for sure.

"Let's go, then." She grabbed her purse and led him out to the parking lot.

Keith hopped into his SUV and followed her the mile and a half to the house. When she got out, the two cartons, a bit worse for wear, sat on the front porch. Keith bounded up the steps and picked up the larger one while Campbell unlocked the door.

"Thanks." She picked up the second box, carried it inside, and set it on the coffee table.

"Where do want this one?" Keith asked.

"Oh, right there on the floor is fine."

"Didn't have room for these when you packed to come home?"

"Yeah, my car was stuffed full, so this friend told me I could leave a few things." She shoved her hair back. "If I remember correctly, I have a few of Katherine Tyler's novels in one of these boxes."

"You were a fan before this all started?"

She nodded. "Can I get you some iced tea?"

"No, I really do need to get going." Keith hesitated, as though he'd actually rather stay where he was than go back to work. "Listen, I probably shouldn't tell you this, but we've accessed Tatton's computer files. He has a lot of old articles about Katherine Tyler archived."

Campbell shrugged. "So do I, since I've been researching her continuously since Thursday."

"But you're being paid to find out about her."

"Yeah." She puzzled over it for a moment. "I don't know what to think about that."

"Me either. But it's one more link between them, besides the chores he did for her." He smiled. "Can I call you later?"

"Sure. I'd like that."

"Good," Keith said. "We've both been so busy the last couple weeks ..."

"Too busy."

"Maybe we'll get in that hike at Land Between the Lakes sometime."

They'd mentioned the possibility before.

"I'd like that, if we ever get the same day off." She walked with him to the door. "I'm going to open those cartons before I go back to the office." She laughed. "Not that I have anywhere to shelve the books. Guess the next thing I need to put together is a bookcase."

Keith smiled. "Let me know if you need help with that."

"Okay. Thanks." Campbell watched him hurry to his SUV. He turned to wave, and she lifted her hand and smiled.

She reluctantly closed the door and went to her father's desk for a pair of scissors. One box was so beat up, it seemed only her generous packing tape job held it together in transit. She knew the larger box held her textbooks, a few favorite classics, some teaching methods books, and half a dozen literature anthologies. Leaving them for a later time, she turned to the second box. It was filled with contemporary novels, and she rummaged through it to locate Tyler's books.

"Thought so." She pulled out one with a satisfied nod and riffled to the title page. "Nope." She skipped over to the back material. "Aha." *Acknowledgements* read the header for a full page of text. She skimmed through it for a moment, then grabbed her purse and pulled out her notebook and a pen.

She glanced at the clock. Still too early for lunch. Five minutes later, she was back at True Blue, and she carried the novel inside and strode to her dad's desk.

Bill's eyes widened. "What's this?"

"One of Katherine's earlier books. It was in my box. In the acknowledgements, she names not only her agent, but the editor who worked on it and a researcher who did some digging for her, to find information she needed."

"Good."

"Not just good. Dad, I think it's the same researcher Xina mentioned, and I think he could be local. This book takes place in southern Illinois."

His eyebrows twitched. "You got a name?"

"Lee Dorman."

"Male or female?"

She shrugged. "I couldn't tell from the comment."

"I guess you know what to do next," Bill said.

"I sure do." Campbell sat down and opened her laptop on her new desk.

9

C ampbell jotted down a few items on a fresh page of her notebook as a shopping list for their supper.

"Do you want salad with that, Dad?"

Bill pushed back his chair. "How about some broccoli or something?"

"Okay, sure."

"Here, give me the list and I'll go to the store. You go on home." He looked over at Nick. "How about you? Do you want to join us for supper?"

"No, thanks," Nick said. "I've got a date."

"Whoa." Campbell eyed him carefully. "Anyone I know?"

"Doubt it. I just met her Saturday."

"She must have been at your gaming group," Bill said.

Campbell felt adrift, left out of something shared. "Gaming, as in a poker game?"

Nick smiled. "No, role playing games."

"Oh, okay." He was out of the adolescent phase she'd relegated him to when she first met him, but she hadn't realized he was still into things like that. A lot of her college students had formed gaming groups—a waste of time, to her way of thinking.

"It's fun. You should try it." Nick snapped his laptop shut and stood.

"I'll see you at home," Bill said. "Don't stay out too late, Nick."

"Don't worry. I'll put in a full day tomorrow." He gathered some papers into a folder and laid it on top of his computer case.

"So, do you play every week?" Campbell asked.

"Usually. Last weekend was the first time I'd been since I got out of the hospital."

She nodded. "You must be feeling pretty good."

"I'm back to normal. And my friends brought me pizza and doughnuts at the hospital, so I had to go back as soon as I could. We're meeting at my place this week."

"Well, I hope tonight goes well."

Just for a second, Nick looked uncertain. "Yeah. She's a nice girl. I mean, as far as I know."

Was he thinking it could be awkward at the next gaming session if the date went awry?

"Be yourself," Campbell said, though Nick's persona wouldn't attract her personally. "And let her talk."

He scowled at her. "What? I don't let people talk?"

She chuckled. "I'm not saying that. Just try to listen as much as you talk on the first date."

"Is that what you did with Steve?"

She snatched up a rubber cow eraser she'd brought from Iowa and threw it at him. "Steve was never my boyfriend." There'd been two dates before the semester and her job ended, but no way was she admitting that now. And she *had* let him talk about himself. If Steve had seemed like the right man, she'd have kept in closer touch with him since her return to Kentucky.

Nick laughed and picked up the little blue cow. "Take it easy, Professor. I'm glad you didn't hit me in the eye with this. And that's no bull." He tossed it over onto her desk, where it bounced and came to rest beside her laptop.

Torn between apologizing and snapping back at him,

Campbell clenched her teeth. Finally she let out a big sigh. The cow eraser was something Steve had picked up at a farming showcase they'd browsed on their second date.

"Look, we'll be working together a lot now. I'll try not to lose my temper at you. In return, could you lay off the jabs about Steve?"

"Sure. But I reserve the right to tease you about Keith."

She glared at him.

Nick gave her a smug smile. "And you can come to my RPG group any Saturday you want."

"No thanks." She wished she had a poetry reading or a book club to invite him to in retaliation—anything in stark contrast to his Dungeons and Dragons or whatever. But she hadn't been in town long enough to find one of those. Besides, knowing Nick, he might accept just to annoy her.

"Okay. Well, I'm heading out. You locking up?"

"Sure." She checked the time. Her dad had a short shopping list, and if she didn't get out of here, he'd beat her home. As she stood, the desk phone rang, and she snatched the receiver. "True Blue."

"It's Xina Harrison."

"Oh, hi, Xina." Campbell sank back into her chair.

"Just wanted you to know I'm here. Rita Henry let me in and showed me to the guest room. Looks like she's got a nice supper waiting for me, and the fridge is stocked for breakfast. She'll be back on Wednesday to cook and clean. I told her to keep her regular schedule until we know what's going on with Aunt Katherine."

"Sounds good. Dad and I are done for the day. In fact, I was just about to leave the office. Did you want to get together?"

"Why don't I come there in the morning, if you have an opening. I'd like to go over to the hospital tonight. I was going to stop there first, but I was so tired I decided to come here and freshen up first. Rita's plying me with homecooked food."

"Sure, morning's fine," Campbell said. "Is nine convenient?"

"Perfect."

"Call one of our cell phones if there's any change, won't you? The last we heard from Detective Fuller about Ms. Tyler's condition was not very encouraging."

She'd barely gotten home and set the table when her father arrived with several grocery sacks.

"Hey," she said, "Xina's at Katherine's. She'll come to the office at nine in the morning."

"Good." Bill set the bags on the counter and pulled out a tray of pork chops. "Those look okay?"

"They look great."

Bill put the groceries away while Campbell cooked supper. They'd just sat down and asked the blessing when Campbell's cell phone rang.

"It's Xina. I'm sorry to bother you again so soon."

"Oh, no, it's fine." Campbell mouthed *Xina* to her dad across the table. "What is it?"

"It's just—I'm at the hospital, and they've got her in ICU. I guess you knew that. Anyway, she looks so awful."

"I'm sorry," Campbell said softly. "They haven't let us see her. They said family only."

"The on-call doctor spoke to me, and he said—" She sobbed. "Oh, Campbell, I shouldn't lay this on you, but I don't know anyone else in town. I knew she was unconscious, but—but he says it's a coma, and she may not ever come out of it."

"I'm so sorry. Maybe her regular doctor can tell you more tomorrow."

"Yes." Xina sobbed again. "They won't let me stay here all night. Twenty-minute visits they said, for all the good it does. She has no idea I'm here."

"You should go back to the house and rest."

"I suppose so. But I never sleep well in a new place, and that big old house creaks. I'm not sure I'll be able to relax, knowing the neighbor was murdered."

Campbell pulled in a deep breath. Her father didn't have an extra room to offer. Should she suggest a hotel?

"Would it help you if I came over there?" She looked helplessly at Bill.

"You'd do that? Could you stay at the house with me tonight? I'm sure I'd feel much better if I wasn't alone."

Campbell could see no reason not to commit. "Yes, I can stay."

Bill nodded to her and cut into his pork chop.

"There are just a couple of things I need to do here," Campbell said. "I'll be over by seven."

When she put the phone down, her father said, "Eat, honey. I'll do the dishes."

She sighed. "I was going to try to contact Bruce Waverly again. He may not know Katherine's been injured."

"Good thought. I can try to call him if you want, while you pack."

"I did speak to him before. He'll remember, and maybe he'll loosen up a little."

"Okay. By the way, dinner is delicious."

"Thanks, Dad."

Fifteen minutes later, she tried the literary agent's number. He picked up after three rings, and while she was glad, Campbell was hit by a splash of nervousness.

"Mr. Waverly, this is Campbell McBride. We spoke the other day."

"I told you, I can't give out any information about Katherine Tyler."

"I'm calling to give *you* information," she said. "Ms. Tyler has been badly injured in a car accident, and I thought you should know."

"Really? How awful. When did this happen?"

"Late Saturday or early Sunday. She's hospitalized in Murray, Kentucky, where she lives. She hasn't regained consciousness."

"I don't know what to say." Waverly's voice had picked up a tremor.

"Her niece is her next of kin," Campbell said. "She's staying at Katherine's house now, to be close to her. I can give you her telephone number if you'd like."

After a pause, he cleared his throat. "Yes, thank you. I should perhaps speak to a family member about her business arrangements. She was working on a project for Krata Press."

"We're aware of that." Campbell put as much confidence in her voice as she could. "I'm sure Ms. Harrison, her niece, would appreciate knowing the details and what the publisher expects. It might be good for one of you to inform the publisher of her accident."

"Yes. And royalty statements will be out soon. Is this niece able to handle her finances?"

"I believe so. Let me give you her contact information." Campbell gave him Xina's cell phone number and email address.

"Thank you," Waverly said. "I'll contact her first thing in the morning. Oh, and Ms. McBride, I'm sorry if I was curt when we spoke on Friday."

"It's all right. True Blue Investigations deals in client confidentiality as well, so I understood."

"You don't know if Ms. Tyler's current project is ready for me to look at, do you?"

"I'm sorry, I have no idea. I was at her house this morning, but that wasn't on my mind."

"And you didn't see any unfinished manuscripts or anything like that?"

"No. I imagine all of that is on her computer. Speak to her niece, but I honestly don't think Ms. Harrison knows about anything like that, either."

He thanked her and signed off. After summarizing the conversation for her father, Campbell went to her room to pack. She added minimal supplies and clothing to her overnight bag. Surely Xina wouldn't expect her to stay more than one night, and if she did, it wasn't far away. Campbell could dash home anytime to expand her wardrobe options.

Her cell phone rang, and she smiled when she saw Keith's name on the screen.

"Hi. You just caught me."

"Oh?" he asked.

"Yeah, I'm going over to Katherine Tyler's house. Xina wants me to spend the night with her. Big old, creepy house, you know?"

"Yeah, I know. Take care, will you?"

"I will."

"Listen, I was wondering ..." He paused.

She waited. Keith didn't usually hesitate to put things out there.

"Could we have dinner tomorrow night? If you're not too busy with Xina, I mean."

Campbell's pulse accelerated. "She should be settled in by then."

"If she's not, it's okay. I mean, I was going to ask you this weekend, but, hey, I don't want to wait that long."

Campbell didn't, either. She grinned at his eagerness. For the past week or two, she'd seen him in snippets, like sound bites on the news. She wanted to spend some leisurely time with Keith.

"Sure. I'd like that."

"Great." The tension had left his voice. "Can I pick you up at the house? Sixish?"

"Sounds wonderful."

Bill was closing the dishwasher when she entered the kitchen with her purse, laptop, and overnight bag. He walked over and placed a hand on her shoulder.

"I'm sure you'll be fine, Soup, but keep in mind Xina's afraid for a reason."

Campbell nodded soberly. "If we hear anything that can't be explained by old pipes or a temperamental air conditioning system, I'll call you or the cops, depending on how loud it is.

He chuckled. "Okay, but I'm serious. This isn't a pajama party you're going to. It might be good to distract Xina with upbeat stuff, but keep in mind you're acting as a bodyguard tonight."

Campbell shivered. "You can't think someone would attack Xina."

"Why can't I?"

"Well ..." She shrugged. "The attack was on Tatton, not Katherine."

"Yes, but a killer was in the neighborhood just a few days ago, and he struck only a few yards from where you and Xina will be sleeping."

His sinister declaration didn't boost her confidence.

"Should I stay awake all night?"

"I don't think that's necessary, but keep your wits about you." He huffed out a breath. "I'm going to put in an application for you to carry a concealed weapon."

"What? No, Dad. I don't need to carry a gun."

"How do we know?"

She gulped. "I guess we don't."

"Think about it. I'll reserve some time for us at the shooting range later in the week."

"I've never fired a handgun."

"You need to learn. If nothing else, you could have a pistol in your room at night. You don't need a permit for that."

"Okay." She wasn't sure she liked the idea. Maybe she should have taken that part-time teaching job after all.

He smiled. "See you at the office in the a.m.?"

"I'll probably be there by eight. We've got a lot to follow up on."

"Great." He leaned in and kissed her cheek. "Take care."

"You too."

10

"I hope you don't mind, I'm putting you in Aunt Katherine's room," Xina said apologetically as she guided Campbell up the stairs.

"Oh, I—uh—" This was definitely outside Campbell's comfort zone.

"Rita had already gone for the night, and I hadn't realized the room I'm sleeping in is the only other one with a bed set up." Xina stopped outside an open doorway. "I'm sure she used to have another room that could be made up for guests. I stayed here once with my parents, and we had separate rooms."

"Maybe you should be the one to stay in her bedroom." Campbell's stomach roiled, threatening to tie itself in knots. "I mean, I'm a stranger."

"I thought about it, but I wasn't sure she'd want me to. Not after the frigid way she treated me last week. I don't want her to be even more angry with me when she wakes up and learns I'm here."

Campbell swallowed hard. She could ask for the couch in the living room, but it looked older and less comfortable than Dad's hide-a-bed.

"I guess it's all right."

Xina's face cleared. "Oh, good. Rita told me she'd made the bed up fresh, in case Aunt Katherine improved and was able to come home."

She flipped on a light switch and they stepped inside. The furnishings were so old-fashioned they'd qualify as antiques—a full bed with a high, oak headboard and a matching dresser with an attached beveled mirror. A white-painted mantel topped a brick fireplace, and a small painting of daffodils in a glass vase hung above.

Campbell glanced up at the brass and glass fixture overhead. Its rays gleamed off the bedside lamp and the finials on a quilt rack. A small oriental rug lay on the pine floor near the bed. Wide baseboards and the deep window frame were painted matte white, which brightened the room. The soft gray wallpaper with a subtle floral design probably hadn't been changed in forty years or more but was still in good shape.

"It's a lovely room." Campbell set her overnight bag on the bed.

"The bath is across the hall," Xina said. "I'm afraid we'll have to share in this old house."

"No problem."

"Oh, and I'm the next door down, after the bathroom. There are two more rooms on this floor, but as I said, Aunt Katherine doesn't seem to have kept them as guest rooms. I don't think she's had many guests since my folks passed away. Anyway, I'm glad there was one."

"What's in those rooms now?"

"One is nearly empty. The other has some old furniture and boxes. Extra storage, I think."

Campbell nodded. "I spoke to Mr. Waverly tonight."

"Who's he?"

"Your aunt's agent."

"Oh!" Xina's features brightened. "What did he say?"

"He was very sorry to hear of Katherine's accident, and he'll phone you in the morning to discuss her business affairs. I hope you don't mind, I gave him your number."

"No, that's good." Xina's eyebrows drew together. "Do you think I should look at some of her papers before I talk to him? I didn't like to touch anything personal, but maybe I should."

"It might be a good idea." Campbell and her dad had discussed the possibility of her gaining access to Katherine's records with Xina's permission. He'd felt they might find answers to some of their many questions if she got a chance to look over documents such as contracts and royalty statements. "I understand about not wanting to snoop, but really, with your aunt at death's door, you'd be better off knowing where things stand."

"Let's do it," Xina said.

"Where are her desk and her files?"

"Downstairs. There's a room she's used as an office for as long as I can remember. It's behind the living room, next to the kitchen."

Xina led the way down the stairs. "Rita set aside today's mail on the entry table. I didn't like to open it. One looks like a bill."

"Let's see how she's doing tomorrow. If her condition doesn't improve, you may have to consider taking over her household finances, but it's early yet." Mindful of her father's cautions, Campbell said, "I noticed that you locked the front door when I came in. Are all the other doors locked?"

Xina paused in the kitchen doorway. "Yes. Rita told me the back door and the door into the garage are both deadbolted."

"How about windows?" Campbell didn't say anything about the break-in at the True Blue office nearly a month ago, but she was fanatical now about making sure windows were locked.

"I don't know." Xina's eyes widened. "Do you think we should check them?"

"I can do it. I'd just like to make sure we're secure before we settle down for the night."

"Thank you. I probably wouldn't have thought to check the

windows. Rita seems very conscientious, but with what happened next door ..."

"Agreed. Just relax for a few minutes, and I'll make the rounds."

"I could fix us some tea," Xina said. "Actually, I don't know what's in the kitchen yet. Aunt Katherine used to give me hot chocolate. There may be some cocoa mix."

"Whatever works for you." Campbell patted her shoulder. "You poke around the cupboards. I'll be back in a couple of minutes."

She started in the entry and worked her way through the first story, flipping on lights as she entered each room and checking every single window. All seemed to be latched tightly. The rooms all felt outdated but cozy. When she was satisfied that she'd been around the entire perimeter except for the kitchen, she made her way there.

"I think we're all set."

Xina turned from a cupboard and smiled. "Great. There are several kinds of tea here, but I don't see any coffee or cocoa mix."

"I think I'd like this one." Campbell tapped a box of lemon ginger tea.

"Mm, that does sound good."

Xina already had a teakettle on a burner. While she took down two mugs, Campbell ambled around the kitchen and checked the latch on the window over the sink.

"Does this house have a basement?"

"Uh, yeah, I seem to remember it does. Dark and creepy." Xina gave a self-conscious laugh.

"Where's the door?"

"Out there." With a wave of her hand, Xina indicated the doorway to a side room.

Campbell flipped on the light and found an oversized laundry room with modern appliances. A fold-down ironing board was mounted on one wall, next to a clothing rack. On the inner wall was a door with a sliding bolt lock.

"I think Aunt Katherine told me that was a bedroom in the old days." Xina came to stand beside her. "She called it a birth and death room, because they put old, frail people or new mothers with their babies here. Since it was next to the kitchen, it was warmer than the upstairs bedrooms." She gave a little shiver.

"Be thankful for central heating." Campbell smiled, trying to transfer some confidence to her. Xina seemed quite nervous just being in the old house. "Our generation forgets the quirks and discomforts our ancestors lived with."

"Oh, I know," Xina said. "We're spoiled. When I was a teen, Aunt Katherine took my mother and me to see what they call the Home Place, over in LBL. It got me thinking about the pioneers. Sometimes I wonder how the women back then stood it here without air conditioning in summer."

Campbell laughed and slid back the bolt on the door. "I'm going to take a quick look in the cellar, okay?"

"Sure, if—Oops! There's the teakettle. You go ahead, and I'll get our tea ready. There's a light switch on the right."

It was easy to find, and it activated a couple of bare light bulbs in the cavernous space below. A flashlight also sat on a narrow ledge beside the steps, and Campbell picked it up. She clung to the railing on her way down the narrow stairs. The dirt floor gave the cellar a damp, earthy smell. Her skin tightened in goosebumps and her heart pounded.

"You're being silly," she said aloud. Forcing herself to go on, she walked all around the basement. In the far corners, the overhead bulbs' rays didn't do the job, so she played the flashlight's beam over the old stone walls and the joists overhead. The electric heating and cooling unit looked fairly new.

A small space was partitioned off beneath one of the high windows, and a few pieces of coal on the floor glinted when her flashlight beam hit them. The coal bin. This house had once contained an older furnace. Campbell made herself walk calmly around. She jumped as a machine in one corner came on. The pump. She stood still and breathed slowly and deeply.

The original owners of the house must have been quite wealthy, she thought, to afford a furnace and an in-house water pump. A hundred years ago, this place would have seemed luxurious. Many of the town's homes were small, basic brick or wood-frame dwellings. Maybe she could find out more about the people who'd built this one.

Xina stood at the top of the stairs waiting for her.

"Find anything good?"

"No, it seems pretty sparse down there." She returned the flashlight to its perch and closed the door behind her, sliding the bolt snugly into place. "There are three windows at ground level, but they're very small, and they all seem secure."

"Good to know." Xina handed Campbell a mug of tea and picked up her own. "What sort of papers do you think we should look for?"

Campbell took a sip of the fragrant tea. "Ooh, that's good. Dad suggested I look for correspondence with her publisher. And when I spoke to Mr. Waverly, he asked if she had any unfinished manuscripts."

"Okay. But she's used a computer for at least twenty years. Wouldn't her current projects be on that?"

"That's what I told him."

Xina ambled across the kitchen, carrying her cup of tea carefully. "I'd kind of like to see her bank statements myself. It's not really any of my business, but if she stays in the hospital long, I may need to start paying her bills."

"True." Campbell trailed her into Katherine's home office.

"I guess she used that desktop computer for most of her work." Xina nodded toward the setup on the desk. "I haven't seen a laptop anywhere."

"Hmm. Is it password protected?"

"I'm not sure. I haven't touched it. It seemed—I don't know, intrusive."

Campbell nodded. "I understand. And we don't have to look at it yet. But do you know what sort of insurance she has? I think you said she's old enough for Medicare."

"Sixty-eight, so yes. She may be drawing Social Security too, since the last time I stayed with her."

"She may have insurance supplements. We should look for paid bills with a private insurance company, and copies of her policies. You need to know what her benefits are, and what expenses will be covered. Oh, and look for a living will."

"Yeah." Xina plopped down in the desk chair, her shoulders drooping. "They already asked me about that at the hospital. They wanted to know if she had an advanced directive. I told the clerk I'm sure she did, but they didn't have it on file."

"If she's been generally healthy, she may not have been hospitalized for years." Campbell wanted to comfort her, but she wasn't sure how best to do that. Maybe a change of tone would help drive the gloom away. "Okay, so why don't you go through the desk, and I'll take a peek in these file cabinets."

"Sounds good." Xina pulled open the flat, center desk drawer.

Campbell approached the two oak, double-drawer file cabinets on the wall opposite the desk. She started with the top drawer closest to Xina's chair, thinking the most important documents might be kept in the handiest place.

Sure enough, she quickly located a thick folder of correspondence with an editor at Random House. She pulled it out and opened it on top of the cabinet.

"This looks like a couple of unpaid bills," Xina said. "She must tuck them in this drawer until she pays them."

"Anything serious?" Campbell asked.

Xina drew a paper from one of the envelopes and unfolded it. "This looks like the current electric bill."

"It's not past due?"

"No. Oh, wait. Looks like she has an automatic payment set up with her bank. It says not to pay it. They'll withdraw it from the bank next week."

"Great. You won't have to worry about that one. Provided there's a healthy balance in the bank account, that is."

"Yeah." Xina opened the second one. "This looks like a statement, not a bill. It's from her health insurance company. No claims last month."

"That might help you as you deal with the hospital," Campbell said. "Now you know what company's policy to look for."

She scanned the first few documents in the publisher's file. "This is a bit painful."

"What?" Xina swiveled the chair toward her.

"The editor wrote Katherine a letter—well, it's by email, but she's printed it out and filed it—when they rejected a book from her."

"What?" Xina's brow wrinkled. "Hadn't she been with them for years and years?"

"That's right. We wondered why she'd left Random House. Well, this may be the answer. Listen to this. 'While we respect your work and are proud of your past canon, we cannot accept this book without major changes. It does not have the splendid plot twists or sparkling writing of your past works. You are welcome to overhaul it and submit it again.'" Campbell met Xina's gaze. "Wow."

"Yeah. Imagine your longtime boss saying that to you."

"Was Katherine a proud woman?"

"I'd say so. I mean, she was always civil with people, but she knew she was at the top of the heap when it came to romantic suspense. That letter must have hurt incredibly."

"Such a shame." Campbell gazed down at the paper. Her stomach felt a bit unsettled, as if the criticism was for her own work. "I wonder what happened between the previous book and this one."

"I'm starting to think it was a medical problem." Xina's expression was bleak.

"She's such a great writer. Do you think she lost her touch because of—I don't know. She's not that old." Campbell searched her brain for medical possibilities. "Some people do get early onset Alzheimer's. Or maybe she had a mini-stroke."

"I would think Rita would have noticed something like that."

"Yeah. Especially if it was sudden." Campbell skimmed the letter once more. "Unless it happened before Rita started working for her."

Xina's chin rose slowly. "Some medical conditions make people depressed. Maybe she was sick, and she couldn't get the manuscript ready in time. I mean, they did buy it eventually, right?"

Campbell shuffled the most recent documents. "I'm pretty sure they did. Hold on." Farther back in the drawer, she found a folder labeled with the title of Katherine's last book with Random House, *You'll Be Sorry*.

"Here's the contract. Yes, she signed it about five—almost six —months after that letter came. It took her a long time to revise it."

"But they liked it then." Xina's troubled eyes seemed to plead for reassurance.

Campbell riffled through the rest of the papers in the folder. "There are notes from the editor—suggestions for changes."

"After the contract?"

"Yeah. The editing process seems to have gone on for weeks." She glanced at Xina. "I'm sorry."

"Did you read that book?" Xina asked.

"Yeah. I, uh, didn't think it was as good as some of the others. But it wasn't terrible."

"High praise." Xina couldn't hold a smile.

"Sorry. I admit I liked some of her earlier ones better."

"You know what? So did I. But they can't all be terrific, can they?"

"I would think not."

Listlessly, Xina pulled open one of the desk's side drawers. "Still, I did wonder at the time. It was so long since her last one had launched. All that revising! Normally she'd do two or three books in the time it took to make that one publishable."

"You're right." Campbell looked through the Random House folder again. "Looks like they passed on the next one too, with no invitation to resubmit it." She checked the dates. "They cut her loose almost four years ago. The outline she'd sent them didn't have the zing they were looking for in her books, and they flat-out rejected it."

"Ouch."

"When Katherine's agent calls you in the morning, why don't you ask him about all this? He'd probably be more forthcoming with you than he was with me."

"Good idea. Is there anything I should have handy when I talk to him?"

Campbell blew out a breath. "You said you have a copy of Katherine's advance directives."

"Yes, I brought it with me. But that's for medical issues."

"Did she give you a power of attorney?"

"Not for her finances."

"But still, you're her closest relative. And her heir, right?"

"Well ..." Xina's face twitched. "She never gave me a copy of her will. I think I am. She implied it to me several years ago. But I can't really count on it until I see it, you know what I mean?"

"I think so." Campbell mustered a smile. "Well, let's see what else we can find. Maybe we can get explanations to some of the things that don't seem quite right."

———

THE SMELL of fresh coffee smacked Campbell in the face when she entered the True Blue office in the morning at five after eight. Her father was working at his desktop computer.

"Hey, sweetheart!" He grinned at her.

"Oh, that coffee smells so good. There wasn't anything but tea at Katherine's place."

"Are you going back tonight?"

She laid her laptop and purse on her desk and headed for the coffeemaker. "I don't think so. Xina's going to let me know, but she thinks she'll be okay."

"No creepy noises during the night?"

"Oh, yeah, plenty, but I'm pretty sure they were all house noises—that and sporadic traffic. Mostly it reminded me of the sounds our old house in Bowling Green used to make."

He laughed. "That house had its quirks. Did she talk to the agent yet?"

"No, she's waiting at home for the call, then she'll go see Katherine. She hopes she can talk to the primary care doctor this morning. And then she'll come straight here and update us." Campbell savored the scent as she filled her special mug with coffee. Her dad had bought her one with the Campbell's Soup logo on both sides the week she started working with him, and she always used it now at the office.

"Where's Nick?" She flicked a glance at the empty workstation.

"I told him to come in at nine."

"You think he's doing okay?"

"Oh, yeah, but I want to make sure he gets his rest." Her dad sat back in his chair. "Besides, I wanted to talk to you."

"Privately?" That set off a little discomfort. She took her coffee to her desk and sat down facing him. "What's up?"

"I have to go to Frankfort Thursday."

She arched her eyebrows but managed not to protest. She'd just got him back! It didn't seem fair for him to go away so soon.

"It's an old case of mine. The defendant has appealed, and it's at the state level now. I knew it was coming up, and I'd been told they wouldn't need me. But something's going on with one of the other witnesses. The prosecutor phoned me this morning and very apologetically told me they need me after all. I'll get a letter to confirm it today or tomorrow, but I'm afraid I can't get out of it."

Campbell swallowed hard. "Okay. So, that's like an overnight trip, right?"

"It's a good four-hour drive, so yeah. I expect I'll only have to stay one night, though. If they want me back in court next week, I'll come home for the weekend."

She nodded. "I guess Nick and I can hold the fort for a couple of days."

"Sure you can. And Keith will be there for you. I've texted him to let him know." He leaned forward and smiled. "Look, we've got today and tomorrow. Chances are we'll be done with Xina's case by Friday."

"You think so?"

"I do. I'm praying Katherine comes out of the coma and things resolve. Even if she doesn't, well, Xina should have a better idea of how things will go. She probably won't need us after this week. Now, tell me what you two found out last night."

Campbell sucked in a big breath. "Okay, we did some discreet looking at papers in her study. We found print-outs of correspondence with her publishers and her agent."

"And?"

"As we'd thought, Katherine's regular publisher rejected the last book she submitted to them. They turned down the one before that too, but they finally bought it after she revised it. They required a lot of changes. And the next one they said wasn't up to snuff."

"Do you think it's just because she's getting older?"

"No. Lots of writers keep going into their eighties. Unless she has a serious health condition, I don't think that's the answer. And Xina did turn up some notes from her last couple of doctor visits. Her blood work was fine, and it seems like she was okay. They scheduled another checkup six months after the last one.

If she had something going on, they wouldn't wait that long, would they?"

"I wouldn't think so. So, her agent sold the rejected book to that new publisher?"

"Right. Krata Press. But they haven't bought any more from her yet. I'm eager to hear what Waverly tells Xina about that. Dad, Katherine's been struggling with the last two books. Badly."

Her father rubbed his chin. "Okay. What about her personal expenses?"

"Xina found a couple of unpaid monthly bills in her desk, but nothing out of the ordinary. There's a second file cabinet that seems to hold the bulk of her household records, but we didn't get into that last night. It was getting late, and we agreed to leave off and go to bed around ten thirty."

"How about her computer?"

"We didn't try to get into it. Xina found it a little intrusive. As long as she has what she needs to deal with Katherine's doctors and her normal household bills, she felt she should wait."

He nodded. "It makes sense, although I wish she'd gone ahead and had a peek."

"Katherine had a regular online payment set up for her electric bill. She may have paid all her bills that way."

"And if she went paperless, you might not find much of use in the file cabinet."

"I don't know, Dad. I glanced in the top drawer, and I could see folders of bank statements and that sort of thing. I pulled out one on her health insurance. Xina was going to look it over this morning before going to the hospital."

"Well, if she's paying her bills online, she's got to have had her wits about her, at least until recently. I mean, it's not like she has children helping her set up computer stuff."

Campbell nodded. "And Rita has nothing to do with that. So far, it looks like Katherine's personal and business records are well organized and up-to-date. But that's after just a quick survey."

They spent a few minutes going over the leads they wanted to follow up on for Xina, then her father steered Campbell in a new direction.

"I haven't taught you to do background checks yet."

"Is that something you do a lot of?" she asked.

"Yeah. It comes in spurts. We have several companies that have us check out prospective employees for them. We got a couple of names this morning from a local pharmacy. Unless Xina has something more pressing, I'd like to spend a couple hours with you on that. It's something you and Nick could finish while I'm away, but it's not urgent."

"Okay. I'd like to learn that."

"The agency subscribes to several websites that most people can't access. You need to get up to speed on using them."

The door opened and Nick walked in. "Morning, Bill. Morning, Professor. What's new in the private eye world?"

They had just finished filling Nick in on the developments in Xina's case and Bill's upcoming trip to the capital when the door opened once more.

"I hope I'm not interrupting anything." Xina surveyed them from the doorway, her face pale and her smile a little shaky.

11

"Have a seat, Xina." Bill pulled an extra chair over for their client to sit in. "How's your aunt?"

"The same. Still in the coma, and still hitched to a profusion of tubes and wires."

"Let me get you some coffee," Campbell said.

"Thank you. I could use some."

While Campbell fetched it, her father introduced Xina to Nick.

"So, how's the other guy look?" Xina stared pointedly at his cast.

"He's in the county jail, so I figure I won," Nick replied with a laugh.

Xina's mouth formed an O. She accepted the coffee from Campbell. "Someday I'd like to hear that story," she whispered.

Campbell smiled. "Nick's our muscle." It wasn't really true, but she could tell Nick was pleased by the red tinge on the tips of his ears and the way he concentrated on his computer screen, not looking their way.

"So, did Bruce Waverly get in touch with you?" her father asked.

"He did."

Campbell sat down beside Xina and set her mug on her dad's desk.

"He was very concerned about Aunt Katherine," Xina said. "He said she'd been struggling with her writing the last few years. He didn't want to call it writer's block, but he said she'd had trouble plotting and getting stories on paper—or on the computer, I guess. But he said her name is still golden in the genre. If she can put another book together in a coherent and cohesive form—his exact words—he's sure he can sell it."

"Hmm. That's encouraging, in a way," Bill said.

"Except that there's no guarantee she'll ever be able to do that, and now she has a brain injury." Campbell wished she hadn't spoken, as a pall seemed to settle over them.

Xina blinked rapidly. "Mr. Waverly did say that Random House had made the break final."

"We figured that from the letters we found last night," Campbell said.

Xina nodded. "And then he told me that Krata Press was cagey about buying another book too. They published one, but the editor told him she despaired of ever getting it into shape to release it. Apparently, she said she had to heavily rewrite a lot of Katherine's scenes."

Bill sighed. "Not so encouraging."

"I'm wondering if it's like you suggested, a mini-stroke. Something along those lines." Her gaze at Campbell seemed a plea for contradiction.

"Maybe we should study up on that," Campbell said. "Find out what the symptoms would be and then talk to Rita Henry about it. She may have seen subtle signs and not realized it."

Bill shifted in his chair, frowning. "You should bring up the subject with the doctors, Xina. See what they have to say. Urge them to give her a thorough workup."

"That sounds good to me," Campbell said. "They should be able to tell if her brain is getting a good blood flow, things like that."

"I think they've done some of those tests, but I didn't talk to them about her changes in behavior. I confess, I didn't want them to question the advanced directive and think she didn't want me to help her."

"That wouldn't matter," Bill said. "If she hasn't changed it, the directive is still in place. And that's part of why we make them. So that when the patient can't make the tough decisions, someone who cares about them—and usually someone younger and of sound mind—can do it for them."

Xina let out a long breath. "Thank you both. This is a bit overwhelming."

Campbell patted her shoulder. "Of course it is." The time when she'd feared her father was dead had almost paralyzed her, and she understood the helplessness Xina was going through. "Keep in mind, she was a smart lady and a brilliant writer, and she picked you. You're the one she wanted to do this for her."

"That's right," Bill said. "She may not remember now, but she chose wisely when she could."

They sat in silence for a moment, and then Nick spoke up.

"So, Ms. Harrison, I was wondering, with all this talk about your aunt's books, was she working on something new?"

"I don't know," Xina said. "Mr. Waverly seemed to think she had something in the works, but he hadn't seen any of it. He asked me if I knew of any unfinished manuscripts, but I had to tell him I didn't."

Campbell thought about it. "If you decide to try to get into her computer, there may be something there."

"There might. But I think I should wait a while longer." She lifted her gaze hopefully to Bill's face. "The doctors say she could wake up at any time."

"We're praying for that." Bill leaned forward and picked up his favorite Racers pen. "And, Xina, I understand you may never need to open her computer, but if you do, Nick is very proficient with that sort of thing. If you need cyber help, he's part of the team."

"Thank you." Xina glanced over at Nick and he gave her a little wave. She turned back to Campbell and Bill. "If she has started on a new book, how will I know if it's any good?"

"By reading it, I guess," Campbell said. "If it seems like an interesting story, and it draws you in, then it's probably worth reading."

"You told me last night you were an English professor."

"That's right."

Xina frowned for a moment. "You would be a better judge of that than I would. If we were to find something, maybe you could take a look at it and give your opinion."

"I'd be happy to," Campbell said. "I'm sure I'd recognize her usual style. I got some of her books from the county library a few days ago, so I could catch up on the ones I'd never read. That's where I got that last one. I finished it over the weekend."

"Now, Xina," Bill said, "what exactly did Waverly say about your aunt's last few books? He mentioned she was struggling to produce them. What else?"

Xina let out a long, slow breath. "Well, he said the last one for Random House, *You'll Be Sorry,* required a lot of revisions. He thought that was the first time she had to do that extensive of a rewrite for them. And then, when he sent them her next book, they rejected it. But you knew that."

"But Krata, the new publisher, bought it," Bill said.

"Yes, but she had to revise that one a lot too, and it took her a long time. Mr. Waverly was really disappointed when she left Random House. Apparently Krata Press doesn't pay nearly as much. And he said it took her ages to make the next one acceptable. He emailed her to ask what was wrong. I think he suspected by then that she might have personal or medical problems."

Campbell nodded. "That seems reasonable. Did he tell you how she responded?"

"She said she was just having a slump. When he got her manuscript of *Crying Shame,* he looked it over, and he thought it wasn't up to her usual quality, but he tried to put a good spin on it and sent it in. He sold it to Krata three years ago, mostly on the basis of Katherine's name and publishing history, but the new editor wanted a lot of revisions, and they changed the title."

"*Ice Cold Blue,*" Campbell said. She couldn't see how that title fit with the story she'd read.

"Yes. After that, he wasn't sure she'd be able to produce another one. He said she'd told him in the past that she had one or two she'd finished and put away, and he wanted her to send him those, but she wouldn't. So he told her to send him something when she was ready. I don't think she's sent him anything in almost two years."

"So, her income's dropped," Campbell mused.

"A lot, from what he said. She was getting huge advances from Random House, but no more. They've reissued all of her books in mass market paperbacks, eBooks, and audiobooks, so she's still getting some royalties from them, but not like ten years ago. Nowhere near as much."

Bill nodded soberly. "I hope she put some away and invested well."

"I haven't been to the bank," Xina said. "I didn't think I should unless it becomes necessary."

"That's probably wise." He picked up his coffee mug. "So, have you heard anything about a researcher who used to work for Ms. Tyler? Someone named Lee Dorman?"

Xina's eyes crinkled at the corners. "I don't think so. You mean since I've been here?"

"Or in the past," Campbell said.

She shook her head. "I knew there was a researcher for at least one book. Aunt Katherine told me once, a long time ago, that she had someone researching for her, but ..." Her chin jerked up. "Wait, there was something. It was for the book about the buried treasure. She had somebody researching treasure hunters and old, forgotten caches that were discovered years and years later."

"Were there many of those around here?" Bill asked.

"I think that book was set out West. And, no, I don't suppose there were many in real life—not nearly so many as there are in books and movies."

Campbell chuckled. "I think you're right about that. I ran across Lee Dorman's name in the acknowledgments in another of Katherine's books, and I wondered if they still had a working relationship. I thought he—or she—might live in this area."

"Oh." Xina's mouth tightened. "I don't recognize the name. Aunt Katherine seems to have let go of a lot of old relationships."

"Yes, she has." Bill pushed his chair back and stood, holding his mug. "Would anyone else like more coffee?"

"None for me, thank you." Xina picked up her purse. "I should get back to the house."

"Do you need me today?" Campbell asked.

"Oh, I don't think so. I apologize for my jitters last night."

"No problem," Campbell said.

"Well, I was awfully glad you were there. But I should be okay now."

Campbell hesitated. "I have a dinner date tonight, but if you feel nervous, please do call. It's not a bother, really." Not to mention, if Xina decided to dive into Katherine's computer files, she wanted to be there.

"Thanks." Xina stood. "I think I'll go through some of the household accounts this morning, and I plan to go back to the hospital this afternoon. Is there anyone in particular I should try to contact?"

Campbell looked to her father for input.

"Nothing special right now," Bill said. "If you find Katherine's bank statements and tax return for last year, make a note of where they are. You may need those if she can't take care of her own finances."

"But you should concentrate on your aunt's health care," Campbell said. "We're praying she makes a good recovery."

"That's right." Bill headed for the coffeemaker. "If she comes out of this coma, you may not have to do another thing."

"Well, I appreciate all you're doing now. If I need to meet with her attorney, I may need some moral support." She looked plaintively at Campbell.

"Don't worry, we're here for you." Campbell touched her sleeve and walked with her to the door. When Xina had gone, she swung around. "Dad, do you still want to work with me on profiles?"

"Yeah, let's put in a couple hours on that. Then I thought I'd help Nick with Jacob Gray's case. I can do some more background work on Benjamin Tatton and Katherine's other neighbors, but a lot hangs on whether her condition improves."

Campbell nodded. "I feel like we're stalled on Xina's case too, until either Katherine wakes up or Xina decides to open that computer. After lunch, I believe I'll make another visit to the library."

"Done with your books so soon?"

"Not all of them, but I'm thinking the librarians might know Lee Dorman."

KEITH ENJOYED WATCHING Campbell savor her steak dinner. She did everything with enthusiasm, even eating. He wished they weren't both so busy and could spend more time together.

"Playhouse in the Park is doing *Yankee Doodle Dandy!* this weekend. Would you be interested in going?" he asked.

"Are you kidding? I love musicals. Thanks."

"Terrific." Her eyes sparkled, and his heartbeat picked up.

"Friday night? Or Saturday?" he asked. "I may need to work Saturday, but I should have the evening free. Barring an emergency, of course."

"Want to aim for Friday night? That way, we can reschedule for Saturday if something comes up."

"I like the way you think. Thanks for being flexible."

"No problem. Anything new on the Tatton case? That is, anything you can tell me?"

"Not really. We're still interviewing neighbors, family, and other contacts."

"Something has me curious. You said he ordered a lot of stuff online, and he was usually right there when the deliveryman brought it. Didn't Tatton have a job?"

"He retired early, and his parents left him the house and some money. Not a huge fortune, but probably enough to keep him going if he was careful."

She took a sip of water.

"So what did you do today?" he asked.

"I went to the library, for one thing. I thought the librarian might know the researcher who used to work for Katherine Tyler. But it turns out she didn't. So I went back to the office for Dad's help in tracking down Lee Dorman."

"Did you find her?"

"Him. Yes, I did. He lives just outside Paducah, so most of his library work was done up there. I drove to Paducah this afternoon."

"You guys put a lot of miles on your vehicles. Why didn't you just phone the library?"

"Oh, come on. You're a detective. Dad says it's always better in person. You get more information out of them, and you can read their body language, which you can't do over the phone."

"That's true. So, was it a productive visit?"

"Not really. Dorman wasn't home. But I'm pretty sure he's the right guy."

"How?"

"Well, for one thing, I went to the McCracken County Public Library. One of the librarians said he's a regular patron, but he wasn't there today. And it's a fairly unusual name. Online I found some bits about him. He used to be a teacher. That's a likely start for a professional researcher. And he's published some articles and short stories."

"Hmm. Find any connection to Katherine Tyler?"

She frowned. "Nothing definite. I hope I can track him down tomorrow and ask some questions."

Keith finished his steak and then asked, "How is she doing—Ms. Tyler?"

"About the same. Xina went to the hospital again this afternoon, and they said she'd been restless for a while, but she's still out of it. Xina's going back tonight. She's probably there right now."

"Well, the house is only a mile or so from the hospital," Keith said.

"Right. They only let her stay a little while, but she wants to be there as much as she can. She's hoping they'll let her stay longer tomorrow. And that Katherine will wake up, of course. I'm sure everything will change if she just regains consciousness."

"Keep praying."

"Dad and I are doing that. It seems like nothing's happening, you know?"

"Well, it's only been two days. The body needs time to heal." Keith smiled. "How about some dessert? Their cheesecake's really good."

"I love cheesecake. Are you going to have some?"

"I might, if you will."

She laughed. "Let's go for it."

CAMPBELL WAS ONLY half awake when her phone rang Wednesday morning. She grabbed it from the nightstand, rolling to a sitting position.

"Xina! Good morning."

"Hi," Xina said. "I hope I'm not calling too early."

"What's up?"

"I wanted you to know I called the police last night."

Campbell caught her breath. "What happened?"

"I heard noises outside, around the garage. I almost called you and your father, but I decided not to bother you. It seemed like a police patrol was in order."

"Did they find anything?"

"Some footprints around the side of the garage. It rained last evening, and the ground was squishy."

Campbell recalled leaving the restaurant with Keith in a downpour.

"They said it was probably just someone cutting through to the next street," Xina said.

"There's a fence across the back yard."

"I mentioned that. The officer didn't seem very concerned."

Campbell swallowed hard. "Xina, the next-door neighbor was murdered last week."

"I know." Her voice trembled.

"That's it," Campbell said. "I'm staying over with you tonight."

"Would you?"

"Of course."

"I hated to ask."

"Don't be silly. If we had more room, I'd invite you to stay here." Campbell's mind raced through her planned schedule. "I'm going to try to find that researcher today. Dad and I thought we might talk to some more of the neighbors. We can ask if anyone saw someone lurking about. After we're done with our interviews, I'll come to the house."

Campbell took a quick shower and joined her father in the kitchen. He didn't look happy when she told him about Xina's nighttime disturbance.

"I'll give one of the guys at the police station a call and see if I can get a full report on the prowler incident." He set a pan of scrambled eggs on the table between them. "Bacon?"

"I don't think I'll take the time." Campbell helped herself to eggs and reached for a muffin.

"You might want to call the old housekeeper before you strike out for Paducah." He set a mug of coffee on the table before her.

"Thanks. Why Doris Conley?"

"She may have met Dorman back when she worked for Ms. Tyler."

"True. It wouldn't hurt to touch base with her."

Her dad topped off his coffee and sat down opposite her. "If there's any funny business over there tonight, you call the police first, and then call me."

"Okay, Dad. I will."

She ended up going to the office with him so she could use the landline. They arrived early, and at quarter past eight she put in the call to Doris Conley about the researcher.

"Oh, yes, I met that fellow a couple of times when he came to the house to help Katherine," she said. "What was his name— Lee something."

"Dorman," Campbell said.

"Yes, that was it."

"What do you remember about him?"

"Not much, sorry. It was a long time ago."

"How long?"

"Oh, eight or ten years, I guess. He looked well fed."

Campbell chuckled, but she was a little discouraged. She wound down the call and gave her father a noncommittal shrug. "Mrs. Conley remembered Dorman, but barely. I'm heading for Paducah."

He sighed. "Okay. I wish I could go with you, but I promised Nick I'd work with him today. He's got a few leads to follow on Gray's daughter. But I don't like you roaming around places you don't know alone."

"Oh, Dad. I'll be fine. I just hope the guy is home today."

12

"I don't understand your interest in my work." The graying man in his fifties had a slight paunch. He stood in the doorway of his suburban ranch house, dressed in dockers and a button-up shirt.

Campbell gazed into Dorman's appraising blue eyes. "Ms. Tyler was recently injured, and her family has asked my agency to look into her recent business contacts."

"Injured?" His eyebrows quirked. "Seriously?"

"Yes. It was a car accident. She's in the hospital in Murray."

"I'm sorry to hear that. But you said recent contacts. I haven't done any work for Katherine Tyler for several years."

"How many years?"

His lips pressed together for a moment, and his eyes lost focus as he considered her question. "I'd say five or six. She had me looking into some old tales about river pirates and treasure seekers once."

"I read that book." Campbell smiled. "It's neat knowing your research helped make it so interesting."

"Well, thanks."

"Do you still do research for authors?"

His chest seemed to swell a bit. "Actually, I'm writing my own book now. I hope to have it out by fall." His eyes narrowed, and he looked at her closely. "So, would you like to come in and sit down and talk about it? I've got a bottle of wine."

Was he coming on to her? Campbell pulled back a little, trying not to show her unease. "Oh, no thanks, I can't really stay long."

He was suddenly less affable. "Well, if you're looking for people who are close to Katherine Tyler, I doubt I can help you today."

"All right, thanks."

She turned and hurried away. When she was safely in her car, she locked the doors and slumped down in the seat. Somehow, she should have kept control of the conversation. She hadn't even given him a business card.

But she was pretty sure Dorman was correct—he couldn't help her. All she wanted was to get home.

Her dad's slight overprotectiveness came back to her, and she smiled wryly as she started the engine. She still didn't think she needed a bodyguard, but maybe he was right in thinking she shouldn't go to interview strange men alone.

When she taught at the university, she'd been careful about relationships, but she'd never had the creepy feeling she'd experienced at the researcher's door. Maybe some self-defense classes were in order. Were there courses in self-confidence?

XINA THREW the door to her aunt's house wide open. "I'm so glad you're here."

"I took off a little early." Campbell carried in her overnight bag and set it by the foot of the stairs. The muffled hum of a vacuum cleaner came from somewhere overhead. Rita, no doubt. "How is Katherine doing today?"

"The same." Xina's cheeks tightened. "The doctor isn't happy. He thinks she should be making more progress."

"I'm sorry."

"I went this morning and again about an hour ago. I was hoping they'd see some improvement, but not yet."

"I can go over with you this evening, if you're planning another visit."

"That would be good. I don't think they'll let you see her, but just having someone along would be a little less depressing." Xina swallowed hard. "Dr. Drummond mentioned the possibility of having her transported to Nashville."

"I'm surprised they didn't do that right after the accident."

Xina shrugged. "I don't know what their reasoning was. But I get the feeling they can't do much more for her here."

"There might be some specialists there who could help."

"I hope so. I'd like to give her every chance possible." Xina sobbed. "I'm afraid she'll end up in long-term care, just the way she is now."

"She's not on life support, is she?"

"No."

Campbell rubbed her shoulder. "Xina, I'm sorry this is so hard for you. Seeing someone you love in this condition ..."

"It is, but I want to be here. Still, what do I do if nothing changes? I can't move to Nashville."

Campbell sighed. "That would mean making some hard decisions. You have the rest of the week off. Let's see how things go."

"Thank you." Xina pulled a tissue from the pocket of her pants and wiped her eyes. She faced Campbell with a determined smile. "So, supper won't be ready for an hour or two. Shall we dive into the rest of her files?"

They went into the study, and Xina showed her a drawer of neat folders containing paid bills and bank statements.

"I'd like to look through those later, if you don't mind," Campbell said. "Is there anything you haven't looked at yet?"

"That bottom drawer." Xina pointed to the lower righthand desk drawer. "It's locked. Or stuck."

Several of the file drawers in the room had locks, but those they'd looked at before had opened easily.

"I saw a couple of small keys in the desk the other night."

Xina opened the shallow drawer in the middle. "There are extra car keys and house keys in the kitchen, but—Oh, here they are." She held out two small keys linked by a loop of twine. "Would you?"

Campbell knelt on the carpet and tried each one. The second one fit, and she turned it and slid the drawer out. Several folders stood in the back, with a small metal box nestled in the front of the drawer. She fingered the tabs on the folders.

"Here's the deed to the house. This one has her car's title and registration." She paused and looked up at Xina. "There are two that say *Will* and *Medical Directives*, and one for a financial advisory chain. She probably has a retirement account or other investments with them." Campbell recognized the name of the company her father used for his 401k account.

Xina pulled in a deep breath. "Do you think we should look?"

"How do you feel about it?"

"I'm not sure. She might wake up and not like it that I've gone through her personal records. I don't want to upset her worse than I already have."

"Then let's wait," Campbell said. "At least you know where they are now."

"Maybe we should check the medical one, just to be sure it's the same as what I gave them at the hospital. My copy was ten years old."

"Okay." Campbell took out the folder in question and opened it. She leafed through several pages of typescript and then handed it to Xina. "The date seems right. Why don't you check?"

Xina looked at the first and last pages. "Yes. Mrs. Conley witnessed it. It's just like the one I have, only this looks like the original, and mine's a copy."

"Great." Campbell smiled and put the folder back where she'd found it. "Should we look in this box?"

Xina's brow wrinkled. "This may sound silly, but would you mind looking and telling me if it's something important or not?"

"Okay." Campbell lifted the box out and set it on the desk. She tried the sliding latch, but it didn't give. "Locked," she murmured. The first key she'd tried on the drawer earlier fit it, and she opened the box. Inside were three cardboard boxes, smaller than bricks. "Looks like checks and deposit slips." She opened them one by one and noted the bank information. "They're all from the same bank. It's probably for her checking account."

Xina stepped closer and looked over her shoulder. "We could check the statements in the file cabinet, I guess."

Campbell looked up at her. "Did the police give you Katherine's purse after the accident? I'm thinking there'd be a checkbook or something in there."

"They brought it over yesterday, and I put it in a drawer in her bedroom."

"You didn't look inside?" Campbell asked. How could anyone not be curious about something like that?

"I took a quick peek, and I didn't see anything unusual. I think you're right, there was a checkbook. I'll go get it."

"Get the whole purse," Campbell said.

Xina hurried out of the room, and her footsteps pattered up the stairs. Campbell lifted out the other check boxes to be sure she hadn't missed anything. A small red envelope was lodged under the final box. She picked it up and examined it, then gingerly slid out a squarish key.

"Oh, Katherine." The deed and her last will and testament were here. Campbell didn't think the author owned expensive jewelry. What would Katherine store in a safe deposit box?

When Xina returned with the purse, Campbell held up the key in its envelope. "Looks like your aunt has a safe deposit box."

"Wow. I had no idea." Xina set the purse on the desk and took the key. "From the same bank?"

"Yes. I'm thinking we should put it back in the same place we found it, but if the worst happens, you'll know it's there." She placed the key in the cashbox and returned the boxes of checks and deposit slips. After locking the box, Campbell put it away, but she didn't lock the drawer, in case Xina wanted to look over some of the documents later.

The desktop was clear except for the computer, a cup of pens, and a box of tissues.

"Okay, let's dump out the purse."

"Really?" Xina stared at her.

"We'll do it gently." Campbell took the brown leather bag from her hands and unzipped the main compartment. She lifted out the bulkiest item—a matching leather wallet—and poured a variety of small items on the desk.

"There's the checkbook." Xina grabbed the maroon leather holder and opened it. "The last check was written almost three weeks ago, to the garbage collection company."

"I'm surprised she didn't have an automatic payment set up for that," Campbell said.

"Well, it looks like she paid for six months ahead, so it wasn't an every-month thing."

"Okay." Campbell separated the remaining items on the desk, pushing them aside one by one. A pack of Kleenex, three pens, and a small hairbrush.

She picked up the wallet and opened the compartment for cards. "Here's her debit card on the same account as the checkbook." She scanned the other cards. "She's got three credit cards, a Medicare card, a drug plan card, dental and eye care, and a couple of store discount cards." She glanced in the slot for currency and set the wallet aside. "Only forty-two dollars."

"She didn't like to carry a lot of cash," Xina said.

Campbell took a quick look in the zippered change compartment but found only a few coins inside. She set the wallet aside and put the other items back in the purse. In one of the side compartments she found a lip balm, breath mints, and another pen. From another pocket she pulled a pill box and a stain removal pen.

She handed the old-fashioned, enameled pill box to Xina. "Would you mind opening that?"

Xina depressed the catch and lifted the lid. "Hmm, I think that's ibuprofen, but I don't know what those other two pills are."

"We can check them with the ones in the bathroom upstairs," Campbell said. "She may be carrying an extra from her prescriptions. Or maybe they're for stomach acid or something like that. I doubt it's anything to be concerned about."

She fingered the pockets carefully to be sure she hadn't missed anything and then replaced all the items.

"So, no surprises," Xina said.

"That's good." Campbell smiled and handed her the purse. "Maybe we should put this in one of the drawers that lock."

Xina's eyes widened. "You're thinking of the prowler?"

"Just general precautions."

The bag just fit in the bottom drawer with the cashbox and documents. Campbell locked it this time and handed Xina the key to the drawer.

"Are you ladies ready for some sweet tea?" Rita said from the doorway.

Campbell turned with a smile. "Hello, Rita. That sounds wonderful."

They followed her to the dining room, where Rita had set out a pitcher of iced tea, glasses, and a plate of homemade gingersnaps.

"Thank you, Rita. This looks great," Xina said.

"You're welcome. I'll be leaving in an hour, but I'll put that chicken pie in the oven before I leave."

"Perfect." Xina looked over at Campbell. "Unless you want to go out for dinner."

"No, I'd love the chicken pie." So far, she loved anything Rita cooked.

Xina smiled. "I guess we're all set then."

Rita nodded. "There'll be salad in the fridge, and there's plenty of ice cream in the freezer if you want dessert."

"She's trying to fatten me up," Xina said with a chuckle.

"I love cooking for people who actually like to eat. And Ms. McBride, I put your suitcase in your room."

"Thanks so much."

Rita nodded and disappeared into the kitchen.

"She's a treasure," Campbell said.

"I think so. Aunt Katherine only has her coming three days a week, though. I'll be on my own tomorrow."

"Well, I'm here at least for tonight. If you don't want to be alone, I can just plan to come over after work every day and sleep here."

"Oh, I don't ..." Xina looked disconcerted.

"Don't worry, I won't charge you for sleep hours," Campbell said with a chuckle.

Xina's expression cleared. "Sorry. I don't want to put you out, but I'm afraid my budget will run a little thin because of this trip. I'm okay so far, but—"

"Don't worry," Campbell said. "The retainer you gave my dad will cover whatever work we do for you this week. If things haven't resolved by then, we'll sit down with Dad and talk about it."

"Thank you." Xina squeezed Campbell's wrist. "Frankly, I'm not sure how I could have gotten through this without you and your father."

"Speaking of whom, I should call Dad and update him on what we've found."

"Go ahead," Xina said. "I'm going to run out to the car. I think I left my readers out there, and I'll want them if we're going to look at bank statements."

Campbell put in the call to her father on her cell phone, and as it rang, a scream tore the air.

"Hello?" Bill said.

"Hold on, Dad! Something's going on." Campbell ran to the front door and threw it open.

Xina stood on the walkway, several yards from the steps. "Look out," she cried. "Snake!"

Campbell swung toward the side where Xina pointed and froze. A huge snake slithered slowly across the porch. Her heart slammed into high gear as the tan snake wriggled and lifted its triangular head. Darker brown markings along its body formed hourglass shapes.

She swallowed hard. "It's a copperhead."

13

"Soup? You all right?" her father said in her ear.

"No, Dad. There's a gigantic copperhead on the front porch. I've never seen one this big."

"Are you sure it's a copperhead?"

"Absolutely."

"Well, keep away from it."

Campbell leaned out the doorway a little. "It's on the move. I'm afraid it will go under the porch and lurk there to ambush people."

"I'll be right over. Call Animal Control. Or call 911—that's easier. They can send Animal Control. But try to keep an eye on it if you can."

Campbell gulped. "Okay. Hurry." She looked at Xina, who still stood a safe distance away. "Dad's coming."

"What can he do?"

"I'm not sure." She punched in 911. "Hi. I need animal control asap. We have a great big copperhead on the porch." She gave the address and hung up after assuring the dispatcher she'd stay on hand.

The snake wriggled its way to the edge of the porch and

eased between the decking and the bottom of the railing. "Can you get a flashlight? Dad said to try to keep an eye on it."

"Hold on." Xina pulled her phone from a pocket and tapped it a few times, then put it to her ear. "Rita? We've got a big snake on the front porch. Can you bring a flashlight?"

Half a minute later, the snake was on the ground, sliding along the edge of the porch's skirting. It was looking for an escape, Campbell figured as she stared at it over the railing. She took no comfort in the thought that the copperhead didn't like her any more than she liked him.

The door opened behind her, and Rita appeared with a flashlight in one hand and a butcher knife in the other.

"Where is the monster?"

"Down there." Campbell pointed and eyed the knife uneasily. "You don't want to get close enough to use that. It's a copperhead."

Rita joined her and peered down at the snake. "My, my, my. Can you keep it from going under the porch?"

"Doubt it."

"I can get a hoe from the garage."

Campbell doubted so much as the tip of the copperhead's tail would be in sight by the time she returned. Rita left the flashlight and knife on the porch floor, but neither one looked like an appropriate weapon to Campbell.

"It's going under the steps," Xina said.

Campbell watched helplessly as its body disappeared. She'd seen a few of the species when she was a kid, growing up in Bowling Green, but never this large. She shivered.

The garage door went up at the same moment her father pulled in a little too fast. He slammed the car to a halt and jumped out.

"Where is it?" He ran past Xina toward the steps and pulled out his pistol.

"It just went under there."

Cautiously, Campbell tiptoed down the steps and joined him.

She pointed to the spot where the snake had wriggled through a small opening. Rita joined them, carrying a garden hoe, but Xina kept her distance, a few yards down the walk.

Bill crouched and stared at the hole.

"We have a flashlight, if that helps." Rita laid down the hoe and scrambled up onto the porch. She passed the light over the railing to Bill.

"There's no way it can get in the cellar, is there?" he asked.

"Not that I know of," Rita said.

"Have you ever seen this guy before?"

"Never."

Bill took the flashlight and shone its beam beneath the steps.

"It's probably long gone," Campbell said.

"Nope." Bill rocked forward and put his face so close to the opening, she was afraid the copperhead might strike and bite him. "I see him."

"Really? Is he moving?" she asked.

"No, he's looking at me." After a moment's silence, he said grimly, "Now that's a snake."

"I hate snakes," Xina said. "I'm worse than Indiana Jones."

"Anyone should be afraid of that one," Campbell told her. "And you don't want it hanging around the place."

Bill glanced at her. "Okay, everybody stand back, and plug your ears."

As she retreated, Campbell noticed a patrol car cruising down the street.

"Dad, the cops are almost here."

"Then I'd better do this quick."

He fired two shots rapidly, louder than Campbell had expected.

"Did you get him?" Rita yelled. "What's he doing?"

"You don't wanna know."

Officer Denise Mills and Sergeant David Andrews hurried toward them.

"Yo, Bill," Andrews called, "are you firing a gun in a residential area?"

"You bet I am," Bill roared back.

From beneath the steps, Campbell heard thrashing and rustling.

Her father let off another shot and jumped to his feet. "That oughta do him." He turned to meet the two police officers. "If that's not the biggest copperhead you've ever seen, I'll buy you a steak, Dave."

Andrews grinned. "As long as it's not snake steak."

Bill handed him the flashlight. "Take a look. I think I got him in the head with that last one. If he's done flopping around, let's haul him out of there."

Andrews peered into the opening, wielding the flashlight and tilting his head to get the best view. He let out a whistle.

"He's big, all right."

"Here." Denise Mills handed him some nitrile gloves.

"What, you don't want to do the honors?" Andrews asked.

Mills shuddered. "No, thanks."

Andrews pulled on the gloves and gingerly reached under the steps. He got hold of the snake's body and began drawing it out.

Bill glanced around and nudged Campbell. "Hey, get that box over there."

When she looked behind her, she spotted an overturned cardboard carton lying between two boxwood bushes. She strode over to it and picked it up.

"Yeah," her father said when she got back to his side. "Looks like a good size for a granddaddy snake."

Campbell turned up one of the box's flaps and frowned at it. "Dad, look at this label."

"What?" He leaned closer and studied the shipping label. "Huh, it's addressed to a gift shop in Paducah."

Looking around at the others, Campbell singled out the housekeeper. "Rita, do you know where that box came from?"

She shook her head. "I'm pretty sure it wasn't there when I came back from Kroger this afternoon."

Bill held out the carton as Andrews tugged on the monster snake and lifted it.

"Wow." Xina took several steps backward. "Keep it away from me."

"Put him right in here," Bill said.

Andrews lowered the snake's grisly body into the box, folding it so that it would fit inside. It had stopped twitching and wiggling and lay still.

A pickup truck rolled to a stop at the curb in front of the house, and the county animal control officer got out.

"You took your time, Eric," Andrews shouted. "Bill McBride did your job for you."

"So I don't need my snake-catching tools?" Eric asked.

"Nope. Bill used his .38." Andrews laughed.

Eric ambled up the driveway and peeked into the box. "Shazam! I've never seen one that big—especially not in town. What's it doing here?"

"Who knows? But he's a biggie all right," Denise Mills said.

"Know what I'm thinking?" Bill asked.

Everyone looked at him expectantly.

"What if someone brought that snake here in this box and turned it loose on the front porch?"

They all stared at him.

"Why would they do that?" Andrews asked.

"Well, your people came here the other night when someone had been prowling around. Ms. Harrison called 911." Bill nodded at Xina. "This is her aunt's house, and she's staying here. But I'm pretty sure someone would like to scare her away so the place would be empty at night."

Xina's face paled. "Oh, come on, Bill. Snakes and creaky noises in the night are bad enough, but you think someone wants to drive me out?"

Bill shrugged. "I don't want to scare you any worse than you already are, Xina, but this box is pretty well snake-sized, and it's addressed to a business in Paducah, an hour away, not to anyone on this street."

"Aw, that's a pretty big leap," Andrews said.

"You're right. I'm speculating," Bill said.

Denise looked over at Ben Tatton's house. "You think it's a warning?"

"Maybe so." Bill locked eyes with the animal control officer. "Have you got something else you can put the snake in? I don't want anyone else touching the box, okay?"

"Sure. I'll get a trash bag." Eric headed for his vehicle.

"Dad, what are you going to do with that box?" Campbell asked.

"Call Keith. I want him to take it and see if he can get any fingerprints off it besides yours and mine. Anyone could have gotten it from the store's recycling bin." He eyed Campbell and Xina. "Are you two sure you want to stay here tonight?"

Campbell met Xina's gaze. "I'm game if you are."

"Yeah," Xina said. "But you can be sure we'll look carefully the next time we open the front door."

"I'm sorry, Ms. Harrison."

The doctor's grave expression torpedoed Campbell's hopes.

"Isn't there any change?" Xina's eyes glistened with unshed tears.

"She seems to be resting quietly now."

"Do you expect to keep her here?" Xina asked. "Or will she go to Nashville?"

"There's not a lot more they could do for her there. I spoke to a couple of doctors at Vanderbilt. They advised me to give it another day or two before making a decision like that."

"But she's still in the coma, not natural sleep?" Campbell asked.

He sighed. "We aren't monitoring brain activity constantly, but I think it's a case where she's on the edge. She could wake up anytime, or she could sink deeper and never emerge. I'm so sorry. But don't give up hope."

"Does it help if Xina talks to her?" Campbell asked.

"It may. We never know." He perused the clipboard in his hand. "Tell you what, I'm going to expand the visiting times for her. You can stay with her as much as you like through the day, but we'll still ask you to be out by 8 p.m. That will give her an uninterrupted twelve hours each night."

"But she's had that."

Xina's woeful tone tugged at Campbell's heart.

"Do you think it will make a difference if I stay most of the day?" Xina asked.

"I don't know, but it may. Talk to her if you want, sing to her, read to her. Whatever you think might get through to her. I understand she's a writer."

Xina nodded. "A very famous writer."

"Well, maybe if you read one of her books to her, or another author she likes."

"That's a thought." Xina's shoulders quivered.

"I'll help you pick out something." Campbell put an arm around her and gave her a little squeeze. "Do you want to go in now?"

Xina nodded. "Thank you, Doctor. Will I see you tomorrow?"

"I'll stop by in the morning. If you're here between nine and ten, you'll probably see me."

"I'll make sure of it."

An hour later, they were back at the house, sipping tea in the living room. Campbell sensed Xina's low spirits after the discouraging visit to the hospital, but she couldn't think of a way to buoy up her new friend. She'd been just as blue, or worse, when her father's condition was in doubt.

Xina pulled some papers from her purse and studied them.

"What have you got?" Campbell asked.

"The living will. There's something about it. I'm not sure what it is that bothers me. The hospital didn't have a problem with it."

Campbell moved from her chair and sat beside Xina on the couch. "May I?"

"Please."

Xina thrust the papers in her hands, and Campbell quickly scanned the document. Everything seemed in order, from dates and provisions to the signatures at the end. She flipped back to the first page.

"It looks all right to me."

She started to give them back, then froze, staring at the letterhead.

"Let's get those folders out of Katherine's bottom desk drawer again."

"Why? Is something wrong?"

"I'm not sure."

They both hurried into the study, and Xina unlocked the drawer. Campbell reached behind the metal box and lifted out the folders.

"House deed, auto—here we go." She separated the will and medical directives folders from the stack and put the others back.

"Show me the letterhead on your living will again."

Xina laid the papers on the desk.

"Okay." Campbell sat down in the wheeled office chair an opened the folder. "Here's Katherine's copy of the medical directive. It's the same as yours, right?"

Xina squinted at it and nodded.

"Now look at the return address on the envelope that says *Last Will and Testament.*"

With a gasp, Xina reached for the envelope. "It's from a different law firm. How did I not notice that before?"

"It didn't strike me, either," Campbell admitted. "She might have used different lawyers for the two, but it seems more likely she'd have them made at the same time, by the same attorney."

"She told me about her bequest to me when she gave me the living will." Xina stared at her with wide eyes. "Do you think we should open the will?"

Campbell hesitated. The thick envelope wasn't sealed with glue but was held closed by an elastic band attached to the envelope. If they were careful, there was no way Katherine could know they'd looked, but she could sense Xina's misgivings. She had qualms herself.

"What if we call my dad and ask him?"

Xina let out a pent-up breath. "Yes. I trust Bill's judgment." She grasped Campbell's shoulder. "Not that I don't trust you, but—"

"I understand. Older and wiser."

"Well, yes. Because of him, we didn't have to sleep with a poisonous snake under our front porch, and we had a policeman watching the house all night."

Campbell smiled. "Let's call. If Dad says open it, we'll open it. If not, we'll put it back in the drawer and walk away."

Xina nodded firmly. "Agreed."

Campbell took out her phone and keyed in Bill's number. As she waited, she swallowed hard.

"Hey, Soup," came his warm, reassuring voice. "What's up?"

With his permission, she set the phone to speaker mode so Xina could hear what he said. Then she explained how they had found an envelope of legal documents in Katherine's desk.

"But the return address of the law firm isn't the one Xina's familiar with, Dad. It's not the same lawyer who drew up the advance directive for medical care."

"Hm. So, you think it's a newer document?"

"We don't know."

"And Xina didn't have a copy of the will?"

Campbell raised her eyebrows at Xina.

"No, I didn't, but Aunt Katherine told me about it at least ten years ago. She said I was her heir."

"Would we be in legal trouble if we looked inside this envelope?" Campbell asked.

"Let me think about it. I'm not sure Xina has the authority for that. Is there a power of attorney document?"

Campbell quickly scanned the papers in the folder that weren't inside the envelope.

"Only as far as medical decisions go, I think."

"Okay, then I'm not sure. Who's the attorney?"

"The envelope says Dunn & McGann."

Bill chuckled. "I know them. I do profiles and background checks for them fairly often. In fact, Nick and I did some work for them last month."

"Oh, right. I thought that name sounded familiar."

"I could call Barry McGann if you like and ask him—in general terms, of course. He wouldn't violate client confidentiality about the contents," Bill said.

"What do you think, Xina?" Campbell asked.

"That might be good. Bill, do you know him well enough to call him in the evening?"

"I think so. Sit tight and I'll see if I can get hold of him."

Ten minutes later, he called back. Campbell quickly answered and set the speaker phone feature.

"I got a little more information than I expected," Bill said. "According to Barry, his firm did do some business for Katherine Tyler a few years ago. He said she wanted her will reworked, but she didn't ask for changes in her advance medical directives—her living will, that is."

"Okay," Campbell said, watching Xina's troubled face. "So, Xina is still in charge medically, but we don't know about the will."

"Right. And since he couldn't tell me about the contents of the will, Barry gave an off-the-record opinion. He said that since Katherine's health is so precarious right now and she may never regain consciousness, he didn't think anyone would pass judgment on her niece—who is her closest living relative and go-to medical person—if she took a look."

"Thanks, Dad."

Xina cleared her throat. "Bill, would you want to stay on the phone while I do that? I admit I'm a little skittish."

"Sure. But, Xina, you don't *have* to open it. If it will make you feel better not to, then just put it away for now."

Closing her eyes for a moment, Xina exhaled. "My scruples tell me to wait, but I'm not sure I could sleep, knowing this envelope is here in the house."

They sat in unbroken silence for several seconds.

"Okay." Xina flung up her hands. "I'm going to do it."

Campbell held out the envelope, and Xina took it. She bit her lip and worked the elastic closure off. From the envelope, she pulled several sheets of paper stapled together and unfolded them. She stared down at the first page for half a minute. Her face twitched, and she turned the page.

Campbell wanted to say something, but she didn't want to break Xina's concentration.

"You still there?" Bill asked.

"Xina's reading, Dad."

"Okay. Take your time."

Finally, Xina turned to the last page. After a few seconds, she lowered the papers to her lap and gazed over at Campbell, her lips parted.

"Are you okay?" Campbell asked.

"I think so. But ..."

Campbell held her breath.

Xina glanced at the will and then shoved it toward Campbell. "You read it. She's left her entire estate to someone I've never heard of before."

14

Xina's face crumpled as she waited. Campbell skimmed to the bequests and found it as Xina had said. Katherine left everything to a Janice Sandler. There were no charitable gifts or small bequests for Xina, the housekeeper, or anyone else.

"I don't get it," Campbell said.

"What?" Bill asked.

Campbell leaned toward the phone. "Ms. Tyler is leaving everything to someone named Janice Sandler."

"Spell it," Bill said.

As Campbell spelled out both names, Xina's lower lip quivered and her eyes filled with tears.

"We'll figure this out." Campbell gave her shoulder a pat.

"I'll do some quick online research and see what comes up," Bill said. "I'll call you back."

"Thanks, Dad." Campbell disconnected the call and turned to Xina. "Don't get upset. Dad will find out what's going on. If nothing else, you can call this attorney in the morning and ask if he'll speak to you. Mr. McGann sounds like a reasonable man. I'm sure he could advise you on your standing as far as the estate goes."

Xina's lips skewed. "It's not so much the estate—this house, and any money she might have. But she's disowning me. I always thought she loved me."

"I'm sure she does." Even as she spoke the words, Campbell had doubts.

"I shouldn't be here in her house," Xina said. "Should I go to a hotel?"

"Oh, I don't think you need to rush into that." Not for the first time, Campbell wished her dad had a bigger house and they could invite her to stay with them. "Nobody else knows what's in the will. At least, I don't think so."

"What about that Janice woman?"

"Well, she might. But she probably doesn't know you're here. If it comes up, just tell her you're Katherine's next of kin, and you're looking out for her health."

"What about the people who witnessed the will?"

Campbell studied the last page of the document. "I don't recognize the names. Do you?"

Xina shook her head.

"It could be people who work in the lawyer's office," Campbell said. "Let's just relax and see what Dad finds out."

Running a hand through her hair, Xina said, "I'm not sure I can ever relax again."

Campbell stood. "Let's go freshen our tea. Come on into the kitchen." Even a change that small might distract Xina.

She put Xina's mug in the microwave with fresh water and tea bag, to speed the process. As they waited, her thoughts churned.

"What am I going to do?" Xina wailed.

"Do you have any idea about your aunt's net worth?" Campbell asked.

Xina's eyes snapped to hers. "I—no. We found the deed to the house. It's a fairly large lot and the house is in good repair, so it must be worth quite a bit. She had a few thousand in her bank account."

The microwave's timer dinged, and Campbell took the mug out and put in the second one and then carried Xina's tea to the table.

"Here. Would you like something to go with it?"

"No, thanks," Xina said. "We didn't find anything like a mortgage. If she didn't own the house outright, we'd have found something, right?"

"Right. And you said she inherited this house from her parents. I'm sure it's been debt-free for years."

"Unless she borrowed on it."

"As you said, we found no evidence of that."

Xina sipped her tea, and her hand seemed steady.

Campbell took that as a sign she'd calmed down a little, and she went back to the counter to wait for her own cup to finish heating.

"We can look at those bank statements more closely," Xina said. "I don't know what else to look at for her net worth."

"There's a folder from a financial advisory company in the drawer with the bank statements."

"I think you're right."

"I didn't look closely at the investments, but they didn't look huge to me, not for someone of Katherine's stature in the popular fiction world. Do you know if she owns any other property?"

"If she does, it's news to me."

"Okay." Campbell retrieved her tea, grabbed a plastic container of cookies from the cupboard, and sat down with Xina.

"I thought she was well off," Xina said, "but now that we know she didn't have a new contract in two or three years, I wonder."

"Surely she invested a good chunk of what she earned over the years. She's a very popular author."

"Was," Xina said bleakly and reached for a cookie.

Finally Bill called back, and Campbell put the phone on speaker and set it on the table between her and Xina.

"Okay, I came up with at least eight distinct women named Janice Sandler online. There may be more. None of them lives in western Kentucky."

"That's odd," Xina said.

"Well, are you sure your aunt never lived outside the area? I know you said her parents owned that house when they were living."

"So far as I know, she lived here her whole life," Xina said.

"And she never married," Campbell put in.

Xina nodded. "That's right, Bill. She was engaged once, but the young man died a couple of months before the scheduled wedding. I don't think she ever got close to another man after that."

"Do you know his name?" Bill asked.

"Hmm. David, I think. Sorry, but I don't remember his last name. It may surface when I give my brain a rest."

"And was he from this area?"

Xina hesitated. "I think maybe she met him in college, but I'm not sure."

"Where did she go to college?"

"Vassar. I'm certain of that."

"Okay," Bill said. "Do you know what year she graduated?"

"No, but I'm sure I can work it out, or at least come close. Or maybe her diploma is here in the house."

"I think it might be in with her personal papers in her office," Campbell said. "I seem to recall seeing something like that."

"Good. If you can find that or at least get me a probable graduation year, I'm pretty sure I can access yearbooks and alumni records online. If you remember David's last name, we can look for him in her class or the two or three classes ahead of hers, but I expect there were quite a few Davids."

"Were they admitting men when Katherine attended?" Campbell asked.

"Yes, I'm sure of it," Xina said. "I don't think they had been for very long, but I know there were male students when she was there."

"Good," Bill said. "I'll double check when Vassar opened admissions to men, but it sounds about right to me. It's remotely possible this Sandler woman is related to the man Katherine was engaged to."

"Do you really think so?" Xina asked.

"I don't think anything yet, but if we want to find out who she is, we should consider every possibility. Well, thank you, ladies—uh, women."

Campbell laughed. "Dad, I don't think a couple of southern women like us will be offended if you call us ladies."

"Well, you've both forayed out to work in other parts of the country," he said sheepishly.

"Thanks for being socially conscious," Xina said with a chuckle.

After Bill signed off, Xina stood. "Your father's a hoot. But I don't think I can sleep until I look for her diploma. And she must have yearbooks around here somewhere." She frowned. "I don't remember seeing them, though. Maybe they're in the attic."

"Well, it's pretty late to be braving the attic." Campbell picked up their cups and headed for the sink. "But we can see if her diploma's in one of the drawers in the office."

While Xina sorted through the folders that weren't work-related, Campbell did a quick survey of the items in the desk.

"Are you sure it's not framed and hanging somewhere?"

"Not that I'm aware of." Xina pulled a folder from a bottom file drawer. "This is labeled *Education*." She opened it and thumbed through several documents. "Report cards, a couple of term papers. Oh, here's a high school transcript." She riffled the folders again and took out a padded folder and opened it. "High school diploma. Uh—here it is! Magna cum laude, no less."

"Bingo." Campbell pushed the desk chair back. "What year?"

When Xina told her, she called her father's cell phone.

"Great," Bill said. "Can we assume that was the end of her school career?"

"I think we can," Xina told him. "I don't know that she got any advanced degrees, although later on she received a couple of honorary ones."

"I wonder why she doesn't have them framed and hanging in here." Campbell looked around at the walls. A few plaques celebrating Katherine's awards hung about the room, and a poster-sized cover flat from *You'll Be Sorry*.

"Don't forget I'm leaving for Frankfort in the morning," Bill said. "I'll work on this awhile, and if I find out anything tonight, I'll call you before I leave or send you a message."

Campbell winced. She'd forgotten he was leaving for a couple of days. "Thanks, Dad. Drive safe."

"I will. If you need help, talk to Nick or Keith," Bill said. "Now I'll leave you and try to connect Katherine-the-student to a young man named David, or the mature Katherine to a female named Janice Sandler." He ended the call.

"I've known a couple of women named Janice." Campbell swiveled the desk chair back and forth. "None of them were named Sandler, though."

"And I've never known any Sandlers," Xina said.

"Sandler could be a married name, though."

"Or a maiden name for a woman who's now married."

Campbell sighed. "Think you can sleep tonight?"

"Maybe. But I do think I should move to a hotel tomorrow."

"If I were you, I'd call one of the lawyers first. We may be able to untangle this."

Slowly, Xina nodded. "What if I go to the hospital first thing, then try to connect with the lawyer?"

"Sounds like a good plan. Then you might have enough information to help you make a sound decision." Campbell rose. "Come on, let's make the rounds and check all the locks."

Campbell accompanied Xina to the hospital on Thursday morning and was allowed to go with her into Katherine's room in the intensive care unit. The pale woman lying on the bed looked small and fragile.

"She's so gaunt," Xina whispered. "I hardly recognize her."

"I'm sorry." Campbell squeezed Xina's hand. "Do you want to sit here a while, and maybe talk to her?"

Xina sniffed. "I guess I should."

"Well, she used to go to church. We could read some scripture to her."

"Maybe." Xina sounded doubtful. "I just wish I knew if she wanted me here. I don't want her to wake up and be furious to see me."

"Being here lets her know you care about her."

The small room held only one visitor seat. Campbell went out to the desk, and a nurse found another chair that wasn't in use and brought it in for her. Xina was sitting at the bedside, holding Katherine's hand that didn't have an IV line.

"I spoke to Mr. Waverly," Xina said in a semi-cheerful voice. "He was very sorry to hear you'd been injured, Aunt Katherine. He wanted to know if there was anything he could do to help you. I told him I didn't think so, but that I'd ask you as soon as you were able to talk to me."

She glanced over, and Campbell gave her a nod of encouragement.

"I do wish you'd wake up," Xina said. "There's so much we need to talk about."

Campbell's cell phone rang, and she started. Signs admonished visitors to turn off their cell phones in the unit, but she'd forgotten this morning. She ducked out of the room and past the nurses' desk, into a wide hallway near the waiting room.

"Dad?"

"Yeah. Thought you weren't going to answer."

"Sorry. I was in the ICU with Xina."

"I didn't think of that. How's Katherine?"

"She looks the same. We haven't seen the doctor yet. Xina's talking to Katherine, but there's no sign that she hears." Campbell let out a sigh and leaned against the wall.

"Any chance of you going into the office this afternoon?" Bill asked. "Keith called. He forgot I'd be out of town, and he wants to come by at one and update you."

"Sure. Should Xina be there? We plan to see Mr. McGann about the new will after her visit with Katherine."

"Hmm. You may learn something then. Better take her along to the office, unless she's really stressed."

"I think she'll want to be there. But she also wants to stay here at least until the doctor does his rounds."

"You'd better call the law firm now and try to set up an appointment. It may be hard to get in without one."

"True," Campbell said. "Has Keith got something pertinent?"

Bill chuckled. "Or maybe relevant? Or just plain important?"

"Oh, Dad."

He laughed. "Well, I just stopped for gas. I'll try to call you once I get to my hotel and run through my notes on Janice Sandler."

"Did you get something last night?"

"Nothing definite, but I have a few leads you can follow up on. Call you later."

She pushed off from the wall and tucked her phone into her purse as she made her way back to Katherine's room. She had meant to check over her dad's dress shirts before he left, but she hadn't gotten a chance. But then, he'd been looking after his own wardrobe for years. Unless she was mistaken, he'd make a presentable appearance in court.

Xina sat where Campbell had left her. Tears ran down her cheeks as she stared silently at Katherine's face.

Campbell tiptoed over and rested a hand on Xina's shoulder. "Would you like to pray together?" Asking felt odd, because she hadn't prayed out loud in a long time, but Campbell had no doubt that God was real, and that He cared about his children. He'd brought her father home.

Xina grasped her hand. "Thank you. Let's."

Sitting side by side, they each offered a short, heartfelt petition.

When Campbell said amen, she opened her eyes to find the doctor standing in the doorway.

"Didn't want to interrupt you," he said.

Brushing a tear from her cheek, Xina stood. "Please come in, Dr. Drummond."

While Xina talked to the doctor, Campbell remained in her seat and listened, watching her client's worried face.

"I'm still hopeful," Dr. Drummond said. "The tests we did yesterday showed good brain activity. She may be fighting her way back to consciousness."

"Do you really think so?" Xina asked.

"I do. And I'm praying for Ms. Tyler myself. We don't usually bring it up, but since you and your friend were praying when I came in ..."

"Thank you." Xina's voice cracked.

Katherine's eyelids fluttered but then remained closed.

"Doctor," Campbell said softly, "she blinked."

He stepped to the other side of the bed and studied Katherine, then put his stethoscope to her chest. After several seconds, he straightened and looked at the monitors.

"You'll see that now and then—probably more often now. I truly think she's improving."

"I was going to go talk to her lawyer," Xina said. "Maybe I should stay here."

The doctor tilted his head to one side, gazing at the patient. "It can be a long process. She could wake up soon, or it could be several more days. But I think it's coming, barring any setbacks. Why don't you keep your appointment and come back afterward? I can ask the nurses to call your cell phone at once if there's a big change."

Xina glanced at Campbell then back to the doctor. "That sounds practical. Thank you."

He laid out a bit more information on the test results. Campbell kept watch, but she didn't see any more movement from Katherine.

When Dr. Drummond left the room, Xina came to stand beside her.

"Anything?"

"No," Campbell said. "But my dad suggested we call ahead to the lawyer's office. That way we won't truck over there and be disappointed if he can't see you."

"Good idea."

Campbell stayed in the room while Xina went out to the hallway to place her call. She was soon back, her eyes gleaming.

"He'll see us now. In fifteen minutes, if we can make it."

"We can."

Xina stepped to the bedside. "Goodbye for now, Aunt Katherine. I'll be back later." She took a thick paperback from her bag and laid it on the bedside table. "Almost forgot I brought that along," she said. "I'll leave it here to remind me to read to her."

Campbell recognized the book as one that had been on Katherine's nightstand when she settled into her room. From the cover, she thought it was romantic suspense, and she'd heard of the author, Amelia Richfield. A bookmark was stuck in it, about a third of the way through the pages.

She followed Xina to the elevators and out to her Fusion. On the way, she told Xina about Bill's possible leads and the scheduled meeting with Keith.

"I think I should go back to the hospital after this," Xina said. "You can tell me about it later."

When they walked into the attorney's outer office, the

receptionist called McGann and then showed them into his office.

Pretty spiffy, Campbell thought. McGann had a huge desk. The carpet felt thick and cushy, and the drapes and furnishings screamed *money*. An array of built-in shelves held lawbooks and art objects. McGann seemed to have a love of sailing and the Kentucky Derby.

"Ms. Harrison?" he extended his hand to Xina.

"Yes, and this is Campbell McBride."

"McBride?" He smiled questioningly.

"That's right," Campbell said, shaking his hand. "Bill McBride is my father. I work with him now, and we're representing Ms. Harrison."

"Interesting. Have a seat, won't you?" When they were all settled, he gazed at Xina. "I understand you're here about Katherine Tyler's will."

"That's right," Xina said.

"Bill told me she's in the hospital, and I'm very sorry about that. But you do understand, since you aren't named in her will, I can't discuss its contents with you."

Xina hesitated then squared her shoulders. "It's just that I had no idea this will existed. She had a previous will in which she named me as her heir. She also had an advanced medical directive." She held out her copy of the document. "I believe this is still in place."

McGann took it and looked it over briefly. "I double-checked after Bill called me, and this firm did not make a new or revised advance directive for Ms. Tyler. All we handled was her will."

Xina looked helplessly at Campbell.

"Did she mention her niece to you?" Campbell asked.

"Not that I recall."

"But you were the one who drew up her new will."

"That's correct."

Campbell frowned. "Were you aware that it was a

replacement for an older document—one drawn up by Woodrow Stallings?"

"No, but that's not unusual. People grow older, things change, and they decide to distribute things differently."

Campbell wasn't sure where to take the conversation. They might not get anything useful out of this visit.

"I know Mr. Stallings," McGann said. "I wasn't aware that Ms. Tyler had been a client of his. We don't discuss our clients with lawyers outside this firm."

"I see," Xina said.

"She didn't bring in her old will and say, 'I want to change this,' or something like that?" Campbell asked.

"No, we started from scratch."

"You seem to remember it clearly."

He nodded. "It was a couple of years ago, but after I spoke to Bill last night I reviewed my file on Ms. Tyler. I recognized her name at the time, and of course I was interested to meet her. I recall the session very well."

Campbell met Xina's gaze. "I'm sorry. It seems Mr. McGann can't help us."

He picked up the advanced directive papers and held them out to Xina. "If it's any consolation, from looking at that I'd say you're still the right person to deal with her medical affairs."

"Unless a newer directive shows up that was written by yet another lawyer." Xina folded the document and put it in her purse.

"That's always a possibility," McGann said. "But you found a new will and didn't find a new directive, so she probably didn't make another one."

"Thank you." Xina rose stiffly.

As they walked out to the car, Campbell studied her profile. Xina looked calm but disappointed.

"Do you want to get an early lunch before my meeting with Detective Fuller, or go straight back to the hospital?"

Xina's whirled toward her. "Why would she cut off my inheritance but leave me in charge of life-and-death decisions?"

"I don't know. I'm sorry."

Xina let out a big sigh. "Let me off at the hospital, I guess. I'll get something in the cafeteria and go back to her room. I can take a taxi to the house later."

15

After dropping Xina off at the hospital, Campbell drove to True Blue and found Nick typing madly away at his computer and occasionally reaching over for an M&M, which he popped into his mouth.

"You'll spoil your lunch," Campbell said in her best mom-of-naughty-boy voice.

"Hey, Professor. Did you eat yet?"

"No. Want to go out?" she asked.

"Keith Fuller's coming at one."

"Yeah, I know. I could get some takeout, if you haven't totally ruined your appetite."

Twenty minutes later she returned with a carry-out order from Wendy's, and they spread it out on Campbell's empty desktop. She had just sat down when her father called.

"All checked in?" she asked him.

"Yeah." He gave her the name and room number of his hotel. "I have to be at the courthouse at two, and I'll have my phone off while I'm there."

"Got it. Nick's here with me." She put the call on speaker.

"How'd it go with Barry this morning?" Bill asked.

"He's seemed straightforward about the will," she said as she opened a container of chicken salad.

"I'm pretty sure Barry's a straight-up guy," Bill said. "He wouldn't take advantage of old ladies."

"Katherine's not that old."

"Yeah, not that much older than me, right?"

"Oh, come on, Dad. You know what I mean. And you hardly have any gray. Yet."

He laughed.

"He didn't give us any new information, though," Campbell said.

"Okay, so I've narrowed down your Janice Sandler to three possible women. Unless she's totally under the radar, that is."

"Fantastic. I didn't think you'd have time to do much on this."

"I spent an hour or so on it last night after we talked. But first, Nick, how are you doing on Jacob Gray's daughter?"

"I was going to ask you about that lead in Lexington. Her father thinks it might be her, and he's excited about it."

"I'm thinking maybe you should go over there," Bill said.

"To bring her back?" Nick asked.

"Well, to talk to her person-to-person. If we phone her, it might just scare her off."

"It's a five-hour drive, at least," Campbell said.

"I know."

"I can go if you want me to." Nick took a big bite of his burger.

"Well, I think you should stay there close to Campbell while I'm in the capital," Bill said. "She's still green, and I don't want to leave her alone yet."

"Dad," she protested, "I'm right here, you know."

"Sorry, Soup. But the case you're working on is an odd one. Nick may be able to help you out."

"So, I should soft-pedal it until you get back?" Nick asked.

"Yeah, if Campbell doesn't need you, open the file on that insurance fraud case."

"Will do."

"All right. If I end up coming back here Monday, maybe I could make the Lexington run. Anyway, Campbell, I put the details on the three possible Janice Sandlers into one file, and I'm emailing it to you right ... now. If you're all set, I'm going to grab some lunch before I go to court."

"Great," she said. "Thanks, Dad. Call me later?"

"For sure. And don't hold anything back from Keith."

"I won't."

They signed off, and Campbell turned her attention to her salad. When they had demolished their meal, she wiped her mouth and finished her diet soda. With about fifteen minutes before Keith was supposed to arrive, she threw away her food wrappers, took her laptop from her leather bag, and set it on the desktop.

Nick slurped the dregs of his drink through the straw and snatched his wrappers from the desk.

She brushed away a few crumbs, then opened her email. One from Steve Bishop jumped out at her, and she previewed it.

Glad the books got there ok, was all it said.

Next, she clicked on her father's latest. She had barely skimmed through it when the door opened.

"Good afternoon."

"Oh, Keith! Come on in." She jumped up and waved toward Bill's chair. "Have a seat."

"Thanks."

"You want me in on this?" Nick asked.

"If you want to be," Campbell replied.

He wheeled his chair over.

"So, no more wildlife around Katherine's place this morning?" Keith asked.

"No, I'm thankful to say."

Keith nodded. "Glad to hear it. We did go over that box your dad had put the snake in."

"Find anything good?" Campbell asked.

"Well, it would have been better if he had given it to us before putting the mangled snake it." Keith gave her a wry smile. "Then we would have been able to tell if Bill's wild theory holds water."

Campbell grimaced. "Do you think someone really put that copperhead there on purpose?"

"I don't know. We did find your prints and Bill's, and some from the gift shop's owner. She was very cooperative. The box was delivered to the store a couple of days before you found it, along with several others. It was full of merchandise she'd ordered. After she emptied it, she flattened it and put it in her recycling bin. End of story."

"Where anyone could have snitched one," Campbell said.

"Correct. It's just too sketchy to draw any conclusions."

She nodded. "Whereas, if we'd found the empty box and you'd found snake scales inside it before my dad played Butch Cassidy with the copperhead, we might have had something."

"Right. Anyone in the neighborhood could have brought that box home and abandoned it outside, where the wind got hold of it. So, moving right along, what do you have on Katherine Tyler?" Keith sank back in the chair and stretched out his long legs.

"She's still unconscious. The doctor says he's hopeful that she'll come out of it, but frankly, we don't see a lot of change. Xina's back over there now."

"I understand you found a will with a bit of a bombshell?"

She nodded. "That's worrisome, but the medical power of attorney still seems to be in place, so Xina's sticking to the job on that. But she thinks she ought to move out of the house, since Katherine is apparently leaving it to someone out of the blue."

"A stranger?" Keith asked.

"To Xina, anyway. I'm assuming Katherine knows her. Dad did some investigating last night, and he just sent me some details on three women he thinks are good candidates for the new heir. Would you like me to fill you in?"

"Sure."

Nick leaned in too, and both men listened while Campbell read from her laptop screen.

"The first Janice Sandler is seventy, living in Elizabethtown. In a way, she seems unlikely. I mean, why leave your worldly goods to someone older than you?" She looked up into Keith's brown eyes.

"True. But she's not that much older than Katherine, right?"

"I guess not. But it still seems odd."

"Unless she's a relative or an old friend, and Katherine wants to be sure she's taken care of in her old age," Nick said.

Campbell gave a reluctant nod. "Like I said, it's possible. And she is the closest one geographically. But she's not a close relative, or Xina would know her. I suppose she could be a cousin, but my research last week told us Xina didn't have any living first cousins."

"But it could be one of Katherine's cousins, or a more distant relative," Keith said. "Maybe someone Xina didn't know about. So, what do you know about this seventy-year-old Janice?"

"She's widowed and didn't have a career as such. Dad says she used to work at a department store. The other two he flagged are younger. The one in St. Louis is around fifty, and she runs an antiques mall. The one in California is thirty-eight."

"California?" Nick stared at her. "You're not going out there, are you?"

"I don't plan to. Not unless we find out for sure she's the heir, and if Dad thinks it's necessary. This says she teaches at a small private school. Married, two kids." Campbell looked up.

"So she won't disappear on us," Nick said.

"Right."

Keith took out his pocket notebook and wrote in it. "So, you need to find a link between Katherine and one of these women. Do you have any inklings?"

"Not yet. I just got this list. And Sandler could be their married names. If we find out their maiden names, it may help us. So, how are things going on the Tatton case?"

Keith shrugged. "Slowly. I have one neighbor who saw a car parked on the street the day it happened. No plate number, but we're trying to run down the owner."

"Anything more on the time of death?" Campbell asked.

"The medical examiner is pretty sure it happened after 10 p.m. Thursday. Up until his report came in, the closest we had was your conversation with him around three o'clock."

"So, between ten Thursday night and noon Friday?"

"Well, he was found at noon. The M.E. said he'd been dead at least six hours, so between 10 p.m. and 6 a.m."

"That's a much better window of time to investigate."

"Yeah, we're concentrating on that—late evening and overnight."

"What time was the car parked outside?" Nick asked.

"The neighbor came home from a movie around half past ten, and it was there then. He doesn't know when it arrived or how long it sat there. He just noticed because it was on his side of the street, not too far from his driveway, and it was unusual."

Campbell jotted *car 10:30 p.m. Thur* on a memo sheet. "Can you tell us what the car looked like?"

"The witness wasn't sure, but he thinks it was a Ford sedan, and it was dark-colored."

"Not much to go on," Nick muttered as Campbell wrote it down.

"You're telling me." Keith stretched. "That's the most of it. I told you that he wasn't just hit over the head."

Campbell grimaced. "Yeah, you said he was stabbed too."

"In the back," Keith said. "Damaged his heart and punctured his left lung."

"Stabbed *and* coshed. So, not premeditated."

"Who knows? The killer may have planned to do it, or he could have found a weapon of opportunity."

"Like one of Ben Tatton's own knives?" she asked.

"We're not sure."

Nick rubbed his chin. "Less chance of tracing it back to the killer."

"That's if we find either weapon," Keith said.

The door opened, and Xina came in. Keith jumped up, and Nick belatedly shuffled to his feet.

"Ms. Harrison," Keith said. "How's your aunt?"

"The doctor said she's in natural sleep now. I took a cab to the house for my things, so that if she wakes up, I can tell her I'm not staying there. I just ran in to let you know, and I'm going right back to the hospital. I'll be at the Marriott tonight."

"Do you want me to stay there with you?" Campbell asked.

"I'll be fine. No bumpy air conditioning or creaky old floor joists."

"Or snakes," Nick said.

Campbell scowled at him. "Don't hesitate to call us at any time, Xina."

"I won't. And I'll call you if there's a change in Aunt Katherine's condition."

She left, and Campbell turned to Keith. "Let's pray she wakes up. That could solve a lot of these questions."

"Yes, on your end. I doubt it will help with the Tatton murder." Keith glanced at his watch. "I'd better get going. Call me if you need anything, Campbell."

"Thanks."

She saw a glance flash between him and Nick, and she thought Nick gave him a little nod. Were they conspiring to protect her? In a way, it ticked her off. She wasn't helpless. But in another way, it felt good to know they truly cared about her. They both knew about the break-in at her father's house when she was staying there alone. In light of the unsolved murder

Keith was working on, it cheered her to know she had a couple of sturdy young men willing to help her.

Campbell spent two hours researching the three Janice Sandlers. The woman living in Elizabethtown, Kentucky, being the closest, drew her attention first, even though Campbell had serious doubts about her. Still, Katherine may have chosen to bless an old friend or distant relative with an inheritance, as Keith had suggested. But try as she would, she found no connection.

"I am so frustrated with this," she sputtered as she went to refill her coffee mug.

"Why don't you just call her?" Nick asked.

"Well, Dad's always saying we don't want to scare anyone off."

"From what? She hasn't committed a crime, that we know of. You could call to see if she knows Katherine Tyler. Say you're a friend or something."

Campbell scrunched up her face. She didn't like to lie to people. "I guess I could tell her about Katherine's accident, if she doesn't know about it."

"There you go." Nick turned back to his computer.

After getting her coffee, Campbell returned to her desk and looked over her notes about the elderly woman in E-town. She hauled in a deep breath, picked up the desk phone's receiver, and punched in the phone number her father had given her. She was still unsure of what she would say.

"Hello?"

Campbell gulped. She sure sounded like an older woman. "Mrs. Sandler?"

"Yes."

"My name is Campbell McBride. I'm calling about Katherine Tyler. Do you know Miss Tyler?"

"Who?"

"Katherine Tyler. She lives in Murray, over in western Kentucky."

"Hmm, I don't think so. What's this about?"

"Well, Miss Tyler is ill, and I'm trying to contact some friends of hers. I ran across the name Janice Sandler, and I wasn't sure if you were the right one or not."

"I don't think so. I don't know anyone in Murray."

"She's about your age," Campbell said. "I thought maybe you went to school together. And she writes books now."

"Doesn't ring a bell."

Grasping at a rather flimsy straw, Campbell said, "She went to Vassar. I don't suppose you attended there?"

The woman laughed. "Honey, I never went to college anywhere."

"Okay. Well, thanks for your time." Campbell hung up.

"Shoulda given her your number, in case she remembers something," Nick said without looking up.

Campbell pressed her lips together to hold in a scream, or at least a scathing retort. If she could think of one.

"I'm crossing her off the list." She tried to infuse her voice with dignity.

"She might have a bad memory and remember something later." His voice rose almost mockingly in his warning.

Campbell wanted to say *shut up,* but she didn't.

Nick shoved his chair back and stood. "I'm going out and see if I can put eyes on this insurance fraud woman. I probably won't be back before five."

Good! Campbell managed a serene, "Okay."

"Want me to call you at closing time?"

"What for?"

"Bill and I usually touch base at the end of the day if we haven't been working together."

"I guess that's a good practice. Sure."

He nodded. "And remember, if something hot comes up on your case, or if anything wacky happens, you take precedence over my surveillance."

"Thank you, Nick. That's good to know."

He hit the restroom and then left with his camera and binoculars.

Campbell leaned back in her chair and let out a big sigh. Finally, she could work without Nick hearing every word she said or smelling the smoke from her brain when she overheated mentally.

She attacked social media, trying to unearth more hints about the remaining two candidates. Her growing lists of data didn't seem to have anything to do with Katherine.

When her cell phone rang, she looked at the screen. It was nearly five o'clock, and Xina was calling her.

"Hi, Xina. Anything new on Katherine?"

"Not really. I'm going back after I eat. I wondered if you wanted to meet for dinner."

Campbell gave it about two seconds' thought. She had a small income now, as her father had started paying her, and going home to his house alone to prepare a meal for herself would be depressing. "Sure."

"How about that Mexican place?" Xina described the location, about half a mile down the street from her hotel.

"Oh, yeah, I know where you mean."

"Six o'clock?" Xina asked.

"I'll be there." Campbell hung up. Now she had an hour to kill. Xina probably wanted to go to the hotel to change or something. She looked down at the black pants and plaid blouse she'd put on that morning when they left Katherine's house for the hospital. It seemed ages ago. Maybe she'd run home and freshen up too.

Her route took her past the former site of Bella's clothing store. It had closed abruptly after the owner's arrest a few weeks ago, but to Campbell's surprise, a crew was working on the storefront, taking down the huge letters that spelled the name. Had someone new rented the building, or even bought out the business? Interesting.

A few minutes later, she stopped at the end of Bill's driveway to grab the contents of his mailbox. Most of it was for her father, but she frowned over an envelope addressed to her. She hurried into the house and placed Bill's mail on his desk. They'd moved it into the living room when her comfortable double bed had arrived to replace the hide-a-bed in his former den. It was now her room, and she headed there with her letter in hand.

The envelope was business-sized, with a return address for a college in Virginia. Campbell had applied for work there after losing her position at Feldman in Iowa. She tore it open, her feelings volleying back and forth between hoping they'd offer her a job and wondering how to turn them down gently.

"We regret that we have no openings in your field at this time ..."

She sank down on the bed. Relief, that was what she felt. Despite its challenges, she actually liked training to be a private investigator.

Rubbing her temples, she tried to force her mind away from jobs and Janice Sandlers. She wanted more than anything to talk to her father, but if she didn't hurry, Xina would be waiting for her at the restaurant.

She'd just finished changing when her cell rang.

"Hey, it's Nick. I'm still at the subject's house. I don't think she's home, so I'm going to stick around here a while longer. If she doesn't show by seven, I'll knock off for the night."

"Okay, thanks," Campbell said. "I'm going to eat out with Xina, and then go over to the hospital with her. I'll see you tomorrow."

AFTER FILLING up on salad and quesadillas, Xina leaned back in her chair. "I am so stuffed."

"Me too." Campbell drained her iced tea glass.

"I've been thinking," Xina said.

Campbell arched her eyebrows and waited.

"This Janice person."

"Yes?"

Xina's mouth skewed. "I suppose I should forget about it, but ..."

"But you're curious," Campbell said.

"Very."

"We all are. That's why Dad and I are digging into it. We've pretty much ruled out the older lady in E-town."

"Where's that?"

"Elizabethtown. It's between here and Louisville. I mean, she could still be the one, but she says she doesn't know Katherine, and she didn't go to the same schools or anything like that."

Xina nodded, her lips pursed. "Of course, Aunt Katherine met a lot of people when she was younger. She went to writers' conferences and did book signings and speaking engagements now and then, although I don't think she enjoyed it. She was always quiet." She met Campbell's gaze. "What do you know about the other two women?"

"Well, they're both married, so Sandler is the married name for both of them."

"Did you find their maiden names?"

"The one in St. Louis was born Janice Palmer. I haven't found the one in California's maiden name yet."

"Palmer." Xina shook her head. "I can't think of any family connections by that name." Her eyes flared. "Maybe we should go back over to the house and look through Aunt Katherine's address book and phone contacts."

"Now, that is a great idea." Campbell grabbed her purse. "Come on."

When they arrived at Katherine's house, they looked around carefully outside, but saw nothing out of place. Xina unlocked the door, and they went straight to the study.

"I'm pretty sure I know where her address book is." Campbell opened a desk drawer. "Yeah, right here." She held it out to Xina.

"Hmm, nothing under Sandler. Let's try Palmer." Xina flipped back a couple of pages. "Look."

Campbell took the book and gazed at it. "Dwight Palmer. But it's crossed out."

"What do you think that means?" Xina asked.

"Maybe he moved." She held the book closer. "I can still read through the scribbles a little bit. I think it says O'Fallon, Missouri."

"Did you bring your laptop?" Xina asked.

"It's in the car. I'll go get it."

Campbell hurried out and unlocked the car door. As she leaned in on the passenger side, she thought she heard something. She straightened with the laptop case in her hand and looked around. Twilight was deepening, and she couldn't see any movement in the yard. A car slowly rolled down the street and passed the house.

She pulled in a deep breath, closed the car door, and pushed the lock button on her remote.

"Here it is," she called to Xina as she went back inside. She made sure the front door was locked behind her.

"I found O'Fallon on my phone," Xina said. "It's near St. Louis."

"Okay. Let me see what I can pull up on Dwight Palmer of O'Fallon." Campbell opened her laptop on Katherine's desk. After a few minutes, she looked up at Xina. "I'm sorry. It's an obituary."

Xina sighed and leaned in to read over her shoulder. "He died of a heart attack. What a shame."

Campbell nodded. "It says he was born in Illinois ... Oh, wait! Listen to this! He is survived by his son Gilbert and three daughters, Heather (Mrs. John Andrews), Karen, and Janice (Mrs. Todd Sandler), and seven grandchildren."

16

"That's got to be our Janice." Xina's eyes were alight with excitement. "We could drive there in four or five hours."

"Easy, now," Campbell said. "We need to think this over."

"You're right. A phone call would be more practical, I guess."

"I'd like to discuss it with my dad before we do anything. It seems like a great lead, but I want his advice on how to approach a conversation with this Janice Sandler." Campbell pulled out her phone and touched the screen. "It's almost eight o'clock. Dad's got to be free now."

She hesitated. He'd said he would call, and she hated to interrupt anything. On the other hand, he'd told her to call if she needed his advice. She brought up his name and tapped it.

"Hey, Soup." He sounded cheerful, but tired. "How's it going?"

"Good. How about there?"

"I just had dinner with an old colleague who's also testifying. It was a long afternoon in court, and I need to go back at nine in the morning. I think I'll go to the hotel and get some rest."

"You do that," Campbell said. "I'd just like a quick opinion on something."

She heard a car door shut on the other end of the connection.

"Shoot," he said.

"I think I've found the right Janice Sandler."

"Terrific! I knew you'd figure it out. Which one is it?"

"The one in Missouri. I did a little genealogy research on her and found her maiden name, Palmer. Xina and I came back to Katherine's house, and we found a Dwight Palmer in her address book. I found his obituary online, and he's survived by a daughter named Janice Sandler."

"That's good work, sweetheart."

"Thanks. So, we wondered if I should call her. I found a number online. Is there a reason to wait?"

"I wouldn't think so. Just be careful how you say things."

Campbell discussed her approach with him for a few more minutes. Finally, she felt she was ready. "Okay, Dad. Thanks."

"Call me back and let me know how it goes."

"I will." She ended the call and met Xina's gaze. "I guess you heard. He says to do it."

Xina nodded, wide-eyed. "You'll talk to her, right?"

"Sure. I don't even have to mention you if you don't want."

"Let's see if she has any idea who Katherine is first."

"Right." Campbell tapped in the digits for the phone number. As it began to ring, she gave Xina a smile she hoped was reassuring.

"Hello?"

"Hi. Janice Sandler?"

"Yes."

"My name is Campbell McBride. I'm an investigator, and I'm doing some research on Katherine Tyler. Do you know Ms. Tyler?"

"Tyler? Hmm ... I don't think so."

After a moment's silence, Campbell said, "She's a writer, if that helps. A novelist."

"What's this for?"

Patience, Campbell told herself. "I work for True Blue Investigations, in Murray, Kentucky. We represent a family member of Ms. Tyler's. Are you familiar with her name?"

"I've heard the name," Janice said slowly. "Does she write romances?"

"Romantic suspense."

"Okay, yeah, I think I've heard of her. Haven't read any of her books, though."

"She was very popular a few years back," Campbell said.

"Maybe my mother knows about her."

Good idea, Campbell thought. After all, it was Mr. Palmer who was in Katherine's address book, not Janice.

"Would you be willing to share a phone number for your mother?"

"Why don't I call her and see if she's willing to talk to you."

"That's fine," Campbell said, "and you can look us up online in the meantime, if you want to." She gave Janice the URL for the True Blue Investigations website, which Nick maintained for her father.

"Why exactly did you call?"

Campbell swallowed hard. "Your name came up in Ms. Tyler's papers. We were looking for names and addresses of her friends and business contacts. She's had an accident, and we thought people would want to know."

"Oh, I'm sorry. I'll ask my mother if she knows her."

"Thank you."

As she put her phone away, Xina said, "If I'm going back to the hospital tonight, I'd better hurry."

"Okay. Let's put away the things we got out." Campbell slid the gray loose-leaf book back into the drawer.

"Can I touch base with you when I get back to the hotel?"

"Of course."

They turned out all the lights and locked up Katherine's house. Campbell drove back to her father's house. For the first time since Bill's return, she would be alone there overnight. She tried to shake off the bad memories as she opened the front door.

Her old precautionary habits returned, and she made a quick sweep of the house before retiring to her room.

IN THE MORNING, Campbell awoke with a hopeful air. The sunlight streamed in through her window. Dad would be home tonight, and she had a date with Keith. That thought alone kept her smiling as she prepared for work and drove to the office.

Nick wasn't in yet, but her father phoned as she started the coffeemaker.

"How'd it go last night?" he asked.

She told him about her conversation with Janice Sandler. "I hope she'll call me today with her mother's phone number. Meanwhile, I guess I'll do more research on her family. There's got to be some reason Katherine's leaving her entire estate to Janice."

"Did you tell her about the will?" Bill asked.

"No. I just told her we'd found her name in some of Katherine's papers and were trying to contact friends and relatives to tell them about her accident. She said she was sorry to hear it, but she seemed genuinely in the dark. She didn't recognize Katherine's name at first."

"Hang in there," her father advised. "If you dig long enough and hard enough, you're bound to find something that makes sense."

"Thanks, Dad."

"How's Xina doing?"

"Okay. She went back to see Katherine last night, and then went to her hotel. I told her to call me anytime today. I think she'll spend most of it at the hospital, and I'll try to get some work done."

"Sounds like a plan. Gotta go. I'll call you later, when I set out for home."

One of the first things Campbell did was review Janice's father's obituary. She noted with surprise that he'd attended the University of Kentucky for two years before doing a stint in the army.

On her favorite genealogy site, she roughed out a simple family tree, inserting the names of Janice's siblings. By itself, that seemed useless. They were all younger than Katherine, and their parents would have been at least ten years her senior. Not likely casual acquaintances.

She did more searching online for both Janice and her father, the two names they'd found associated with Katherine. She didn't find much on Janice, except for a wedding announcement. Dwight Palmer had been a physical education teacher for most of his adult life. He'd moved his family to the St. Louis area thirty years ago, apparently to be near a new job. He'd retired at sixty-two.

His name turned up as a swimming instructor at a youth club when he was in his twenties. Even earlier, he'd spent a couple of summers lifeguarding at a state park in Kentucky, not far from Lexington, where he'd attended college. At age nineteen, he was featured in a newspaper story as a local hero, having saved a young girl from drowning.

Campbell studied the photos of Dwight Palmer that accompanied the articles. He was a handsome young man, but she couldn't see any connection to Katherine or the Tyler family.

Nick came in and headed straight for the coffeepot. Campbell noted it was nearly ten o'clock.

"How are you feeling?" she asked.

"Great. I think I can wrap up my report on the case I was working on today."

"The Gray case?"

"No, the insurance one. I got some good pictures last night.

And we've got a couple more employee profiles I can work on, unless you've got something I can help you with."

"I'm trying to figure out what to work on myself," she admitted. "I know there has to be a connection between Katherine Tyler and the woman she named in her new will, but I can't find it, and the heir has no clue."

After lunch she was still at loose ends, so she decided to pop in at the hospital. Xina was on duty in Katherine's room.

"Campbell, I'm so glad you're here!"

"Is there a change?"

"The doctor thinks so. I read to her all morning, and she moved more. Her hand twitched, and then her face moved. She didn't open her eyes, that I saw, but I'm starting to believe it will happen."

"That's great. How's the book?" Campbell nodded at the paperback in Xina's hand.

"Oh, it's okay. It sounds a lot like her last book, though."

"Like Amelia Richfield's last book? I didn't—"

"No, like Aunt Katherine's last book. *Ice Cold Blue*."

"That's the one Krata Press published."

"Yeah."

"Odd." Campbell couldn't think what else to say.

CAMPBELL EYED herself in the inexpensive full-length mirror she'd bought at Walmart. Her father would never care to see his full image, but having only the mirror over the bathroom vanity had driven her crazy.

Were the linen pants and subdued top dressy enough for the theater? Of course they were. Probably she'd see patrons in jeans and shorts there. The building was an old train depot that had been moved to the park fifty years earlier and converted into a small community theater.

The doorbell rang and she jumped. He was early, and she still hadn't decided whether to change into a dress. Too late. She hurried out to the front door.

"Hi," Keith said with an apologetic smile. "I'm a few minutes early, I know, but I brought you something."

She looked past him. A four-shelf pine bookcase sat on the porch with a red bow on top.

"I remembered you didn't have anywhere to unpack your books. If you've already got something—"

"No, I don't," she said quickly. "Thanks so much."

He grinned and picked up the bookcase. "Lead the way."

A bookcase of her own. Campbell had meant to pick up one, but she hadn't wanted a flimsy chipboard shelf unit, and she hadn't had time to think too deeply about where to look for a nice one.

She led him down the hall to the den-turned-bedroom and paused in the doorway. Two blouses lay discarded on the bed, the closet door was open, and her cartons of books still sat to one side. At least the bed was made.

"Uh, right in here." She shouldn't be embarrassed. It could be a lot worse. And Keith had seen this room before, after all. Of course, that was the night someone had broken into the house, and there had been several other police officers in here too.

"Where—"

"Oh, sorry. I think I'll put it where the cartons are. Let me just push them out of the way."

He set down the bookcase and grabbed one box while she shifted the other. With a flourish, he moved the bookcase against the wall, under her framed diploma for her master's degree. Keith eyed the certificate for a moment.

"I only ever went to Murray State," he said.

"So? It's a good school. I wouldn't have applied for work there if it wasn't."

His eyes zipped to hers. "Did you hear back on that?"

She shrugged. "They had a part time post open, but I've decided to stay on with Dad. At least for a while."

His smile returned. "Where is Bill? Still in Frankfort?"

"Yeah, he called me when he left his hotel. I don't expect he'll get back for a couple of hours."

"Does he have to go back next week?"

"No, they've assured him his testimony was helpful and lucid, but finished."

"Great. Well, are you all set, or do you need a few minutes?"

"I'm ready." She realized she truly was. Keith sported black jeans and a short-sleeved cotton shirt. Perfect date-wear for summer in Kentucky.

She grabbed her purse from the dresser, and they went out to his black SUV, the ideal, if boring, vehicle for a detective. Her own car was white, a poor choice, she'd learned when she lived and worked in the snow belt. But here, it seemed every other car was white.

So hers wasn't too bad for a private eye. It blended with the herd. She squelched the secret longing she'd harbored for a bright yellow sports car. Maybe when her ten-year-old car gave out. If she wasn't still sneaking around following people and conducting covert surveillance. As long as she worked for True Blue, she had a feeling she was doomed to boring car colors.

THE PLAY CAST wasn't brilliant, but the young man playing George M. Cohan had a true, vibrant voice and tons of energy. Overall, Keith mentally rated the production with a B. The whole show exuded fun, which was what he'd hoped for. Campbell seemed to enjoy it. That counted more than anything else.

When he turned in at her driveway, the first thing he noticed was that the only light on was the porch light. The driveway was empty.

"Looks like Bill's not home yet," he said.

Campbell frowned. "I hoped he would be. Would you like some iced tea?"

"Sounds great." He'd wondered if she would invite him in. Campbell wasn't prudish, but she was a little conservative, and so was he when it came down to it. He wouldn't overstep the rules of propriety.

Inside, she laid her purse and play program on the kitchen table and went straight for the fridge, where she pulled out a big pitcher of tea.

"I think we even have some cookies. Store bought."

He smiled and watched her ferret out two glasses and a half bag of Pepperidge Farm mint chocolate Milanos.

"Ice?" she asked.

"No, it's probably cold enough."

She handed him a full glass and poured one for herself.

"Let's go sit where it's comfortable." She snagged the bag of cookies on her way to the living room. He liked that she didn't feel he needed the grace of a plate.

"Wasn't the play great?" She grinned at him.

"It was pretty good. I thought maybe your standards were higher."

"Oh, I've seen some very mediocre productions at the college where I taught." She frowned.

"What?"

"Oh, I modified *mediocre*. It's either mediocre or it's not."

He chuckled. "Sort of like *unique*?"

"Exactly. Something can't be somewhat unique or very unique. Anyway, this show was a notch above mediocre in my book. Thanks for taking me."

"I enjoyed it. But I may never get the songs out of my head."

She grinned. "I know. H-A-double-R-I-G-A-N spells—"

"Harrigan!"

They both laughed.

"My brain has been beating out 'Over There' ever since we left the theater." Keith picked up the cookie bag she'd dropped on the coffee table and opened it. "How'd you know I love Milanos?"

"They're Dad's favorite."

"Aha. Good taste, Bill."

"Mm." She took out her phone and swiped the screen. Her forehead bunched. "I wonder if I should call him. But I hate to bother him when he's driving."

"He'll be along." Keith hoped he was right. Maybe he'd better stay with her a while, until she knew for certain her father was all right. Bill had given her enough scares lately.

"Hey, what about those books? Want to unpack them now?"

She took a big sip of her tea and set the glass down on a coaster. "I'm game if you are."

They went back to her room, and she knelt on the floor next to the box of fiction.

"Want me to take the other one?" Keith asked.

"Sure. Let's just get them into the shelves, and I'll sort them later. Yours is all textbooks and other nonfiction, and some of them are heavy. Why don't you put them on the two bottom shelves, and I'll put these in the top two."

He could handle that. Keith shoved aside a layer or bubble wrap and pulled out a thick hardcover. "Medieval Literature. Sounds interesting."

"Are you just saying that?"

"No, I meant it. Surely *some* of it is interesting."

"A lot of it is." She hefted three paperbacks and stuck them in the next-to-top shelf, lying down with the spines out.

"You don't want them standing up?" he asked.

"I'll probably put the paperbacks that way later, but it's really easier on the books if they lie flat. Especially those big ones."

"Hadn't thought about that." He carefully positioned the medieval lit book and pulled another volume from his carton.

"This box is so beat up, I was afraid some of the books might be damaged." Campbell lifted out several more paperbacks and put them in the bookcase. "So far, so good."

"This one looks okay." Keith lifted a textbook titled *Grammar and Composition*. How dull could you get?

"What in the world?"

Campbell's brow wrinkled as she stared down into her box.

"What is it?" he asked.

She pulled out a small, blue case, about four inches square, covered in velveteen. "It looks like a jewelry box or something."

Keith watched her closely as she lifted the lid.

She sat very still, staring at what was inside.

He moved closer and crouched beside her. "What have you got there?"

A round, bronze medallion hung from a green-and-black ribbon.

"I can't believe it!"

"What is it?"

"It's Feldman University's Steiger medal."

17

"I take it you weren't expecting to find that medal in there," Keith said.

She stared up at him. "Far from it. This thing was stolen a couple of weeks ago. I read about it on Facebook. The award was given to a very unpopular professor at Feldman during the graduation ceremony in May, and at least half the faculty was furious."

"Why?"

"They didn't think he deserved it."

"Then why did he get it?"

She shook her head helplessly. "The people who decide include the trustees, who aren't part of the faculty. I guess enough of them thought he should get it, so they gave it to him."

Keith nodded, his eyes on the medal. "And how did it get in your box of books?"

"That's the million-and-sixty-four-thousand-dollar question."

He quirked his eyebrows.

"Inflation," she said.

He smiled. "Right."

She scrambled to lift more books out of the box. "I grabbed a few of Katherine Tyler's books out of here the day they arrived, but I didn't see this. It was shoved down toward the bottom."

"Can I help?"

"Sure. I want to make sure there's nothing else in here that shouldn't be."

Keith took stacks of books from her hands and transferred them into the new bookcase. When the box was empty, she stuck her head into it, then stood, lifted the carton, and tipped it upside down. "Anything fall out?"

"No."

He took it from her and righted it, then felt carefully along the creases in the bottom, where the flaps met. "It seems to be empty."

"I taped up that box myself, before I dropped it off at Steve's apartment. Keith, I did not steal that medal."

"I believe you."

She blinked. "Just like that?"

"Of course. You're not a thief. And if you were, you wouldn't have pulled it out of the box with me standing right here."

She exhaled heavily. "What do I do now? Should I notify the school? Or the guy it was stolen from?"

"How about the last person known to have touched those boxes?" he asked.

"Steve." She let out her breath in a puff, grabbed her laptop, and sat down on the edge of her bed.

Keith walked around to where he could see the screen. She pulled up the email program and clicked on "new message."

Is there something you want to tell me?

She jabbed SEND.

"Okay," he said. "Maybe we should retreat and have another cookie."

She threw him a baleful look, but she stood.

They weren't out the door when the computer pinged. Campbell hurried back to it.

"He's answered."

She sat down, and Keith leaned in behind her.

The email said simply, *Like what?*

Like what's in the box with my books, she responded.

They waited, not speaking. Campbell clicked the SEND/RECEIVE icon twice before Steve's reply came in.

I have no idea what you're talking about.

Campbell growled and seized her cell phone. She tapped it a few times and put it to her ear.

"Stephen!"

"Hello to you too, Campbell. What's going on?"

Keith was standing so near, he could easily make out the man's words.

"I was unpacking my book boxes tonight, and I found something that doesn't belong to me."

"Like what?" Steve asked.

"You tell me."

"What do you mean? I don't know what you're talking about."

"You didn't add something to one of my boxes?"

"No way. You had them taped when you brought them to me."

"Yeah."

She sat scowling for a moment. "Who's been to your apartment in the last two weeks?"

"Huh?"

Campbell put a hand to her forehead. "Hold on a sec. I can narrow it down. I know this wasn't in the box when I packed it. What day did you ship it?"

"The same day you sent me the message that you were ready."

She glanced up at Keith. "Look, Steve, I've got someone here who can help me figure this out. Can I put you on speaker?"

"Yeah, go ahead."

She tapped the screen. "Okay, Steve, this is Keith. Keith, Steve. Now, guys, the day Steve's message came in was the same day Xina Harrison came to my dad's office for the first time."

"Who?" Steve asked.

Keith just nodded.

"Oh, it's a client," Campbell said. "I'm only mentioning her to clarify when things happened. But that was Thursday of last week. The boxes arrived on ... Monday?" She arched her eyebrows at Keith.

"Yeah, I'm pretty sure that was the day," Keith said.

"And you're just now opening them?"

Campbell rolled her eyes. Keith had seen her do the same thing when she was exasperated with Nick. He'd wondered if this Steve character was competition for Campbell's heart, but now he didn't think so. He couldn't help smiling.

"I opened them that day, but I didn't start unpacking them until now."

"Okay." Steve sounded subdued. "So what's the problem?"

"There's a small box inside one of my book boxes." Campbell eased down onto the edge of her bed. "Look, Steve, you know the Steiger medal was stolen?"

"Uh, yeah, I heard about that."

"Well, guess where it is now."

"You've got to be kidding me."

"I'm not. It's right here in my hand."

Steve swore, and Campbell winced and met Keith's gaze.

He shrugged. The academic's oath was much milder than things he heard every day around the police station.

"I just read about the theft on Facebook the other day," Campbell said. "Do you remember what day it was actually stolen?"

"Hold on." After a few seconds, Steve said, "Here it is. It was in the paper Wednesday. And the theft was reported on ... yup, Tuesday."

"Okay. So, Keith." She looked up at him. "This medal was probably stolen last Monday night or Tuesday. The paper ran the story on Wednesday. On Thursday, Steve emailed to ask if I wanted him to ship the boxes, which he did that same day."

"Got it," Keith said. He wished some of his colleagues had minds as orderly and logical as Campbell's.

"That means it must have been put in the box between Monday night at the very earliest and Thursday of last week. And I taped up that box at least two weeks earlier—no, it was longer than that. The day before graduation."

Steve supplied the date, and she nodded.

"Almost four weeks," Keith said. He walked over to the box where Campbell had found the medal case and knelt beside it. He closed the flaps and carefully examined the tape that had secured it.

Steve wrangled with Campbell over the possibility of someone adding the surprise to the package.

Keith carried the empty box over to Campbell. "Look here," he said softly.

"Steve, hold on. Just think for a minute who would have been in your apartment during that time period, okay?"

She turned her attention to the box in Keith's hands.

"There's a lot of tape on this box," he said. "It's your usual clear packing tape, but notice how some of the top layer of cardboard is lifted. But you slit the tape open."

Her eyes lost focus for a moment. "I used scissors."

"Did you recycle the box?"

"No. Well, I got both boxes from the school cafeteria's recycling, but they weren't beat up."

"Then I'd say someone lifted the original layer of tape and then redid it."

"You hear that, Steve?" Campbell said clearly, staring at her phone.

"I hear you. And I just remembered, you didn't answer my message until Thursday night. I shipped the boxes Friday morning, a week ago today."

"Okay," Keith said, "can you tell us who visited your

apartment that week?"

Steve sighed. "Molly Tanner was here a couple of times."

"Are you still dating?" Campbell asked.

Keith tried not to show his elation when Steve said, "Yeah. Kind of." If these two were discussing Steve's dates, that pretty much ruled out Campbell as his love interest.

Campbell gave a little *hmpf.* "Who else?"

"Uh ... Chris Blye was here. Gary Tokildsen, and Anna what's-her-name came over Wednesday night. You know Anna— Gary's girlfriend. We all went to a movie together."

Keith took notes.

"Who else?" Campbell asked.

"Uh ... I think Chris came back the next day. I'm not sure if it was ... Yeah, okay, Chris Blye came again on Thursday."

"What for?" Campbell met Keith's eyes.

"Mm, not sure. He thought maybe he'd left something here. Not his phone or his keys. A jacket, maybe?"

"Isn't it pretty warm out for a jacket?"

"Well, it was a little cool the night we saw the movie."

Keith cleared his throat. "Steve, think about the night those friends came into your apartment. Did they know Campbell's boxes of books were there?"

"Yeah, they were right near the door, ready to go to UPS. Anna saw the address and asked what I was doing with Campbell's stuff."

"Okay, so those three people all knew you were going to ship some boxes here to Campbell."

Campbell met Keith's eyes and nodded slowly. "Steve, did any of them come back a second time besides Chris?"

"Uh ..."

"And did Chris have anything with him when he came?" Campbell asked.

"He brought his gym bag. Said he was going to work out and asked if I wanted to go with him. I said yeah."

"So you had to go change clothes, or what?"

"Absolutely right. You think he might have put the medal in the box then?"

"He had an opportunity. He could have had packing tape in his bag, providing a means." Campbell looked at Keith. "How do we find out if he had a motive?"

"Good question," Keith said. "It could have been someone else who saw the boxes that week and returned, but Steve doesn't remember it." Steve's girlfriend, Molly, he thought, but he didn't say it aloud.

"Or even someone at the shipping company that delivered them," Campbell said with a weary air.

Keith understood her discouragement. He didn't want to look down that road, either. It opened up too wide a field of suspects.

After a few seconds, Steve said, "Now that I think about it, Chris had called me Wednesday morning. He said he wanted to show me something. He was all excited. That's when we talked about the movie."

"But he didn't say what he wanted to show you?" Campbell's voice rose as she spoke.

"No. He was going to show me that night."

"Did he?"

"No," Steve said. "The other folks came at the same time, and we left for the cinema. I forgot all about it."

"Did they talk about the medal at all that night?" Keith asked.

"Well, yeah. Everyone connected to the college was talking about it. That was the big topic of conversation. The police were going to go around and question everyone who'd been in contact with Dr. Griffin that week."

"Were you one of those people?" Campbell asked.

"No, I hadn't seen him since graduation."

"Did the others say they'd seen him?" Keith asked.

"I don't remember."

"Okay," Keith said evenly. "I suggest you keep this to

yourself. Don't tell anyone the medal has surfaced here in Kentucky."

"Well, what are you going to do with it?" Steve asked. "Return it to the college? Or Griffin?"

"I'm not sure," Keith said. "We'll have to talk to the police there first."

"Huh? You're going to call the Des Moines police? I heard the campus police called them in."

Keith said gently, "Steve, I'm a detective here, with the Murray Police Department."

"Oh. Wow. Like you couldn't have mentioned that earlier?"

"Look, Steve, I'm sorry," Campbell said. "Keith wasn't here officially. He's a friend of mine. But everything you told us tonight is the truth, right?"

"Well, yeah."

"Just keep quiet about it, and expect to hear from your local police," Keith said. "They'll take your statement. Meanwhile, we'll tell them everything we know and ask what Campbell should do with the medal."

It took ten more minutes to calm Steve to where he was willing to keep quiet overnight and talk coherently to the officers who would undoubtedly contact him the next day. Finally Campbell closed the connection.

She gazed up at Keith, her eyes huge. "Thanks. I don't know if I could have handled that professionally if you weren't here."

He patted her shoulder. "I'm glad I was here. Now I should get on the phone and talk to the Des Moines P.D."

"Do you need to go to the station to do that?"

"I'd rather do it here, so that if they ask, you can talk to them right away."

"Okay. I have a feeling we're going to need coffee."

Keith grinned. "Make a pot."

As they entered the kitchen, the front door opened and her father called, "Campbell! You here, Soup?"

She darted through the doorway to the entry. "You know I'm

here, Dad. My car's out front, and so's Keith's."

"I know."

Keith followed her to the doorway and watched Bill park his wheeled suitcase and fold Campbell into a hug.

"Evening, Bill."

"Hey, Keith. What's going on?"

"I'll let Campbell explain while I make a couple of phone calls. Did you have a good trip?"

"Yeah, it was okay. I got hungry and stopped to eat, so I'm later than I estimated."

Campbell took his arm. "It's all right. I'm just glad you're back. Come on in the kitchen while I make coffee."

"I've been drinking coffee all the way here," Bill said. "No more caffeine for me."

"Okay. Sit down and I'll tell you all about it."

"About what?"

"It's right up your alley," Campbell said. "A logic puzzle."

Keith smiled and walked to the far end of the living room, where he could barely hear Campbell's even tones as she explained to her father what had happened. A minute online gave him the contact number for the Des Moines police department, and he clicked the call icon.

THE NEXT MORNING, Nick came to the house bringing a box of doughnuts and sat at the kitchen table with Campbell and Bill, drinking coffee and eating. Campbell and her dad took turns relating the previous night's adventure.

"Keith and Campbell spent almost an hour on the phone with Des Moines," Bill said. "First, Keith had to assure them it wasn't a prank and he really was a police officer, and they really did have the medal here in Kentucky."

Campbell smiled. "Seems the cops there have been chasing around, trying to figure out what could possibly have happened to it. After Keith and I went over it about three times, they finally decided to go talk to Chris Blye, the guy at the top of our suspect list."

"He broke down and confessed to everything," Bill said, reaching for the coffee carafe.

"He stole it as a prank," Campbell said. "Then he heard the cops were questioning people. The college was giving permission for them to search school property, and Chris has an apartment on campus."

"How old is this guy?" Nick scrutinized the doughnuts and picked his second one.

"He's probably twenty-three or -four. He's a graduate assistant, and he was lined up to teach a couple of summer classes."

Nick shook his head. "That's the kind of stunt we pulled in junior high."

"I know. He thought he was so smart when he sneaked into Dr. Griffin's house and swiped it off his dresser, and he was going to tell Steve about it. Then he got scared the police would come after him, and he realized how serious it was. When he saw my boxes at Steve's place, I guess he thought it would be a good way to get the evidence out of Iowa."

"That's crazy. What did he think you'd do when you found it?"

Campbell lifted her hands and shrugged. "Beats me. He could have called and warned me, but no. So he got his visit from the cops last night."

"Is he in jail?"

"I think he's out on bail," she said. "Or he will be soon. The medal's not that valuable. It's more of a symbolic thing."

Campbell's phone rang, and she pulled it from her pocket. "Xina, what can I do for you?" She looked pointedly at her father when she spoke the client's name.

"Campbell, I need you. I'm over at Aunt Katherine's, and it's a mess. I think someone broke in here last night."

18

"Have you called the police?" Campbell asked.

Her father jumped up in alarm. She raised a hand to calm him.

"Not yet," Xina replied.

"Call them. Dad and I will be right there."

She closed the call and reached for her purse. "Xina says someone broke into Katherine's house overnight."

"Let's go."

Nick stood. "Should I come along?"

"Well, she's called the police." Campbell looked to her father for direction.

"Go over to the office, Nick. If it looks like there's something you can do, I'll call you."

Nick didn't look happy, but he picked up the box of doughnuts and the keys to his Jeep. The three of them hurried out the door.

Bill jumped in on the passenger side of Campbell's car, since it was in the driveway and his was in the garage.

"Tell me exactly what she said."

While she drove, Campbell repeated Xina's words, as nearly

as she could remember. "*A real mess*. That's what she said. No specifics."

A couple more tense minutes, and they were there. Campbell parked in the drive, behind Xina's gray Saturn. Xina stood on the front steps, watching them anxiously, and a black SUV was parked at the curb. Campbell glanced at the license plate.

"Keith's here," she told her father.

Xina gave them a wobbly smile as they approached. "Detective Fuller is inside. He said to wait out here."

Campbell climbed the steps to stand beside her. "Are you all right?"

"Yes, now that you're here."

"Let the police clear the house first," Bill said from the walkway. "Then we'll go in with you."

A squad car rolled down the street. Bill waited for the two patrol officers who got out of the car to join them.

"Hey, Mel. Denise," he called.

Campbell recognized Denise Mills and Mel Ferris. Bill gave them a quick rundown on what had happened and introduced them to Xina.

"Thank you for coming so quickly," Xina said.

"I'll go in and help Detective Fuller do a run-through," Officer Ferris said.

Mills stayed with them. "I understand your aunt owns the house?" she asked Xina.

"That's right. She's in the hospital. I have her medical power of attorney, and I'm staying at the Marriott, but I came over to check on some things. When I unlocked the door and went in, I could see that things had been disturbed since the last time I was here."

"When was that?" Mills asked, taking out her notebook.

"Thursday evening. Campbell McBride was with me."

Campbell nodded. "We came over to get Miss Tyler's address book. Everything was fine then."

"My aunt's housekeeper usually comes in on Friday," Xina

said. "I gave her the day off, since I'm not staying here and my aunt is still incapacitated from her accident."

"Oh, was that the car accident last weekend?" Officer Mills asked.

"Yes. She's in a coma."

"I talked to one of the first responders on that call. I'm very sorry about your aunt." She looked toward the entrance. "You said the door was locked when you got here?"

"Yes," Xina said. "I unlocked it when I arrived about twenty minutes ago."

"Well, we'll just wait for the word, then we'll go inside. You can tell us if anything is missing."

———

KEITH TURNED toward the door as Mel Ferris entered the upstairs bedroom. "No one seems to be in the house, but this bedroom's been ransacked."

"Just this one?" Ferris asked.

"That's right. The others don't seem to be occupied. Other than the office downstairs, this is the only place I saw evidence of a burglary." As he spoke, Keith eyed the nearly empty closet carefully. "Check through those piles of clothes on the bed, would you?"

A straight chair stood before the open closet. He examined the seat carefully, but couldn't see any marks on it. He placed one foot on it and tested it with his weight. So far, so good. He pushed up onto the chair and looked along the top shelf. Shoes, boxes, purses, and a tote bags were strewn about the floor below him, and he assumed some of the items had been stored on this shelf. After studying each wall carefully, he stepped down and moved the chair.

Inside the closet, he crouched and ran the beam of his flashlight slowly over every inch of wall. He paused, studying the baseboard at the bottom of the end wall.

CAMPBELL TURNED toward the front door as it swung open. *About time!*

Keith nodded to her, but his gaze settled on Xina. "Okay, we're sure the place is empty. Can you please come in and see if you think anything was stolen?"

Xina's lips trembled, but she nodded.

Campbell drew closer to her. "Do you need to sit down for a minute?"

"No, I'm okay. It's a huge mess inside. I don't know if I'll be able to tell what's missing. Maybe you can help me?"

"I'll try," Campbell said. "And we can help clean up afterward too."

"I don't know what Aunt Katherine will say when she wakes up and hears about this." Xina swallowed hard and went inside.

"Most of the damage seems to be in the study and one bedroom upstairs," Keith said as they walked through the entry.

Campbell caught his arm as the others filed inside. "What does that tell us?"

"What do you think?"

"Either he found what he was after, or he was interrupted—in which case, he may come back."

Keith smiled but said nothing.

Xina stopped in the doorway to the study. "Oh, boy. How am I ever going to sort this out?"

Campbell peered over her shoulder. It was as bad as the chaos she and Nick had found at the True Blue office when it was ransacked, but the file cabinets, chairs, and printer table were moved out from the walls.

"I'll help you," she said. "I remember how the files were, and most of the things in the desk."

Xina clutched her sleeve. "Thank you."

"That bottom right drawer was locked," she told Keith, pointing toward the desk. The drawer she indicated was pulled out all the way, and the front tilted down onto the rug. "We locked Katherine's purse in there, and she also had bank checks and the key to her safe deposit box in there."

"Hold on." He turned toward the doorway. "Denise? Do you have gloves on you?"

Officer Mills came in with a box and gave a pair of gloves to Campbell and one to Xina, while Keith pulled a fresh pair from his own pocket.

After examining the drawer front, he stood. "That wasn't pried open. Check if the safe deposit box key is still there, please, and if you think of anything that's missing, tell me."

Campbell strode to the desk, and Xina hovered nearby.

"There's the purse." Campbell picked it up off the floor under the desk and handed it to Xina. "You look inside and see if everything's there."

She spotted the desk keys on the floor and hooked the loop of twine that joined them with her index finger. "These were in the flat center drawer. One opens the bottom right drawer, and the other opens the gray cashbox inside it."

Keith took a small plastic bag from his pocket. "Just drop them in here, please."

Campbell went back to the desk and knelt in front of the tipped drawer. Carefully, she lifted out the metal cashbox. It opened easily this time.

"This was locked before," she told Keith as she opened the lid. "I relocked it after we looked inside. Hmm, the boxes of checks are still here. There were three before, and there are three now. That looks okay, unless he grabbed a pad of checks out of one of the boxes."

She set each little box on the surface of the desk and grinned in triumph. "Got it. I guess the burglar didn't bother to look underneath."

She took the safe deposit key to Keith, and Officer Mills produced another evidence bag.

"There are also five manila folders in that drawer," Campbell said. "They were there before, but I haven't checked the contents yet."

Xina came over with the purse. "Her checkbook and wallet are in here. The cash that was in the wallet is gone."

"Forty-two dollars," Campbell supplied.

Keith wrote it down. "Anything else? Credit cards?"

"Uh, there's at least one missing." She looked helplessly at Campbell. "Do you remember ..."

"There were three," Campbell said. "At least one was a Visa. I think one was a promotional card—you know, where a small percentage went to a local charity. Schools, I think. It may have been a debit. And one was a ..." She squeezed her eyes shut for a moment. "A blue Mastercard."

"Anything else?"

She shook her head. "I don't remember any more than that, but there should be records of her payments that would have the numbers on them in that cabinet over there." She pointed to a file cabinet that had stood against the side wall but was now two feet away from it. "At least, there will be after we sort out the files that are on the floor."

"Excellent," Keith said. "Ms. Harrison, would you please call the bank immediately and tell them the house has been broken into. They should cancel your aunt's debit card right away, and any other cards they can help with. I suggest putting a hold on her checking account too, until we're sure it's safe."

"I can help her with that," Bill said. "I've got the bank number right here on my own card."

Campbell said, "You might want to grab one of her statements, Dad. Should be in that top drawer, if they're not all over the floor." She pointed, and Bill made his way cautiously to the file cabinet.

"What's in the folders in the desk drawer?" Keith asked. "Are they special?"

"Yes, I'd say so. Her property deed, will, medical directives, that sort of thing."

"If she keeps those here in the house, what's in the bank box?"

"I wondered the same thing," Campbell said.

"Would you check the folders now, please?"

She crouched by the drawer again. After a moment, she turned to him. "As far as I can remember, everything is here."

Keith nodded and made more notes.

Campbell studied Xina's form as she and Bill lifted papers from the floor and sorted them. The bank statements must have been dumped. Xina wouldn't do this, would she? The opportunity was there. But why would she have asked Campbell to stay with her a couple of nights if she wanted time alone to explore the house? And if she wanted to destroy documents—say, the new will—she could have done it quietly and never told them.

No, Campbell wouldn't believe their client would do something like this when she was so eager to please her aunt.

"Let's go take a look upstairs," Keith said. He spoke to Officer Mills, and then Campbell went with him up the stairway.

"That's Katherine's room," Campbell said as she noticed where Officer Ferris was standing watch in the hall.

"We thought so. You've been in there before?"

"It's where I slept the two nights I was here. Under protest, but Xina wouldn't let me sleep on the couch. She slept in the guest room."

Keith went in and stopped in the space between the bed and dressing table. "As you can see, once again the thief moved the furniture away from the walls."

"Why?" Campbell looked up at his serious profile.

"Usually that means he's looking for something he thinks may be hidden behind it. All of the other bedrooms look empty. No clothes in the closets, for instance. And they haven't been disturbed."

"And this closet's been emptied." Campbell eyed the piles of clothing heaped on the bed. Shoes, boots, a small suitcase, bags, and a few cardboard boxes sat on the floor around the open closet door.

"Yes. Either he didn't get to the other rooms, or he knew exactly what he was looking for and started in the most likely places."

"He did go through the files," she said slowly. "Can we assume he was looking for papers?"

"It's possible, but not definite."

"Okay, what then?"

"He took everything off the top shelf," Keith noted, "and that chair was moved over here. The indentations in the rug tell us that it used to sit in front of the dressing table."

"Okay, so he brought the chair over and used it to climb up and move the stuff off the shelf?"

"I think so. We didn't tell Xina yet. But there's something else."

"What?"

"Did you notice in the living room downstairs, the print over the mantel was taken down?"

"I didn't even go in the living room," Campbell said.

"Well, it was leaning against the brickwork at the side of the fireplace."

She frowned. "He moved a framed print. So ... could he have been looking for a safe?"

"That's my thinking. See that picture over there?" He pointed to a small, framed painting that lay on the pillows on Katherine's bed.

Campbell caught her breath. "The daffodil picture." She turned her head and stared at the bare wall over the fireplace. "It was there."

"I figured as much."

"Is it valuable?" she asked. "Remember, the Ramsey downstairs was sold a few months ago. I never thought about it, but this looks like an original oil painting, not a print."

"I don't know," Keith said. "I took several photos of it, and

I'll look into that angle. But if that was what the thief was after, why leave it behind when he left?"

She nodded, trying to make sense of it all.

"Which brings me back to the furniture pulled out from the walls," he said.

"Looking for a safe down low, behind dressers and things?" She shook her head.

"Maybe not a safe," Keith said. "Maybe a hidden cupboard."

"A secret compartment?" Her adrenaline surged. "He could have been tapping on walls, looking for a hiding place."

"I don't think he found one," Keith said evenly, "but I did."

"What?" She put her fists on her hips and stared at him. "You —but how?"

"Once I thought he was looking for that, I started noticing things. He left drawers and closets he'd searched in disarray. If he found a hidden compartment, I don't think he'd close it afterward. And I don't think he found the one I found."

She paused, trying to come up with an explanation. "Are you just smarter than him, or—"

"The closet is dark. There's no overhead light in there."

"It's an old house," she said.

"True. Closet lights were almost unheard of when this place was built, and I don't think Ms. Tyler's done a lot of modernizing outside the bathrooms and kitchen."

He waved toward the left side of the closet. "Take a look."

"Should I use the chair?"

"Nope, you don't need to. Remember, Katherine isn't a tall woman."

Campbell peered into the closet. It extended about three feet beyond the door.

"Here." Keith handed her his flashlight.

One click, and its powerful beam flooded the small space with light. She studied the back wall carefully and then turned the beam toward the end. Again, nothing. She played the light on the wall between the closet and the bedroom.

"Hey, this wall has a baseboard. That's not usual in a closet, is it?"

"I don't think so," Keith said. "And if you're putting one of the interior wall, why not on the other walls?"

"A secret compartment?"

He smiled. "Can you open it?"

She crouched and tried to pry off the board. It seemed secure. Meeting the carpet at the bottom, it stretched from the doorjamb to the end wall. She felt along the white board, and at the end she found a small space in the corner, between it and the wall. She got two fingers in and pulled. The board popped off, hitting her shin.

"Ouch."

Keith laughed. "Your fingers are smaller than mine. Good job."

"When all her stuff is in the closet, it's not noticeable." She played the light over the small space she'd revealed. Only about four inches high, it stretched between two studs.

"I don't see anything in here."

"That's because I took it out."

She stood and sidled into the doorway.

"I found this inside." Keith pulled out yet another evidence bag and held it up. In it was a green-and-black flash drive.

Campbell's jaw dropped. "That was in the cubby?"

"Yeah. He had to have missed it altogether."

She looked back at the board she'd pried off and shook her head. "Katherine must have known about it."

"She lived here all her life."

Campbell's mind was in high gear. "I guess you'll have to take that drive back to the police station to see what's on it."

"I will, but I'll let you know, provided it's not something ultra-sensitive."

"Thanks."

Keith looked toward the bedroom doorway. "And now I want

to get Xina up here, if she's finished talking to the bank. I want to know if she was aware of this compartment."

Xina seemed shocked when he showed her the hiding place.

"Well, I'll take this flash drive with me," Keith told her. "Would you stop by the station later to be fingerprinted, Ms. Harrison? I'd like to be able to eliminate your prints from the ones we're collecting."

"Of course," Xina said.

Campbell walked with him to the front door.

"Mel will oversee the rest of the processing here," Keith said. "I wish we had Katherine Tyler's prints."

"You don't have them? They must be all over this house."

"Yes, of course, but it would make it a whole lot quicker to sort through the many, many prints we've gathered if we had a complete set of hers and Rita Henry's on file. I'll call Ms. Henry and ask her to come by as well."

"Well, you've got mine."

Campbell stayed to help Xina with the cleanup after the police were finished processing the scene. When all the officers had left, they spent another hour straightening the study and Katherine's bedroom, putting everything back in the same order it had been, so far as they could remember.

"I know she'll be able to tell people have handled her things," Xina said with a moan. "I hope that doesn't upset her."

"The police can explain to her about the break-in." Campbell hung the last jacket in the closet. "I'm sure she had everything arranged a certain way, but she'll just have to understand."

Xina's face scrunched up. "I'm not sure she will. She wasn't very understanding before the accident."

Her cell phone went off, and she looked at it. "Oh, no. It's the hospital." She shot Campbell a stricken glance. "I didn't make it there this morning because of this mess. I hope nothing's wrong."

Campbell waved toward the phone with a circular motion,

hoping Xina understood she should move things along by answering.

With trembling hands, Xina swiped the screen and put the phone to her ear.

"Yes? Yes, this is Xina Harrison." She gulped. "All right, I'll be right there. Fifteen minutes. Thank you."

She tapped the phone and looked at Campbell. "She's awake."

19

"What?" Campbell managed not to let it turn into a scream. "Really, truly awake?"

"The nurse said she opened her eyes and groaned and drank a little water. They called the doctor right away, and then they called me." She shoved her phone into a pocket. "I've got to hurry. She could drift off again before I get there."

"Let me drive you," Campbell said.

"No, it's not far, and I'll need my car."

"I'll follow you then."

"Okay, thanks. Oh, where's my purse?"

"I think you left it on the hall table."

Xina broke the speed limit on the residential streets between Katherine's house and the hospital. Campbell didn't try to keep up. She'd seen enough of Murray's constabulary for one morning.

When she reached Katherine's room, Dr. Drummond was inside with Xina and a nurse. Campbell hesitated in the doorway.

"She did speak a few words," the doctor said. "She asked for water, and she asked what day it is."

Xina stared at him for a moment. "That's it?"

"The nurse said she closed her eyes after that. When I came

in, she appeared to be sleeping, but when I touched her hand, she opened her eyes. I told her my name, and she didn't say anything, but she did focus on me. That's about as far as we've gotten."

"Please go ahead with your examination," Xina said. She edged toward the door and reached for Campbell's hand. "You heard?"

"Yes," Campbell whispered. "Is she awake or not?"

"Her eyes are closed," Xina said. "What if she's gone back into the coma again?"

"Let's wait and see what the doctor says."

Xina nodded. They stood together just inside the door while Dr. Drummond moved about at the bedside and spoke to the nurse. He turned and joined the two women with a taut smile.

"When I say her name, she opens her eyes and looks at me," he said. "She doesn't respond verbally. Her vital signs seem good, but she doesn't respond when I ask her to do something—squeeze my hand, for instance, or track with her eyes."

"What does it mean?" Xina asked. "She's not paralyzed, is she?"

"I don't think so. She might not be hearing me, or she might be deliberately ignoring me. I thought perhaps if you stepped over and spoke to her again—I'd like to see her response."

Xina walked hesitantly into the room and rounded the bed to the far side. Campbell followed but stood back a couple of paces.

"Aunt Katherine, it's me, Xina. How are you feeling?" Xina reached for Katherine's hand and gave it a gentle squeeze.

Katherine turned her gaze on her niece and stared at her. Campbell could see that her eyes were wide open, the irises an icy blue-gray. Her brow furrowed.

Xina smiled. "Hello, Auntie."

Katherine turned her head and sought out the doctor. She opened her mouth and croaked out, "Who is she?"

Xina's jaw dropped, and her eyes went wide.

Katherine rasped, "Get her out! Get her out!"

"IF WAS HORRIBLE," Campbell told her father half an hour later. "I didn't know what to do. The doctor took us out in the hall and suggested we let Katherine rest for a while and come back later. Xina asked me to go with her around three o'clock. Dr. Drummond said they'll call her if there's an emergency, and to just give her time."

"Xina went to the hotel?" Bill asked.

"Yes. I went up to the room with her, and she promised to lie down. I told her to call if she wanted to get lunch with us."

"You can do more for her here."

"How do you mean?" she asked.

Bill sighed. "I was hoping we could go to the shooting range this afternoon, but never mind that. I did some more investigating on people we've connected to Katherine Tyler. That researcher for one—Dorman."

"What about him?"

"Well, he's squeaky clean, except for a few traffic tickets over the years. And he's done research work for other writers, and he's also done quite a bit of copy writing in the past."

"Okay, so he's a decent writer himself. He told me he's working on a book."

"I couldn't find any connection between him and Ms. Tyler for the last eight years."

"So, a dead end?"

"Not necessarily, but not a very live one."

"Okay." Campbell pushed her swivel chair back and forth, thinking.

"I also looked at every David in Katherine's class at Vassar," Bill said. "There were three who were there during her freshman year, plus eight more upperclassmen."

"That's a lot."

Bill reached for his coffee mug. "Yes, and if you add in ones who came in over the next three years, there are a couple dozen."

Campbell huffed out a breath. "So what do we do? I never found an engagement announcement."

"True. But remember, Xina said he died a couple of months before the wedding."

"So, obituaries?"

"It was a long shot, but I may have something. One of the Davids who graduated the year Katherine did was killed in an accident two days after graduation."

"Two days—Dad, that's got to be him."

"Hold on, now. It's a possibility, that's all. Not a sure thing. I'm sending you a copy of the obit now."

She brought in his email and skimmed the attachment. "David North. Dad, you're a genius. Now what do we do?"

"Look at the list of survivors."

"... and his loving fiancée, Catherine Taylor." She looked up. "That's got to be our Katherine. They misspelled her name, but it *has* to be her."

"There's a pretty good chance." He smiled and sipped his coffee.

Campbell stared at the screen, frowning. "How could they get both first and last name wrong? I mean, it's only one letter in each, but—"

"Stranger things have happened."

"Meaning?"

"Meaning, there may have been another young woman who was this fellow's fiancée, and whose name was almost, but not quite, the same as our Katherine Tyler's."

"You don't really believe that."

"It was almost fifty years ago, honey. Look, when I was in school there was another boy in my class name Bill McBriarty, and later, at the police academy, there was an instructor named Willard McBride. Almost my name. Almost."

She pulled in a deep breath. "Okay. You're right, we need to be careful and not blow this by making assumptions."

He nodded. "Someone in David's family gave the information for that obituary, and they were upset at the time. It could have been someone who'd never met Katherine. It would be easy to get the spelling wrong."

"So ... we contact the other survivors?"

"Obviously not the parents. They're probably gone now. But David North had several siblings, according to that obituary. I suggest we start there. They'd be about Katherine's age now—late sixties, early seventies. One of the sisters was married at the time and lived in Florida. The other lived in the same town as David's parents. Probably she was still at home. His brother lived in Richmond, Virginia, and his name's a bit unusual."

Campbell returned to the list of survivors. "Royal North. That's a lot better than John Smith."

"Yeah. Now, I haven't begun looking for these people yet, but that might be a good place to start. If we can't find him, or if he's passed away, we'll go after the sisters."

"Sounds good to me."

He nodded. "I vote for take-out lunch. We eat here, and I'll work on this lead."

"What should I do?"

"Well, Soup, this could be a total bust so far as our case goes. I suggest you do some more scrutiny of the Sandler family. Look at Janice's past—the one we think is the new heir. What connection does she have to Katherine?"

"She says none."

Bill shrugged. "She says. There's got to be something. Find out if she's a writer. Maybe she attended a conference or a retreat where Katherine was a speaker. Or maybe she came to Murray at some point. And look at the rest of the family too. Could be Janice's grandma gave Katherine an endorsement thirty or forty years ago that gave her career a boost. We have no idea what we're looking for."

Campbell nodded slowly. "I just pray I'll recognize it if I see it."

He took out his wallet and handed her two twenty-dollar bills. "You get the food, okay? Get whatever you want. Oh, and before I forget, I saw something interesting when I read through the stuff you found on the Sandler family."

"What was that?"

"Well, her father, Dwight, was a phys ed teacher, and he coached the swimming teams at the high school where he worked."

"I remember. He started out as a lifeguard for a summer job." She tucked the money into her purse and zipped it.

"Yes," Bill said. "He was quite the hero fifty-five years ago tomorrow."

"Tomorrow?" What was significant about that? Campbell tried to do the math quickly in her head.

"Hint," her father said with a little smile. "You saw a news clipping about this."

"Oh, the near drowning."

"That's right."

"And you think it's important?"

"Well, it could be. If someone saved your life and you wanted to repay them, what would you do for them?"

Campbell frowned. "The girl he rescued was not Katherine Tyler."

"No, she wasn't. But doesn't it make you curious about her?"

"Yeah, kind of."

"She was almost Katherine's age—within a year."

"Maybe a friend?"

"Not that I can see, but you never know."

"Maybe the two girls went to summer camp together," Campbell said.

"Could be anything. Anyway, her name was Linda Braxton."

"Have you found anything else about her?"

"Not yet. Haven't had time. Go get us something to eat, and you can start on that while I work on David North."

An hour later, Campbell tossed the empty wrappers and cartons from their lunch. Nick had come in and polished off what she and her dad hadn't eaten.

"I'm heading out." Nick picked up his phone and car keys. "I'm meeting Mr. Gray to give him the final report on his daughter."

"Good work," Bill said. "I'm glad she's willing to talk to him. And tell him that if he needs us afterward, we're here for him."

"I will. He's so happy, I think he and his wife are ready to drive to Lexington and get her today."

"If she wants them to," Campbell said.

"Well, yeah. She does have a job there, and she seems to be settled and have friends and an income, so she may not want to come home."

"All we can do is find the person and help them make the contact," Bill said. "The rest is up to them."

"At least they'll know now that she's safe." Campbell sat down at her desk and adjusted the position of her laptop. "Drive safe, Nick."

"Thanks."

He was out the door.

"He didn't drive to Lexington with that cast on his arm, did he?" Campbell asked.

"No, but he had a detailed conversation with Miss Gray, and she was willing to have contact with her parents."

Campbell shook her head. "Are you sure he's okay?"

"You saw him," her father replied. "He's happy to be working again. If his arm's sore, he's got meds for that, but really, I think he's nearly healed."

"The cast won't come off for two more weeks."

"That's Nick for you."

Campbell turned back to her quest for everything Dwight

Palmer. "Dad, I'm thinking about Katherine's new will," she said a few minutes later.

"What about it?"

"She had it drawn up just a few weeks after Dwight Palmer died."

Bill stopped typing and sat back in his chair, a pensive frown on his face. "Okay, that could be significant. Maybe she heard about his death and wanted to do something."

"I don't get it. And besides, he had four children. Why pick Janice as her new heir?"

"There's got to be something else," Bill said.

"Well, if Janice is telling the truth, she didn't know Katherine and wasn't familiar with her work." Campbell puzzled over it. "The connection seems to me to be between Dwight Palmer and the girl he saved, Linda Braxton. Where does Katherine fit in?"

"Maybe she knew the girl, Linda, and wanted to do something nice for the man who saved her."

"Fifty years later?"

Bill shrugged. "You're right. Maybe he did other swimming rescues that we don't know about."

"I suppose it's possible."

"So, you haven't found any connection between Katherine and the Palmers, other than the address book and the will?"

Campbell rubbed her forehead. "I feel like I'm spinning my wheels. Janice says there's no connection between her and Katherine, and I don't even know where to begin with Linda."

"Sometimes it's like that."

She picked up a pen and jotted on a memo sheet *Link Linda B and Katherine?* "But, Dad, we may be wasting time on totally irrelevant leads that aren't really leads at all."

"Why don't you give Xina a call?" Bill asked. "Get your mind off this for a minute or two."

That sounded like good advice, and Campbell placed the call.

"Hi," Xina said in low tones. "Hold on a sec."

Campbell waited.

"Okay, I'm in the hall." Xina sounded a little breathless. "I'm not sure what to do now. She's in and out—she'll wake up for a few minutes, and then she'll drift off again."

"Has she said anything to you?"

"A little," Xina said. "She didn't scream at me when she saw me, so I guess that's an improvement."

"Well, yeah," Campbell said.

"The first time, she kind of squinted at me and said, 'Who are you again?' I said, 'I'm Xina, your niece, Aunt Katherine.'"

"Then what?"

"She got this real scowly expression and said, 'I suppose you're staying in my house.' So I assured her I am not. I didn't tell her I slept there a few nights or about the burglary."

"Wait until you think she's ready," Campbell said.

"I'm trying to stick to neutral topics, but I don't really know what to say to her, other than to ask how she feels or if I can get her anything. I mean, I can't talk about the house or her business or the way she treated me the first time I came over."

Campbell's mind raced. She almost advised Xina to ask her aunt if she remembered some of the people they'd been talking to and researching—Lee Dorman, for instance, or David North, or even Janice Sandler. But that might not be such a good idea. They didn't want Katherine to know Xina had found and read her new will, or that she had detectives poking into her past. And anyway, Campbell wanted to be in the room when those questions were asked.

"What about Ben Tatton?"

"What, you think I should ask if she remembers he was killed?"

Campbell winced. It sounded so grim. "I guess not. That could set her off again. I don't suppose there's any indication of why she had us thrown out this morning?" It was actually only Xina she'd ranted against, but Campbell had been with her, and she was willing to ease Xina's distress by sharing the blame.

"Not really."

"Maybe she was just disoriented at first."

"Well, she still doesn't seem happy that I'm here, but she seems to have accepted it. I did tell her I'm just trying to make sure she gets the best medical care. Oh, and Keith Fuller was here a couple of hours ago."

"Really? What for?"

"To ask her if she remembers the car accident. She said she didn't, really, but she thought there was a deer in the road."

"Okay. Do you want to have supper with Dad and me? I'm cooking spaghetti tonight."

"I'd love to. Thanks."

Campbell tried to encourage her a little more before signing off.

"So, Katherine's awake but not forthcoming?" Bill asked.

"That pretty much sums it up. Xina's afraid to say much or ask her anything that will upset her. She doesn't want to get banned from the ICU. She'll come for supper, though." Campbell arched her eyebrows. "So, back to the grindstone?"

"If you're tired, honey—"

"No, Dad, I'm okay. But I think I'll have some more coffee."

An hour later, she double-checked a snippet of information she'd run across and said cautiously, "Da-ad?"

He'd been very quiet, working away at his desk, only leaving it to get something from a file cabinet and top off his coffee.

"Yeah? You got something?"

"That girl, the one who almost drowned ..."

"Linda Braxton."

"She's the one," Campbell said. "It turns out she had contact with the Palmer family later on."

"Oh?"

"I found Janice's mother's Facebook page, and I skimmed through the archives. I'd almost given up when I spotted a picture of a young woman and a little girl beside a campfire."

"Janice and her sister?"

"No, Mrs. Palmer labeled it 'Janice and friend Linda B.' Dad,

I think Dwight and his family kept in touch with Linda after the rescue, and they actually took her with them on a camping trip with their youngest daughter."

"When you talked to Janice, you didn't mention Linda Braxton, did you?"

"No, just Katherine."

"I think you should call her again and ask about Linda."

"Yeah." Campbell flipped through her notes for Janice Sandler's telephone number. Her stomach fluttered a little, but she told herself not to be silly. If Janice thought she was a nut case, so what? This was her job now.

"Mrs. Sandler? Janice?"

"Yes?"

"This is Campbell McBride. We spoke on the phone yesterday."

"Oh, yes, I remember it well. You told me my name was in some papers belonging to a woman who was in critical health."

"That's right, but I'm happy to tell you that she's a bit better today. She's awake and talking to her niece."

"I'm so glad. Maybe when she's up to it, someone can ask her how she knows me."

"I hope we'll be able to clear that up," Campbell said. "Right now, it's strictly health and family matters."

"Well, I'm glad she's made progress."

"We all are. Could I ask you a question about someone else connected to your family?"

"I guess so," Janice said.

"What can you tell me about Linda Braxton?"

"Oh, Linda!" Janice's voice was more animated. "She was a family friend. I knew her since I was a tiny child. My dad saved her life at a swimming beach where he was the lifeguard when she was young. He kept track of her, and when she was an adult, she would come and visit our family once in a while. But she's gone now."

"Gone?" Campbell's heart seemed to stop for a second. "You mean ..."

"She's dead now," Janice said. "Five years, maybe. Four at least."

"I see. Do you know how she died?"

"No. Someone told me she'd passed away—my dad, I think. Then I saw the death notice online, but I don't think it gave a cause of death."

Campbell stammered out a few more words and a 'thank you' and hung up. She stared across the room at her father.

He just waited, eyeing her quizzically.

"She's dead," Campbell said. "Another dead end, literally. Linda Braxton is dead."

20

B ill tapped away furiously at his keyboard, scowling at the monitor and muttering, "How could we have missed that?"

"We hardly looked at her until today." Campbell got up and went into the tiny bathroom. She soaked a paper towel and blotted her face with cool water. This was not going the way she'd hoped. Not at all. Katherine would probably send Xina home, and they'd never find out what had derailed her relationship with her once-favorite niece.

A few minutes later, she trudged out to her desk, throwing her dad a glance. "Find anything?"

"Yeah. She died, all right. Overdosed on sleeping pills five years ago."

Campbell felt like she'd been punched in the stomach. "She killed herself?"

"Looks like it."

"Why?"

"I haven't found any indications." Bill scratched his chin. "I think I'll call Keith about this. Somewhere there's a police record of when she did it. At least a 911 call or something. He could get the first responders' report."

"What good will that do?" Campbell asked.

"You got anything better?"

"I've got zilch."

Bill reached for the desk phone. After a hold, he got through to Keith and asked him to look into Linda Braxton's suicide. When he hung up, he gave Campbell an apologetic glance.

"He says it may take a while. He'll have to connect with the police in Paducah, which is where the obit is datelined."

"At least it's not a thousand miles away."

"Yeah, maybe we can keep this case in Kentucky. While he's working on it, let's see what else we can find out about her."

Campbell nodded. "I'll go social media. You go for vital records." She paused and swiveled her head to look at him. "Keith didn't say anything about that flash drive, did he?"

"The one he found at Katherine's house? No."

At the end of a half hour, they'd scraped together a scanty biography. Linda was born a year before Katherine Tyler, in Georgia. Her family moved to Paducah, Kentucky, when she was four, and she lived most of her life there. She was employed as an accountant at McCracken Finance, a medium-sized firm that handled a lot of business and personal accounts. She'd died at age sixty-four.

Campbell turned up an online guest book from the funeral home that handled her remains, but only a few comments had been added. It seemed her friends were few and her relatives even fewer. Her bosses left a rather bland comment, saying she would be missed. A few social media posts turned up mentioning Linda shortly after her death, and not all were complimentary.

"I get the feeling she wasn't well liked." Campbell turned to face her dad, an unsettled heaviness in her chest.

"As far as I can tell, she never married," he said. "And I agree. I think she was a very lonely woman."

Keith hadn't called back by closing time, and Campbell left before Bill so she could stop at the store on her way home. Since they were expecting a guest, she wanted to pick up a few extras.

Once she got to the house, she started cooking supper. Her

dad came in a few minutes later, while she was spreading garlic butter on slices of Italian bread.

"Anything I can do?" he asked.

"Feel like setting the table for three?" she asked. "I expect Xina any minute."

But when the doorbell rang fifteen minutes later, it was Keith who stood on the steps, not Xina.

"Is this a bad time?" he asked.

"No, come on in." Campbell couldn't help smiling. It was never a bad time for Keith to show up, as far as she was concerned. "Dad's in the kitchen."

As they passed the dining table, Keith glanced at the three place settings.

"Xina's coming," Campbell said. "Will you stay and eat with us? There's plenty."

"Sure, if you don't mind."

"Dad, throw on another plate," she said with a grin as they entered the kitchen.

"Well, Keith, I'd about given up on hearing from you today."

"I got a report just as I was getting ready to leave the station. Thought I'd come by and give you the news."

"Terrific." Bill opened the flatware drawer and took out silverware for Keith. "What did you get?"

"Well, that Linda Braxton you asked about—the suicide was like you said, except ... well, it seems she was under suspicion of theft by embezzlement when she died."

Bill stood still and eyed him keenly. "A big enough theft to prompt suicide?"

"Her employers had an audit, and they came up more than fifty grand short."

Bill whistled softly. "That's a lot of money."

"More than her annual salary."

"Kentucky wages are still way too low." Campbell pulled the tray of garlic bread from the oven and turned off the stove. "Was she guilty?"

"Looks like it. The investigation went on for a few months after her death, but they're pretty sure she did it. She certainly had the means and opportunity, and it looks like she had motive too. She was living pretty close to the bone."

"Debt?" Bill asked.

"House and car payments, and an old loan. After she died, there wasn't much to recover. Her employers didn't pursue it. They didn't want a lot of negative publicity for the company, and there was no one left to go after."

"Wow," Campbell said. "And the Palmer family thought she was such a nice person."

"Palmer?" Keith asked.

"Yeah, yeah." Bill picked up the bowl of tossed salad and took it to the table. "I told you about how Dwight Palmer rescued her from drowning when she was a kid, right? That's why we started looking at her. She had a connection to the woman in Katherine Tyler's new will."

"Oh, right. The lifeguard's daughter," Keith said.

"The lifeguard being Palmer."

The doorbell rang, and Bill turned toward it. "That's got to be Xina. Is it okay to discuss this frankly in front of her?"

"Oh, I think so," Keith said. "I mean, there's no open case here. I just wish it all had something to do with Tatton's murder, but I'm afraid it's another dead end."

Campbell grabbed a strainer for the spaghetti while Bill went to the door.

"So, what did you find on that flash drive?" she asked.

His eyes brightened. "A manuscript."

"Seriously? An unpublished one?"

"I haven't had time to dive into that."

Campbell shook her head. "Keith, it could be important. Her agent specifically asked Xina if she'd found any manuscripts at Katherine's house."

"Well, I don't know if it's an old one or something she just finished. I've only had time to run a quick search on the title with the author's name, and I came up dry."

"That's exciting. Of course, sometimes they change working titles before publishing a book."

Bill and Xina came in, and soon all four were seated at the table, where Bill asked the blessing.

"How is Ms. Tyler?" Keith asked Xina.

"It's hard to say." Xina frowned. "She doesn't talk much."

"I gathered that when I visited," Keith said.

"Yes, she certainly didn't want to speak to you. I decided to start reading to her after you left, more or less to fill the silence. I followed Campbell's suggestion and took along a paperback we'd found on her nightstand."

"What sort of book is it?" Bill took a slice of garlic bread and passed the platter to Campbell.

"It's another romantic suspense, by a popular author." Xina sprinkled parmesan over her spaghetti. "I'd never read it before. I thought maybe Aunt Katherine would be bored if she'd already read it, but she didn't object. Just lay there with her eyes closed. I had to stop now and then to be sure she hadn't fallen asleep. But when I did that, she'd say, 'Go on.' So I did."

"I'd take that as a good sign," Campbell said. "She approved of *something* you did."

"Yes, I agree." Xina's eyebrows drew together. "But you know, it's funny. I've only read three chapters, but that book sounds a lot like Aunt Katherine's last book." She looked at Campbell. "You know, *Ice Cold Blue*."

"You mentioned that," Campbell said. "How are they alike?"

"Well, the woman's on the run from her ex-husband, and the FBI agent comes to the rescue, and I think he's going to be the love interest."

"Do you think the author may have copied Katherine's idea?" Campbell asked.

"Oh, come on," her father said. "There are only so many plots. Especially for romances."

"That's true."

Xina gave a little shrug and poured dressing over her salad. "There's even a book in Aunt Katherine's study about master plots. I glanced through it the other day, and apparently there are only a dozen or so main story lines, and nearly every book—or at least, every well-written book—lines up with one of them."

"I've heard that," Campbell said. "I should read up on it. If I ever go back to teaching, it might make an interesting class."

"No," Keith said. "You should write a book of your own. I'm sure you could."

"You flatter me."

"How long are you staying, Xina?" Bill asked.

"Well, I had planned to drive home tomorrow, but with things so unsettled, I called and arranged a couple more days off." She sighed. "I've used all my personal leave, and now I've started on my vacation time. I can't stay here forever, but I don't feel I can leave yet."

When Campbell started to clear away the dishes, Keith sprang up.

"I'll help."

"Why, thank you, Kind Sir," she said.

They both reached the kitchen with their hands full of dirty dishes.

"Just set them down anywhere." Campbell put her burden on the counter over the dishwasher.

"I wanted to tell you that the Des Moines police got right on the case about that medal," he said. "Wasn't sure you'd want to discuss it in front of the others."

"Probably not. I mean, Dad knows, but I haven't mentioned it to Xina. Thanks."

He nodded. "Well, I'm not sure if they'll get it cleared up over the weekend, but the investigating officer said if you can express mail the medal to this address, they'd appreciate it." He pulled a slip of paper from his shirt pocket. "It's the main police station, in care of Detective Carter."

"Good. The sooner it's out of this house the better. I'll mail it Monday morning."

Keith smiled. "Are you going to church with your father tomorrow?"

"We usually do, unless he's awfully busy. Which is probably counterproductive, right? Day of rest, and all that."

"Well, I thought maybe sometime you'd like to go with me. I know we go to different churches, but I'd really like you to meet my folks. In fact, my mother told me that even if you couldn't come to our church, I was under orders to invite you and Bill to dinner tomorrow. Sorry I left it so last-minute. I meant to tell you this morning, but we got distracted with the break-in at Katherine's and everything."

"Wow. I'll have to ask Dad. I'd like to meet them." It was true, but even so, her stomach fluttered just thinking about it. She looked up into his eyes. "Has Dad met them before? I know you were friends before I came."

"I don't think so, but I could be wrong. Bill knows a lot of people."

"Okay. Well, I'll ask him after Xina's gone."

"Great."

They went back to the dining area for more dishes and leftover food.

"Who wants pecan pie?" Campbell asked.

Her father stared at her. "When did you make pie?"

"I didn't. Ray at the Barn Owl made it."

"Then I definitely want some. And coffee."

"Of course," Campbell said. "Xina?"

"Just a small piece, thank you. Then I'm going back to the hospital."

"Do you want me to go with you?"

"No, I think I'll be fine. Maybe I'll give you a call when I get back to the hotel."

"We'd appreciate that," Bill said. "I know you can take care of yourself, but with all the odd things happening lately, we want to make sure everything's okay."

AFTER CHURCH THE NEXT DAY, Keith followed his parents' car to their lakeside home. He'd given Bill directions, but he was a little nervous about the visit.

"Keith, can you make a pitcher of sweet tea for me?" his mother asked before they were even in the door.

"Sure, Mom." He didn't mind, as long as she didn't make him put on an apron.

Just as he set the full pitcher in the refrigerator, Bill's blue Toyota Camry pulled in outside the kitchen window.

Somehow, his parents and Bill had never crossed paths, and Keith quickly made the introductions.

"What a beautiful home," Campbell said. She walked over to the large windows on the living room wall overlooking Kentucky Lake.

"Thank you," Keith's mother replied. "This used to be our summer cottage, but we decided to move out here permanently a few years ago, and we did a huge remodel first. Haven't regretted it once."

His dad pulled Bill aside to show him his wide array of fishing tackle, and Keith tagged along with the women as his mom gave Campbell a tour of the house.

"It's perfect," Campbell said.

Mrs. Fuller smiled. "Thank you so much for saying that. Nathan and I spent years dreaming about what we could do with this place. I don't know how many floorplans he drew before we finally decided. It was a royal mess for a year and a half, but it's turned out quite well, I think."

"Mom's just as responsible for the outcome as Dad is," Keith assured Campbell. "And as for the decorating, well, if it were just

Dad, this place would be one big workshop attached to a boathouse."

His mother laughed. "There's some truth to that."

After a leisurely dinner, they had ice cream in folding chairs on the back deck. Keith and Campbell's chairs were separated a little from the rest, and at last he had the opportunity to suggest an outing the next day.

"I'm planning to go to Paducah in the morning, and I thought maybe you'd like to come along," he said.

She blinked at him. "You don't have to work tomorrow?"

"It's business, sort of, but it will be on my own time. Between police resources and True Blue, I'm very curious about McCracken Finance. I made an appointment with the CEO."

"The firm where Linda Braxton used to work." Campbell nodded slowly. "You think it's worth a drive and the loss of several hours."

"I think you were right—there's some connection there with Katherine Tyler, and what connects to Katherine Tyler interests me."

"You think she's involved in the Tatton murder, don't you?"

He shrugged. "She's the only clue I have that hasn't petered out. Neighbors Tatton annoyed, siblings he bickered with—it's all come to nothing. But he and Katherine lived side by side for decades, and they had regular contact. She hired him to do yard work now and then, and she seemed to be on pretty good terms with him."

"Therefore, anything related to Katherine could also be related to Ben Tatton."

Keith sighed. "It sounds pretty thin, doesn't it? But there's been so little evidence in this case. Do you think I'm nuts to follow up on what you and Bill are doing for Xina?"

"Not exactly. We've found some odd circumstances in Katherine's life too. If she'd been a recluse all her life, that would be one thing, but she wasn't. We've learned she was quite social and even gregarious in the past. She was a sought-after public speaker in the writing world, and she kept up with friends and other writers. But not lately."

"Yeah. Now she doesn't seem to want to interact with anyone."

"That's what I mean," Campbell said. "She yells at her niece and sends her away. Her housekeeper barely sees her, even on the days she works in the same house with her."

Keith cocked his head to one side. "She hired Rita Henry when?"

"About five years ago. Right after she fired Doris Conley."

"Yeah. And she fired Mrs. Conley over the phone."

"But Doris had worked for her for a long time," Campbell said slowly. "She'd felt they were friends. What does it mean?"

"Go with me tomorrow. I hope we can get some answers, even if we have to get at them through a back door."

21

Campbell felt a little shy sitting next to Keith the next morning as he drove up the highway.

"I had a wonderful time yesterday," she said. "It's so peaceful out at the lake. And I love your parents."

He smiled. "Thanks. I'm pretty fond of your dad too. What did he say about this expedition?"

"Just to stay alert. He's up to his neck in this case. And he thinks you're right. We'll find a connection if we're persistent."

"I'm starting to trust your judgment. Your hunches have been right a lot of the time."

She raised her eyebrows. "Thanks, but that's a lot to live up to. Next time I'm wrong, you'll be disappointed."

He glanced over at her, still smiling. "I don't think so."

A few minutes later, she asked if he'd had time to look further into the manuscript he'd discovered on the flash drive.

"Not yet. I may turn it over to Matt Jackson to do a little research for me while I sort out this other stuff."

She wanted to shake him and scream, "Give it to me! Dad and Nick and I can find out if it's the same as one of her published books!" But she knew he wouldn't do that, and she kept quiet.

Edward Trainor, the chief executive officer of McCracken Finance welcomed them into his office with an air of wariness. After the introductions, he waved them into padded chairs.

"Frankly, I'm not sure what the purpose of this visit is, Detective. Why are the Murray Police interested in something that happened in Paducah years ago? The person who committed the embezzlement here has been dead for five years."

"Linda Braxton's name came up in connection to another case," Keith told him. "We're investigating anything that seems relevant to the newer crime."

Trainor frowned. "Surely not that murder you had last week?"

"I can't really discuss it, but Ms. Braxton had a connection to someone we're investigating on another matter. Could you please tell me the circumstances of the embezzlement case? I've seen the police report, and I understand you were the one who first reported it."

"That's right." Trainor sat down at his desk, clearly ill at ease. "We had an independent audit, and it turned up a large discrepancy. Naturally, we started looking hard at the people who had access to our accounts. It was a difficult period, because we had to keep everything quiet, but the employees knew something was up."

"Did you interact with Ms. Braxton during that time?"

"Only superficially. I had to manufacture some work for her to do that wouldn't have her going into the accounts we were worried about." Trainor shook his head. "It was a sad business. The very day the auditor nailed down the evidence against her, she didn't show up for work. I called the police, in case she was trying to leave town. They found her dead at her home."

"And the money?" Keith asked.

Trainor grimaced. "It was never recovered. The police had investigators checking all of her personal accounts, but they couldn't find it. Oh, they could see where she'd made deposits over a period of several years—money they couldn't account for without her stealing it. And some of the deposits exactly matched amounts missing from our funds that month. But she'd moved it."

"When?" Campbell asked.

Trainor eyed her curiously. "A few weeks before her death. About the time the audit started, actually."

"So she could have withdrawn cash from her accounts and hidden it."

"I suppose so, but why bother if you're going to commit suicide? And the police claimed they thoroughly searched the property but came up emptyhanded. We never got back a cent."

Keith thought he knew Campbell quite well, but he couldn't read the look on her face.

"So, how did Ms. Braxton get along with her coworkers?" he asked.

"I think she kept to herself. She did her work alone—had a small office down the hall. I don't really think she socialized much. My secretary was here when Linda worked here. Perhaps she could help you with that."

"Okay. One last question," Campbell said. "Do you know anything about her family?"

"She was single." Trainor's brow wrinkled. "I'm not even sure who she'd listed as next of kin, but the secretary would be able to pull that up for you."

A few minutes later, he showed them out into the lobby, where the secretary said she'd be happy to answer their questions.

"Linda wasn't the friendly type," she said. "I asked her to have lunch with me several times, but she never took me up on it."

"Did you ever see her outside the office?" Keith asked.

"No. I invited her to go with my husband and me to a concert once, but she said no thanks. I admit I sort of gave up on her after a while. If a person doesn't want to be friends, that's pretty much that."

"What about her family?" Campbell asked.

A blank look came over the woman's face. "As far as I know, she didn't have anyone."

"Mr. Trainor said you could check the old records for us," Keith said. "We wondered who she listed as her next of kin or emergency contact."

"Just a minute. We've changed software since then." She frowned and tapped away at her keyboard. After a few minutes, she said, "There it is. Hmm." She looked up at them. "Someone named Dwight Palmer. I think the phone number is in a Missouri area code."

Keith copied it down. "Thank you very much. And is there a picture of Ms. Braxton in the file?" He thought he saw a gleam in Campbell's eyes, but she said nothing.

After a few clicks, the secretary shook her head. "No, I'm sorry."

Back in Keith's SUV, he turned to face Campbell as she buckled her seat belt. "What were you thinking when you asked Mr. Trainor about the money disappearing?"

"I was remembering something that came up when Xina first came to see Dad and me."

"Oh? Something I'd be interested in?"

"A painting used to hang in Katherine's living room. She sold it last fall."

He nodded. "I remember your father mentioning that."

"He found it odd that she'd kept it so long and then sold it. We speculated that she had a sudden need for money. But the weirdest thing was, we never found that she'd received the money from the auction house. At least, she didn't deposit it in the bank accounts we know about."

Keith gave a little groan. "How did you access her accounts? I mean, we need a warrant for that. It was Bill, I suppose."

"No, Xina and I found the banking records when we were looking for documents in her house. That was before we found the will that bypassed Xina."

"Oh, right. But, you can't just go snooping in people's bank records."

Campbell raised both hands. "Hey, Xina was her next of kin, remember? We were trying to help her, and she felt she needed a handle on her aunt's finances."

Keith's troubled expression told her he wasn't quite mollified.

"You saw those same bank statements strewn on the floor in her study," she said.

"Yeah, we all did. I suppose it's all right."

"Dad thought so. Xina was our client, and she believed she had a perfect right to be there. She hoped to find documents that would help Katherine, like her insurance policy, for instance."

"Did you find that?"

"Yes. She has Medicare and a supplemental coverage. Xina and I found the policies and statements, but we also came across her bank records and her old tax returns, right there in black and white. So I can tell you for certain, there were no big deposits last fall."

He nodded, still not completely at ease with the privacy issue.

"There were a couple of automatic deposits for royalties from her publishers," Campbell went on, "but nothing from the auctioneers, and nothing unexplained. I don't think she dumped a big bundle of cash in her checking account after she sold the painting."

"I don't suppose you found much cash in the house?"

"Just the small amount in her purse that was recovered after her accident, and about two hundred dollars in a bank envelope in her desk."

"Both of which were missing after the break-in." Keith frowned and started the engine. He was quiet as he pulled out of the parking lot. He drove down the street and stopped at a traffic light.

What was going through his mind? Campbell supposed he

was wondering if Katherine had spent the money in cash? Odd for anyone to do that with such a large amount. And if she hadn't spent it, where was it now?

"So, maybe Linda Braxton is like Katherine in that way," he said. "Influx of cash that doesn't show up on the books."

"Yes, but remember, Linda was an expert at manipulating ledgers. In Katherine's case, I have no explanation." Campbell was silent for a minute as he drove toward the highway. She went back over their conversations with Mr. Trainor and his secretary. "You remember we told you Dwight Palmer is dead?"

"I do. And he was Janice Sandler's father."

"That's right. And Linda listed him as her emergency contact."

"She was a friend of the family," Keith said.

"So, what now?"

"I'm not sure." He glanced at the dashboard clock. "Are you on a schedule? Can we stop for some lunch and hash it over?"

"I'd love to."

"WE'VE KEPT a watch on Katherine's house the last couple of nights," Keith said, "but not tonight."

"Why not?" Campbell asked.

"Budget." Keith grimaced. "The chief thinks I'm spending way too much time on this. He says I need to concentrate on Tatton's murder. But I can't help thinking that's connected to Katherine Tyler. There are just too many things there that don't add up."

Campbell took a bite of her salmon and chewed while she thought. She swallowed and said, "We could do it."

"We? You and me?"

"No, True Blue. Xina hired us to make sure her aunt's okay. Well, someone's been breaking into her house while she's out of the way in the hospital. So why shouldn't True Blue guard the house tonight to make sure he doesn't come back?"

"I can think of several reasons."

She arched her eyebrows and waited.

"Okay, first of all, can Xina afford to pay you for that many man hours?"

"Good point, but I think we're invested enough in this that we'd do it gratis. I, for one, would sit up all night just to make sure that jerk doesn't mess with Katherine's stuff again."

Keith laughed. "Spoken like a true professional. My second point is, she's awake now. No more acting in what you think is her best interest. We can ask what she wants us to do."

It was true. Campbell was having a hard time adjusting from the effective absence of the subject True Blue was investigating to knowing Katherine was awake and opinionated and just a few blocks away from her house.

"Well, what were you thinking when you asked the secretary at McCracken Finance if she had a photo of Linda Braxton?"

Keith eyed her steadily. "What do you think I was thinking?"

"Okay, I've had the same thought, but it doesn't really make sense."

"Doesn't it?" He wasn't smiling.

22

K eith dropped Campbell off at the office and went on alone to the police station.

"I'm sure we could do the surveillance job," her father said when she'd detailed her conversation with Keith and their morning's work.

"But don't we need her permission, now that she's awake?" Campbell asked.

"Technically, no, if we're not actually on her property. But let's see what Xina tells us. Maybe she could help you persuade her aunt that someone should be there—someone prepared to confront any prowlers."

"But what if they already found what they were after?"

"We've no indication of that," Bill said. "It's my opinion they wanted what Keith found in the closet wall."

"Her manuscript? You may be right. I wish we could get our hands on that."

Throughout the afternoon they worked on what details they could find of Linda Braxton's life. Nick came in happy with the results of his missing persons trace.

"Mr. Gray and his daughter had a satisfactory reunion," he

241

reported. "Mr. Gray's not happy that she won't come home, but at least he knows where she is now, and she's safe."

While he wrote up his report, Campbell kept on doggedly pursuing every tiny lead she could. At last, she looked over at her father.

"Dad, I think I found it."

"Oh? What have you got?"

"Before she signed on at McCracken Finance, Linda Braxton spent a couple of years with a franchise financial service here in Murray."

"You're not kidding me, are you?" Bill shoved his chair back and came to stand beside her.

"It was a fairly short stint. She was basically clerking while she finished some training, and then she moved on to Paducah."

"And Katherine Tyler used that service."

"You guessed it."

Bill reached for his cell phone and keys. "Let's go talk to them."

The franchise owner, Donald Wright, was adamant about client privacy, and Campbell grew discouraged.

"What else can we do?" she asked her father.

"Time to call in the big guns. Look, Mr. Wright, the police are extremely interested in this case. I'm going to call Detective Keith Fuller and see if he can meet us here and explain how crucial this investigation is. If necessary, he can get a warrant."

The worry lines on Wright's forehead deepened. "I'm sorry, but I can't—"

"We don't want to know anyone's financial secrets," Bill went on. "We just need you to confirm that you once employed Linda Braxton here. We know Katherine Tyler was a client for many years. We've seen her financial statements. Just tell us, please, when Ms. Braxton was here. Dates, that's all we need."

Wright sighed. "I wasn't here in the period you're talking about. I bought the franchise about eight years ago, and Ms. Tyler has been a steady client. I don't know this Linda person you're talking about, but it should still be in the company files. Let me talk to my office manager."

They went out to the lobby, and Wright stepped into the small, enclosed outer office. Bill and Campbell stood by the Plexiglas window watching, but couldn't make out the quiet conversation that ensued.

After several minutes, Campbell gave up. She sat down and leafed through a magazine, but her father waited by the window, watching Wright and his employee. Finally Wright returned to the doorway, and Campbell joined her father.

"Okay, the company did have an employee by that name for about a year and a half." He held out a slip of paper, and Bill took it. "Those are the dates of her employment. We don't have anything else."

"No performance reviews or anything like that?"

"I'll wait for a warrant, but it looks like she left here on good terms. I really don't have anything that's pertinent to your case, but the birth date matches up with the woman who was here at that time."

The door opened, and a man carrying a briefcase entered. He nodded at Wright and sat down in the chair Campbell had abandoned.

"Okay," Bill said. "Thanks very much for your time."

Outside, Campbell said, "That was like pulling teeth."

"Yeah, it's frustrating, but I don't mind. I mean, if I were the one being inquired about, I'd want my privacy protected too."

Campbell got in the car and buckled up. "So what do we know now?"

"We know Linda Braxton was in Murray for about a year and a half. She had plenty of opportunity to meet Katherine Tyler through her job, or anything else. A library reading group, at church. Anything, really."

"But probably right here." Campbell looked back at the brick building they'd just left. "Too bad we don't know if she worked on Katherine's finances."

Bill shrugged. "They probably don't have that information now. Linda left here sixteen years ago."

"So, what do we do? Do we ask Katherine some questions and see how she reacts?"

"No, I don't want to even mention Linda Braxton's name to her. Not until Keith is done with his investigation. And don't tell Xina what we suspect. I'd hate for her to spill it, even unintentionally."

On the way back to True Blue, he drove past Katherine's house. All was quiet.

"Rita's not there," Campbell said. "I think Xina told her not to bother until she knows Katherine is going home."

"We'll see what Keith's come up with," Bill said, "but I'm planning to sit outside that house tonight. You can join me if you want, but I warn you it will be boring."

"I should get some practice in surveillance."

Bill turned into the parking area in front of the office. "I need to return some phone calls. I think one of the injury claim cases we investigated is going to court, so I may have to testify again soon."

Campbell puffed out a breath. "In Frankfort?"

"No, here in Murray." After a moment's silence, he said, "What?"

"Oh, I don't know. This job isn't how I thought it would be."

"Not as exciting as Magnum or Rockford?"

"Oh, please, Dad. Rockford? You really are old!"

Bill laughed. "Having to lower your expectations, are you?"

"No, not really. It's just different. I can see how we really help people like Xina. But a lot of what you do just seems like … paperwork."

"Or computer work," he said.

"Yeah. It's a lot more of an office job than I realized. But you don't even have many people come to your office. You could do ninety-nine percent of it from home."

"When it comes down to it, I could do it all from home, but

it wouldn't seem as professional to outsiders—potential clients. Perception counts for a lot, Soup."

"I suppose."

He shut off the engine. "So, what do you think so far? Too boring?"

"I don't think so. When I taught literature, I got to talk about something I loved, but I still had to do testing and grades and record keeping. But what was I doing for those students?"

"Helping them get their degrees."

"Yes, but look at what I'm doing now. I'm helping Xina find out if her aunt is really okay."

Her father nodded slowly. "This could be life-changing for Xina. That's why we're going to sit up all night in the car."

"I'm going over to the hospital, Dad."

"How come?"

"I want to tell Xina we're surveilling Katherine's house tonight. Maybe she'll loan us her key, in case we need to go inside for some reason."

"Okay, but be careful what you tell her. I don't want to put her on edge, and I certainly don't want her alerting Katherine to what we're digging into."

"I won't."

When Campbell looked into Katherine's room a few minutes later, Xina was seated in a chair on the far side of the bed. She noticed Campbell and tiptoed to the doorway.

"She's sleeping now, but she was awake earlier."

"Is she talking to you?" Campbell asked.

"Not a lot. She did fret a little about giving Rita her paycheck. I said I could bring in her checkbook so she could sign the check, and I'd get it to Rita."

"She was okay with that?"

Xina grimaced. "She wants to go home."

"What does Dr. Drummond say?"

"He told her she's not ready yet. And he told me privately that he wants to keep her here until he's convinced her mind is clear—maybe a couple more days. If she seems lucid, he'll discharge her then. But the nurses did get her up this morning for a walk in the hall. That seems to have worn her out. She's been sleeping for almost two hours."

Campbell wondered if Katherine was feigning sleep to avoid talking to Xina.

"Well, listen, the police budget won't allow them to keep an officer at the house tonight, so Dad and I thought we'd do a little security duty."

"Oh, I can't ask you to do that."

"Sure you can. We don't mind. It will be a good training exercise for me, and Dad says if nothing happens tonight, we won't charge you for our time."

"That's very generous of you both."

Campbell shrugged and realized she was beginning to think of Xina as a friend, not just as a client.

"So listen, we won't try to go into the house at all, unless we think we need to. But if something happens, I thought maybe it would be handy for us to have a key. What do you think?"

"Oh, Campbell! I trust you and Bill implicitly. Let me get my purse."

BILL PARKED his car on the street, opposite Benjamin Tatton's house, where they would have a good view of Katherine Tyler's front door and driveway. They sat until almost midnight in the dim light from the streetlight down the block. As they watched Katherine's dark house, they talked softly and sipped coffee Bill had brought in a large thermos.

"I really think I want to stay," Campbell said. "I'm learning so much from you."

"I think we make a good team, but, honey, I don't want you to feel pressured. If you want to keep looking for something else, I'll support you all the way."

"No, this may be my niche. I'd like to stick with it long enough to find out for sure."

Her father's smile widened. "Then we'll put in your paperwork first thing tomorrow, and I'll sign you up for an online class in procedure. What do you say to that?"

"Sounds interesting."

"Great." He reached over and patted her arm. "I've been wanting to do those things, but I didn't want to influence you."

"Influence away. I'm ready."

"That's terrific."

Campbell's gaze locked on Katherine's uninviting house, but nothing had changed. "Okay, I need to ask you something. Do I want to know what you do when you're on surveillance and you've had too much coffee?"

Her dad laughed. "Why don't I get out, and you take the car over to the office—or McDonald's if you prefer. I'll keep watch while you're gone."

"Are you sure?"

"Of course. It's no problem. I'll go over and stand near that tree in Tatton's front yard. There'll be a pretty good view from there, and if I get back in the shadows, no one will see me."

Campbell considered that. "Okay, but do you think the neighbors will notice our activity?"

"Mrs. Hill?"

"Yeah, I was thinking of her."

"When you come back, park in a different spot. Just make sure we can still see Katherine's house from where you land." He pointed. "Maybe over there. I'll come to you once you're parked."

"Okay."

Although they'd both had a lot of coffee, she decided to make her restroom stop at McDonald's and return with fresh brew and fruit pies as a surprise for her dad. She put the bag on the front seat and set the large paper cups firmly in the cup holders, then drove back to where she'd left him.

Something was different, and she slowed to about twenty miles per hour. A car was parked in nearly the same spot she and her father had sat in for three hours. A glance toward Ben Tatton's tree didn't show her any trace of her dad, but she didn't see anyone in the newly arrived car, either.

She rolled on past, to the next intersection. At the stop sign, she paused for a moment, wondering what to do. She decided to circle around and head back down Katherine's street in the opposite direction. When she came in sight of the parked car, she slowed and looked for a good spot.

Not wanting to park too near the newcomer or directly in front of Katherine's house, she stopped a little farther down than she wanted, between Katherine's and the next large house. The view wasn't ideal, but an oak tree shadowed her, and she doubted Vera Hill could see her spot from her front windows.

Campbell turned off the engine and sat in the quiet darkness. She felt almost invisible. Her father had undoubtedly seen that new car's arrival. He'd left his binoculars on the back seat. She got them out and trained them on the other car. Still no sign of anyone in the driver's seat.

Opening the glove compartment, she tried to keep an eye on the car, but saw no flicker of movement. She took out a small flashlight and pulled the keys from the ignition. Instead of getting out on the street side, she slid over to the passenger seat and opened the door next to the sidewalk. Since they were using her father's car, the dome light didn't come on. Bill had disabled it so he wouldn't draw attention to himself at times like this, and Campbell was grateful. She made a mental note to do the same in her car.

Letting her eyes adjust, she lingered half a minute in the shadow of the oak tree. Cautiously, she strode down the sidewalk toward Katherine's house, not turning on the flashlight. As she approached, she kept to the side of the walk and ducked low along the shrubbery. She tiptoed up the side of the driveway and paused at the edge of the porch.

There was no sign of her father. He'd said he'd come to the car when she returned, but he was nowhere in sight. Was he still over on Tatton's property, lurking in the camouflage of the shadows?

What was she supposed to do? She didn't want to knock on the door.

She gazed along the front of the house, at the windows, and thought she saw a flicker of light at one, but it was gone almost as quickly as it appeared.

Her heart raced. Someone was inside, but something told her that whoever was in there hadn't entered through the front door.

The air had cooled over the hours since the sun sank, and she shivered. She should have thrown a sweater in the car, but it was eighty degrees when they left home, and that never entered her mind.

Gripped by uncertainty, she hovered in place. A strong urge to call Keith grasped her, but it was after midnight. She wouldn't make the call unless she had something definite to tell him.

Making a quick decision, she hunched down beneath the windows and scurried to the end of the house, where the garage was set back a few feet.

The overhead door to the garage was shut, and she tiptoed around the corner, her hand on the flashlight. A small door faced the side yard.

Campbell hesitated then put her hand to the knob. It turned easily. Had her dad gone inside? Their previous conversations led her to believe he wouldn't do that. She'd entrusted Xina's key to him, but she thought it only fit the front door.

When she pushed gently, the door opened. She stepped inside the garage and turned on her flashlight. Katherine's parking spot was still empty. A quick sweep with her beam assured her she was alone. She swallowed hard. Her dad wouldn't pick the lock, would he? He must have found the door open as well.

Which meant someone else went in the house first. Had flickers like the ones she'd seen drawn him?

On tiptoe, she crossed the concrete floor to the door that gave access to the kitchen. It also swung open at her touch. Rita or Xina would have left it locked from the inside. Campbell distinctly remembered a deadbolt. Her dad had told her those were notoriously hard to pick. Did someone else have a key?

She inched up the two steps that led from the garage to the level of the house and looked into the kitchen. No lights were visible, other than the dim glow from the windows. Holding her breath, she stepped inside and closed the door partway, leaving a gap of a few inches in case she wanted to make a quick retreat.

Standing stock-still, she listened. A creak and definite footsteps came from overhead. She tried to orient herself to the layout upstairs. Someone was in Katherine's bedroom.

More creaking, and a thud. Had the burglar come back to search more thoroughly?

The kitchen table lay to her right, near one of the windows. She eased across the floor carefully, without turning on her flashlight. At the doorway to the dining room, she paused again to listen. Did she imagine she heard someone breathing?

Should she creep up the stairs? Maybe it was time to call Keith. But she'd feel silly if that was her father up there banging around.

A glow at the top of the stairwell startled her, and she shrank back in the doorway. A beam of light traveled down the stairs, accompanied by footsteps and the creak of the old stair treads. She could make out a man's dark form behind the hand that held the light.

Campbell's pulse rioted. He was taller than her dad, wasn't he? The poor light and swirling shadows made her unsure. At the bottom of the steps, he swung the light in her direction, catching her full in the face. She gasped and clung to the doorjamb.

He ran toward her and slammed into her. Instead of being

shoved aside, Campbell was thrown backward and tumbled to the floor, gasping for air. He tripped over her and crashed down on her legs.

"Dad," Campbell croaked out, but she didn't have enough breath left in her lungs to yell.

Suddenly light flooded the room. The man loomed above her, holding his flashlight over his head like a club.

"Hold it right there."

The burglar froze and jerked his head toward the doorway where they'd just collided. Campbell had a swift impression of her father standing with one hand on the light switch and the other training a pistol on the burglar. But her attention was immediately riveted to the intruder's face.

"You!"

23

He crouched awkwardly, squinting at her.

"Put the flashlight on the floor," Bill said tersely.

Slowly, the man complied, his mouth gaping. "Do I know you?"

"We spoke on the phone a few days ago." Campbell struggled to sit up.

"Put your hands up," Bill said grimly. Without looking Campbell's way, he asked, "You know this guy?"

"He's Bruce Waverly, Katherine's agent. I saw his picture on his website."

Waverly lifted his hands, encased in polyethylene gloves, to shoulder height and rocked back on his heels. "Look, I can explain."

"I'll bet you can," Bill said. "We'll let you do that, just as soon as the cops get here. Make the call, Soup."

With shaking hands, Campbell extracted her phone from her pocket and punched 911.

"Hi, this is Campbell McBride. My father and I have apprehended a burglar." She gave Katherine's address and looked to her dad.

"That's good," he said. "Now wake Keith up."

That was an assignment she was glad to complete. The phone rang several times before Keith's groggy voice came to her.

"Hello? Campbell, is that you?"

"Yes. Dad and I are in Katherine's house. We caught the burglar."

"What? You're kidding."

"No, I'm not. There's a squad car on the way."

"I'll be right there."

By the time she'd told him their prisoner's identity, Bill had forced Waverly to sit down at the kitchen table and was securing his hands behind him. Campbell stared at her father. She'd known he carried rubber gloves, small plastic bags, and assorted other items while investigating, but really? Zip ties?

"Da-ad?" The quaver in her voice was mortifying.

"Yeah?"

"Never mind." She went to the cupboard for a clean glass and helped herself to a drink of water.

"You okay?" Bill asked.

"Yeah. He knocked the wind out of me, but I'm good."

A million questions raced through her mind. What would her father have done if Waverly had a gun? Would he really have fired a shot if Waverly hadn't obeyed his orders?

Her knees felt a little wobbly. She needed to sit, but she didn't want to join the man at the table, so she leaned against the counter and took several deep breaths. She caught the wail of an approaching siren.

"Go on out and meet the officers," Bill said, tucking his pistol back in his shoulder holster. "Tell them the situation is under control."

Campbell walked quickly into the hall, flipping on the overhead lights, and went to the front door. She unlocked it and crossed the porch then hurried down to the driveway.

The marked car rolled up, and officers Jackson and Stine got out. Campbell had met them both before, and she was glad to see familiar faces.

"Ms. McBride, what's going on?" Jerry Stine called as he strode toward her.

"My dad's inside holding a prisoner in the kitchen. We were watching the house because a burglar has been here at least twice in the last week."

"I was here Saturday, after it was ransacked," Matt Jackson said.

"Right. Well, this may be the guy who did it, but we're not sure. I recognized him as Bruce Waverly, Katherine Tyler's literary agent."

"Does he live in Murray?" Stine asked.

"No. I think he works out of Chicago. Oh, and Detective Fuller is on the way."

As she spoke, she walked with them onto the porch and opened the front door.

"Go right on through to the kitchen." She waved the way down the hall, and the two officers left her.

Campbell closed the door and leaned against it. She pulled in a deep, slow breath. Another vehicle pulled into the drive, and Keith jumped out of his SUV.

"That was fast," she said as he took the porch steps two at a time.

"Are you sure it's Katherine's agent?" Keith asked.

"It's him." She told him briefly what had happened.

As she finished, her father came out onto the porch.

"Thanks for coming, buddy," Bill said.

Keith grinned at him. "You and Campbell have me well trained. If you think it's important enough to call me, I respond asap."

"Well, this guy was in a hurry to leave when he realized someone else was in the house. He knocked Campbell down. They both fell, and he was about to brain her with a big flashlight when I got to them."

"We'll talk later about you being in here," Keith said.

"He's the one who broke in, not us," Bill said. "And Xina told us we could come in. She even loaned us her key, but we didn't use it."

"So, where is he?"

"The prisoner's in the kitchen," Bill said. "Jackson and Stine are with him. I told them you were coming."

"Thanks." Keith walked down the hall.

"You coming in?" Bill asked Campbell.

She nodded. "Wouldn't miss it."

A moment later, they entered the kitchen together.

"So, Mr. Waverly, what are you doing here?" Keith asked their prisoner.

"I came to try to help Katherine."

"By breaking into her house?"

Waverly said nothing.

"I'm pretty sure you don't have a key, do you?" Keith took hold of the back of Waverly's chair and shifted it so he could look him in the face.

"As a matter of fact, I do. She gave me permission."

"Oh, when was that? She's been unconscious for more than a week."

Campbell flicked her father a glance, and he gave her a solemn nod. She interpreted that as instructions to keep quiet. Keith was no doubt fishing for information on how much Waverly knew about Katherine's condition.

When Waverly didn't respond, Keith asked, "Have you ever been here before?"

"I ... No."

Keith looked over at Stine. "Call in a couple more officers. We need to see what damage he did this time."

Stine nodded and stepped into the hallway.

Keith bent down and said, about six inches from Waverly's face, "And how did you get to Murray? Ms. McBride told me she called you in Chicago last week."

"I drove down."

"When?"

He hesitated. "Yesterday."

"Where's your car?"

"Around the corner."

"What's the license plate number?"

Waverly scowled. "It's a rental."

"Is the paperwork from the rental company in the car?" Keith asked.

"Yes."

"So, we'll find that you rented it yesterday in Chicago?" After a long pause, Keith assured him, "In case you're wondering, I will check up on every single detail."

"Okay, I rented it here."

"Oh, you rented it here." Keith paced halfway across the kitchen and turned back to glare at him. "What happened to your own car?"

"It's in Chicago. I flew down to Paducah."

"And what day was that? Because you know I will find out within minutes."

"Yesterday. That is, Sunday."

"You mean Friday."

"No. I just came down yesterday."

Keith scowled at him. "You were here in this house Friday night, searching the place."

"No, I wasn't." He looked up at Keith. "I think I want a lawyer."

Keith raised both hands. "Okay, fine. Is that your Chicago lawyer? Or do you want someone local?"

Waverly's bottom lip trembled.

"Where are you staying?" Keith asked.

"The Holiday Inn."

"Where are your car keys, Mr. Waverly?"

Waverly hesitated.

Don't make me search you." Keith sounded annoyed, beyond being woken up in the middle of the night.

"In my left pocket," Waverly said.

Keith crouched and pulled the keys out and handed them to Stine. "Check out the paperwork and take the car to the station, Jerry. Call the Holiday Inn and get the registration info, then call the airport and check out his recent travels." He turned to Jackson. "Matt, take the prisoner in and book him."

"Right," Jackson said.

"After that, help him connect with a lawyer of his choosing."

The two officers hauled Waverly to his feet and herded him toward the front door.

"Oh, by the way," Keith called after them, "Ms. Tyler came out of her coma. You can bet I'll ask her if you have permission to come here and strew her belongings all over the place."

Waverly's face tightened.

"Come on," Jackson said.

When the prisoner was out of the house, Campbell exhaled and closed her eyes for a moment.

Her dad touched her shoulder. "You sure you're all right?"

She looked into his eyes. "That was pretty intense."

"Yeah. What do you say we go home? Keith and his people will finish up here."

"You can both come by the station tomorrow to give your statements," Keith said.

"Okay." Campbell touched his arm. "Thank you so much for everything."

"Thank *you*. It's a relief to have the burglaries solved. Now maybe I can focus on Tatton's murder."

CAMPBELL DIDN'T SLEEP MUCH. The overdose of coffee and the harrowing events of the evening kept her tossing on her bed for hours. As dawn broke, she drifted off, and she awoke at 9:30 a.m. with a headache and a sore hip.

Bill had left her a note on the refrigerator door: *Gone to the office. Come in when you're ready and we'll go to the PD.*

Grateful for a short respite, she fixed herself a caffeine-free breakfast and took a couple of ibuprofen. After a shower, she blew her hair dry and dressed in pants and a short-sleeved blouse. The headache had receded, and she felt almost human again.

When she finally arrived at the office, Nick and Bill were both at their desks.

"Hey, Professor," Nick said. "You get all the action around here."

She put on her most disdainful expression. "Says the man with his arm in a cast."

"Yeah, well, it's coming off next week."

"Good news on all fronts," her father said. "Waverly is talking, and Xina phoned to say Katherine seems more alert. Keith hopes he can talk to her, at least for a few minutes, this afternoon." He pushed back his chair and stood. "Ready to go make our statements?"

"Sure. Let's get it over with."

Nick grinned. "Don't worry about a thing, boss. If the new client comes early, I'll be right here."

"New client?" Campbell threw Nick a frown and followed her father out the door. "We have a new client?"

"Prospective," her dad said. "He's supposed to come in at eleven and talk. Wants us to find out if his son-in-law is really where he says he is."

Campbell raised her eyebrows.

"Hop in. I'll explain on the way."

Fifteen minutes later, they were both sitting at a table in a conference room at the police station, writing out their versions of the previous night's events. When Campbell read over what she'd written about their encounter with Waverly, she shivered.

"Having second thoughts about your new career?" Bill asked.

"Not really. But sometimes doing good is hard."

"That's true. Thank the Lord you weren't seriously hurt last night."

"I've got some major bruises on my hip and my arm, but I think everything else is okay."

"Good."

She eyed him across the table. "Dad, next time I go on surveillance, remind me not to drink a gallon of coffee."

He laughed. "I'd say 'occupational hazard,' but some people tolerate caffeine better than others."

"Well, I'm starting to wonder what it's doing to you."

"Don't worry about me, kiddo. So, you done?"

She nodded and stacked the papers she'd filled with longhand. "We should have done this on the computer and emailed it to them."

Bill smiled. "Next time."

When they got to the hallway, she turned toward the front desk, but Bill started in the opposite direction.

"Where are we going?" Campbell whispered as she scurried to catch up with him.

"Keith's office. The detectives are over here."

They walked into a large room with several desks. Keith spotted them and stood.

"Hey, McBrides. All finished?"

"Yeah. What's the word on Bruce Waverly?" Bill handed him his statement.

"He's still in a cell. I learned some very interesting things about him."

"I'll bet," Bill said.

Keith took Campbell's papers. "For one thing, this wasn't his only recent trip to Murray. He stayed at the same hotel last week."

"You're kidding," Bill said.

Keith shook his head. "Apparently he made a quick flight down here the day you first phoned him, Campbell."

"What? The day he hung up on me? That was like—the same day Xina hired us."

Bill frowned at him. "Are you saying Campbell's call to Waverly had something to do with Tatton's death?"

"It might. But he says he didn't do it."

"Well, sure," Bill replied. "Who's going to cop to murder when the only thing you have evidence of is him breaking into a house?"

"I'm eager to talk to Katherine Tyler." Keith locked his hands behind his head and looked up at the ceiling. "Waverly says he came down the first time to see Katherine. But he won't say if he saw her or what they talked about, if they did talk."

"Interesting," Campbell said.

"Yeah. His lawyer is with him now. I hope they'll give me some more information after they consult. And I'm heading for the hospital right after lunch. Ms. Harrison cleared it with the doctor, but I'm not supposed to stay long."

"I hope you can get something out of her," Bill said.

"Well, we haven't told Ms. Harrison about Waverly's arrest yet. I want to keep that quiet until I see her aunt."

"We haven't told her," Bill said. "I didn't even give Nick the details. I told him this morning we'd caught a prowler at Ms. Tyler's house, but he knows he's to keep that to himself."

Outside the police station, Campbell said, "Dad, I think I'll go over to the hospital now. Xina's there, and she may have more information."

He nodded. "Remember, don't mention Waverly."

"What if she asks about the prowler?"

"Tell her to ask Keith when he goes in later. Play dumb, or just tell her you can't give out the details until the police do."

Campbell rode back to the office with him and took her car to the hospital. Xina looked relieved to see her and joined her at the doorway to Katherine's room.

"She's awake, and I read to her for a while before Dr. Drummond came in, but then she told me to quit reading it."

"Is she friendlier than she was before?" Campbell asked.

"A little. I assured her again that I'm staying at a hotel, not her house. I haven't told her anything about the break-in or the snake."

"Good. It's probably best to hold off on that. So what did the doctor say today?"

Xina's brow wrinkled. "It was a little odd. He asked her about a scar on her abdomen."

"They removed her spleen," Campbell said, frowning.

"No, not the new one. An old one. Aunt Katherine said it was from when she had her appendix out as a teenager, which is what she always told me, so I didn't think anything of it."

"So why was that odd?"

"Because when Dr. Drummond was done examining her, he said they'd like to do a few more tests and make sure she's steady on her feet. They want to keep her a couple more days."

"Was Katherine agreeable?"

"She didn't look happy, but she didn't argue with him. But then Dr. Drummond said something like he wanted to speak to me about her home care when she leaves, so I followed him out to the nurses' desk. He was still wondering about that scar. He claims there's no way it's fifty years old. He said it's much more recent."

Campbell just stared at her for a moment. "So ... do you think she had another surgery more recently?"

"I said the same thing, but the doctor said there's no other scarring that would indicate an appendectomy. And he said the one she's got doesn't look professional. I'm not sure what he meant."

Campbell drew in a long, slow breath. "Detective Fuller is coming in to see her later, right?"

"In about an hour. I think I'm going to stay with her."

"You should eat lunch."

"I just feel as though it's a bad time to leave her."

"Okay. I'll pop down to the coffee shop and get you a sandwich and a cold drink and bring it up to you. Don't tell her I'm here. She might start asking questions."

"Yeah, she doesn't know I hired investigators to look into her situation. I don't think this is a good time to spring that on her."

"If she asks about me, just tell her I'm a friend, because I am." A staffer was wheeling a cart stacked with lunch trays along the hallway. "Looks like Katherine will be getting her meal soon, anyway. You can eat together."

"Good. They're letting her have a little solid food today. Thanks, Campbell."

"No problem."

Xina when back into her aunt's room, and Campbell headed for the elevator. When she got off, she found a nook within sight of the coffee shop and pulled out her phone.

"Detective Fuller."

Hearing his deep, steady voice gave her courage. "Keith, can you get DNA samples from things at Katherine's house? Toothbrush, hairbrush, things like that?"

"We could, but that could be problematic, now that she's awake. I'd probably need a warrant."

"Well, my advice is to apply for a warrant immediately and then compare her DNA to Xina's. Keith, I am almost positive that woman is not Katherine Tyler."

24

K eith sat at the table facing Bruce Waverly and his lawyer, Earl Nyman, who had driven down from Paducah at the request of Waverly's personal attorney in Chicago, with whom he had a professional connection.

"Tell me why you flew down here the first time, Mr. Waverly," Keith said. He gave the date of the agent's flight, on the same day he'd done the initial wellness check on Ms. Tyler.

"We'd been corresponding by email and talking on the phone. I got the feeling something wasn't quite right. The quality of Katherine's work had declined drastically over the last few years, and I wanted to see her face-to-face."

"Was this the first time you'd seen her?" Keith asked.

"No, we used to see each other at least once a year, usually at a conference or seminar. I take appointments to meet potential new clients at these events, and if Katherine was attending, I always made time to sit down with her. We enjoyed our meetings, and they were constructive for both of us so far as her career was concerned. She also came to my office once, when she was in Chicago for a speaking engagement."

"When was the last time you'd seen her?"

"Not for more than five years." Waverly shook his head.

"That told me something was off. She'd stopped attending professional conferences and doing public speaking. I don't think she's done a book signing in the last five years, either."

"Did you learn why that was?" Keith asked.

He sighed and glanced at his lawyer. Nyman nodded.

"I think it was a medical issue," Waverly said. "She's getting older, and when I asked her about some things we'd discussed on the phone earlier, she didn't seem to remember them. I didn't stay in Murray long on that trip, but after I got back to Chicago, I contacted someone we both knew who could check up on her and perhaps find out if she was up to doing another book. I was having my doubts."

"And you made a second trip," Keith prompted.

"Yes. After I was told she'd had an accident and was hospitalized, I flew down again."

"Did you visit her in the hospital?"

"I learned she was in a coma, so, no, I didn't get to see her yet. I hoped she would improve, and I could talk to her soon."

"And while you stayed in town, you decided to poke around her house."

"That's not—I—"

"Oh, come on, Waverly. You were caught red-handed."

Waverly's head sank. "She'd told me several years ago that she had a complete manuscript ready, but then her computer crashed. She said she'd saved it on a flash drive and would send it to me as soon as she got her new computer set up. She also claimed she had other story lines—plots she'd developed. And partial manuscripts. I thought she'd go on producing books for the rest of her life."

"So, what happened?" Keith prompted.

"I didn't hear from her for months. When I finally called her, she didn't seem to remember what she'd told me. I was sure she had another bestseller for me, but ..." He raked a hand through his hair. "The next book she sent me was terrible."

"Was it the one she'd salvaged from the old computer?"

"I don't know. I couldn't believe how awful it was. Katherine and I had a good working relationship for several years, and I fully expected that to continue. But if she was ... no longer lucid ... well, I wanted to know. I flew down and had a brief meeting with her. She seemed okay, but she denied having a complete manuscript she was sitting on. I went back to Chicago that same night."

"But after you heard she was in a coma, you came back here. You thought you could find those other manuscripts and produce something with Katherine Tyler's name on it. *The long-awaited and much-anticipated new work of the bestselling author.*"

"It wasn't like that."

"What was it like?" Keith asked. "Because we know you burglarized her house twice."

"No. I met with her that first time, and I didn't come back here until tonight. That other time you're talking about—that wasn't me."

"Then who was it?"

"I NEED TO GO HOME." Katherine glared at her niece. "They can't keep me here against my wishes."

"The doctor thinks it's best, Auntie," Xina said. "It's for your own good."

"Rubbish. Get me my clothes."

"Why do you need to go home so soon?"

Campbell watched from the doorway as Xina pleaded with her aunt.

"This will cost me a fortune," Katherine snapped.

"But you have Medicare."

"There are always things that aren't covered. Besides, I need to speak to my agent."

"Mr. Waverly?" Xina asked.

Katherine frowned at her. "Yes. How did you know that?"

"I—I spoke to him last week, after your accident. I thought you would want him to know."

Katherine was silent for a moment.

Xina flicked a glance toward the doorway. Campbell drew back a little, hoping Katherine wouldn't see her if she followed her niece's gaze.

"I suppose it's best that he knows," Katherine said. "Have you told him I'm better now? Maybe I should call him."

"Uh, well, you can use my—"

Campbell shook her head decidedly. Xina caught her gaze for a moment.

"Oh, well, I don't think—um, how about if I bring in your cell phone tomorrow? You can try to call him then, but we're not supposed to use phones in here."

"There's a phone right there." Katherine waved toward the nightstand.

"That's the hospital phone," Xina said. "I don't think they'll allow long distance calls on that."

"Why ever not?" Katherine grew more cross by the moment.

Xina looked helplessly at Campbell.

"Well? Why not?" Katherine persisted. "Or I can use your cell phone. It's a smart phone, isn't it?"

"Uh, yes, but—uh—I'd have to take you in a wheelchair out into the hallway and outside the ICU."

"Nonsense."

Slowly, Xina drew her phone from her purse. Campbell waved frantically, shaking her head.

"Oh, it's not charged up. Besides, I don't know Mr. Waverly's number."

"You said you called him once already. His number should be in there somewhere."

Someone touched Campbell's shoulder, and she looked around into Keith's face.

"What's going on?" he whispered.

She drew him away from the doorway, toward the nurses'

station. "Katherine's upset. She's insisting she needs to call her agent. And she wants out of here, badly. Xina's trying to keep her from calling Waverly."

"Does Xina know he's in the county jail?"

"No, but I signaled her not to let Katherine try to call him."

"It won't matter if she does. We confiscated his phone and took out the battery."

"So, what now?" Campbell asked.

"Time to have another chat with Ms. Tyler." Keith strode into her private room.

KEITH LEFT Campbell hovering in the doorway and entered the glassed-in unit just as Katherine screamed at her niece, "Get me my clothes. Now!"

"Hello, Ms. Tyler," Keith said smoothly. "I see you're feeling stronger."

She scowled at him from her perch on the edge of the hospital bed. "The policeman."

"Yes, I'm Detective Fuller. I have some information for you, and I hope you have some for me."

"You'll have to wait until later. I'm going home." She held a cell phone to her ear, and her lips curved downward. "Stupid message. Not available. This is ridiculous."

She tossed the phone onto the bed, and Xina snatched it up.

"Sorry, Aunt Katherine. Maybe you can get hold of him later. Why don't you just lie down and relax."

"I told you, I'm going home. Get my clothes." Katherine fixed Keith with an icy glare. "And you, get out."

"No, Ms. Tyler. That's not going to happen," he said.

Xina stepped forward, her hands extended in supplication. "Aunt Katherine, the doctor says you need to stay a bit longer. I'm your medical caregiver, and—"

"I'll appoint someone else," Katherine snapped. "The

housekeeper will do." She pulled in a deep breath and squared her shoulders. "Actually, I'm sure I can speak for myself. The hospital can't keep me here against my will, and neither can you." She turned her angry gaze once more on Keith.

"That's where you're wrong," Keith said smoothly. "I can keep you here, under guard, or I can take you to the police station."

Xina gasped. "What—?"

Keith focused on the patient. "Your agent, Bruce Waverly, is in Murray."

"He's here?" Katherine's voice cracked. "Where is he? I want to see him."

"I'm afraid you can't do that right now. He's in a cell at the Calloway County Jail."

Her chin rose half an inch, and she held his gaze with icy eyes. "What's the charge?"

"There are several, including the burglary of your house last night."

Her lips parted, but she said nothing.

"Don't you want to know if he stole anything?" Keith asked.

She turned her face away.

"He was also here a couple of weeks ago," Keith went on. "The day after Ms. Harrison arrived in town. But you knew that, didn't you?"

Katherine's jaw clenched.

Keith said evenly, "Linda Braxton, you're under arrest for the murder of Benjamin Tatton. Now, I suggest you settle back into bed, and I'll read you your Miranda rights." As he spoke, he clipped a handcuff bracelet around her left wrist and fastened the other side to the bed rail.

———

XINA STRODE past Campbell with tears streaming down her cheeks. Campbell hurried after her and touched her back.

"Hey."

Xina whirled around.

"Oh, there you are!" She sobbed and reached out.

Campbell folded her in her arms. "There, now. It's going to be all right." She led Xina out to the waiting room, which was mercifully empty. They sat down in vinyl-covered chairs, and Xina broke down, her body wracked with weeping.

Campbell found a box of tissues and brought it to her.

"Here, friend."

Xina snatched at the box and pulled out a sheet.

Campbell sank down beside her, ready to supply whatever comfort she could.

"I know we both thought it was possible, but ..." Xina gasped in a breath and let out a series of piteous whimpers.

"I didn't want to say it, but with what Dad and I uncovered and what Keith learned about Waverly—"

"You told me they'd arrested the burglar, but you didn't say it was her agent." Xina's red-rimmed eyes widened. "Why didn't you tell me?"

"We didn't want any chance of you telling Katherine. I'm sorry. It's not that we didn't trust you, but you saw how persuasive she can be."

Xina nodded slowly, staring across the room at nothing. "She talked me into giving her my phone so she could call him." Her eyes jumped to Campbell's. "But she didn't get hold of him."

"No, the police have his phone. He broke into Katherine's house, and my dad caught him."

"Were you there?"

"I was." Campbell winced. "If Dad hadn't been carrying his gun, Waverly probably would have killed me, the same way ..."

"The same way Mr. Tatton was killed?"

"Almost." Campbell thought about that. "He was hit over the head and then stabbed. I don't think the police took any weapons off Waverly last night, but he sure would have whacked me with his flashlight." She shivered.

"Maybe that's what Ben Tatton was hit with," Xina said.

Movement at the doorway caught her eye, and she jumped up as her father walked in.

"Dad, what are you doing here?"

"Keith called me and told me to get over here. What happened?"

"He's arrested Kath—I mean, Linda, and handcuffed her to the bed," Campbell said.

"She wanted to leave, against the doctor's orders," Xina said. She wiped her eyes with a tissue and held out a hand to Bill. "Mr. McBride—Bill—thank you so much for everything. Campbell was just telling me about last night, and how Bruce Waverly attacked her in my aunt's house."

Bill clasped her hand for a moment. "Everything's okay now." He glanced around. "Where's Keith?"

"Still in the ICU with Linda," Campbell said.

"Good. I saw two uniformed officers heading that way. Let's sit down and give them some space." Bill pulled a chair around to face them.

Xina reached for another tissue and swabbed her cheeks. "I'm a mess. Sorry."

"You're fine," Campbell said and rubbed Xina's back lightly. "You have a right to be upset."

Xina gave a little hiccup, her eyes full of fresh tears. "It's just—I mean, if that's Linda Braxton, where's my Aunt Katherine? And why didn't I know it wasn't her?"

Bill sighed. "I suspect we'll learn your aunt is dead. I'm sorry to be so blunt, but that's the logical solution. As to why you didn't realize the deception, there are several contributing factors."

"That's right," Campbell said. "You hadn't seen her in five years, and you didn't see her often before that. And Linda Braxton has a strong superficial resemblance to Katherine. That first night you went to her house, it was dark in there. You said so yourself."

"It was pretty gloomy," Xina admitted. "And she kept her distance."

"You said she'd aged a lot," Bill added.

"She had. I mean, I thought she had. That was my explanation, I guess. I thought her age had caught up to her. But that seemed reasonable."

"Each time you saw her, your brain accepted the way she looked a little more."

"Did you feel like you hardly recognized her?" Campbell suggested.

Xina gave a bitter chuckled. "I did. I didn't come out and say that. I just thought she'd had a decline—whether physical, mental, or both. But yes, I felt as if I was talking to a different person."

"Her personality had changed," Bill said.

"Radically. And when she woke up from the coma, I thought her eyes were dull. They weren't as blue as they used to be. But I thought that was age too. No wonder she treated me so shabbily."

"Katherine loved you," Campbell said firmly. "She would have welcomed you with joy and invited you to stay with her."

The tears spilled over and ran down Xina's face. "That's what I hoped for. I was so hurt."

"I know." Campbell put an arm around her and drew her close. "Your instincts were right, Xina. Something was dreadfully wrong."

"You just didn't know how wrong," Bill said.

"It's—it's unthinkable."

"That's why you didn't think it," Campbell said gently.

Xina sniffed. "I should have said something."

"On that first visit, your mind refused to even consider something like this," Campbell said.

Bill's gaze flickered. "Here's Keith." He stood.

Campbell gave Xina a squeeze and rose.

"How's it going?" Bill shook Keith's hand.

"We're almost home on this," Keith said. "I've got two officers watching her, and no one else is allowed into the room except her nurse and doctor."

"You've alerted Dr. Drummond?" Campbell asked.

"I told the charge nurse to call him." Keith stepped over to Xina's chair. "I'm so sorry, Ms. Harrison."

She sniffed and nodded. "What can you tell me? Do you know what happened to my aunt?"

"I have my suspicions, but we don't have the full story yet. My best guess is, she's in the grave marked Linda Braxton."

25

"How could she have carried that off?" Campbell asked.

"It would be hard, but I think that's what she did—murdered Katherine and took her place."

"Sit down, Keith." Bill indicated the chair he'd vacated and pulled another over for himself.

When they were all seated, Keith said, "I think this was something Linda planned for a long time. Months, maybe longer. While she worked at McCracken Finance, she began to fear her embezzling would be discovered. She realized she needed a way out. Somehow she'd fixated on Katherine Tyler. She'd probably met her through the financial advisor in Murray, where Linda had worked for a year and a half, or some other event here in Murray."

Campbell said slowly, "And way back then, she learned that Katherine looked like her—or she looked like Katherine."

"That's right. People may have remarked on it at the time, but that was years ago. When she moved to Paducah and started stealing from her employer, she remembered that. And she hatched a plan. Somehow, she lured Katherine into a situation where she could drug her. Maybe she asked her to be a writing mentor or something, I don't know. But she'd arranged everything to make it look like she committed suicide, and she left her car and her papers the way they'd been—everything. And she drove away in Katherine's car, with Katherine's purse, her I.D., and her keys."

"She became Katherine Tyler." Campbell could barely believe the audacity of it.

"Apparently she didn't show up for work the next day. The office couldn't reach her. On the second day, they asked the police to check on her, and they found her dead. No one questioned the corpse's identity. She was in Linda's house, wearing Linda's clothes, and an empty prescription bottle with Linda's name on it was lying next to her."

"Incredible," Bill said.

"Her lawyer is on the way."

"Barry McGann?" Bill asked. "He's not a criminal lawyer."

"He'll probably recommend someone who is," Keith said.

Xina looked up at him. "Now we know why she went to a different lawyer to get the will changed. She was afraid Katherine's lawyer would realize she was a different person."

"Could be. But the longer Linda posed as Katherine, the easier it got. More people accepted her as Katherine. She kept away from people Katherine had known well. Stopped going to church, put off visiting her friend Pamela Rogers."

"And she kept making excuses not to see Xina," Campbell said.

"That's right. It's also why she fired Doris Conley over the phone and hired a new housekeeper."

Xina's jaw dropped. "Of course! When she first replaced Katherine, Doris would have known immediately. They'd been close for years."

"And someone else figured it out," Keith said.

"Who?"

Xina gave him a blank look, but Campbell's mind was racing.

"Ben Tatton," she said.

Keith nodded. "I finally got the story out of Waverly.

Katherine called him in Chicago the night Xina visited her. He said she sounded panicky. Not at all like her old self. Waverly decided to fly down and calm her and see if he could get a handle on all the changes he'd sensed in her—the way her work had suddenly dropped in quality five years ago, her forgetfulness, her inability to produce a manuscript she'd promised him."

"Did she know he was coming?" Bill asked.

"He says he didn't tell her, and it was a spur-of-the-moment decision after they'd hung up." Keith settled back in his chair. "This is where it gets really interesting."

"That was the night Ben Tatton was killed," Campbell said.

"Yes. When Waverly arrived at Katherine's house in his rental car, no one answered the door. But as he turned back to his car, he saw someone walking across the back yard to the house next door—Tatton's house. It was after dark, but he had the impression of an older woman carrying a cane."

"A cane?" Campbell stared at him. "Tell me it was an antique ebony cane with a duck head for a handle."

Keith smiled. "All right, I'll tell you that. Waverly followed her. When he got to Tatton's back door, two people were arguing. He recognized Katherine's voice—the voice he'd been hearing on the phone for several years. The man said something, and she screamed at him that she was not going to pay him and she had other ways to shut him up."

The listeners sat in utter silence, waiting for him to resume.

"And then it gets fuzzy."

"What do you mean?" Bill asked.

"Waverly insists he didn't kill Tatton."

"But she had the cane," Campbell said.

Bill nodded grimly. "Yeah. Who had the knife?"

"Waverly says Tatton had it. He was menacing Ms. Tyler with a large kitchen knife. Waverly's words, not mine."

"Well, he didn't stab himself in the back," Bill said.

"No. But Waverly won't say he did it. He says Katherine—

that is, Linda—cracked Tatton over the head with the cane when he was distracted by Waverly's entrance."

"I can't picture her dropping the cane, picking up the knife, and stabbing him," Campbell said.

"Neither can I," Keith admitted.

"Where are the weapons?" Bill asked.

Keith leaned back in his chair. "That's still a mystery, but Waverly says he put them in a trash bag there in Tatton's kitchen, gave it to Katherine, and told her to get rid of them. Then he drove back to Paducah, cool as a cucumber, and flew back to Chicago that night."

"That's his story," Bill said.

"Yup, that's his story."

"Wait," Xina said. "Why did she hit him with the cane?"

Keith shrugged. "Waverly claims Tatton was threatening her. When he saw she was in danger, he stepped in to defend her. That will probably be his defense. That, or he'll blame it all on Ms. Braxton."

"And she'll blame him," Bill said.

"Probably. Reasonable doubt for both of them. But as to the reason for the argument, it's pretty clear that Tatton was trying to blackmail his neighbor."

"He knew she wasn't Katherine," Campbell said.

"That's right. And Waverly overheard enough to realize the truth."

"But he didn't come forward."

"No. We finally got into Tatton's cell phone, and he had some close-up photos of Katherine. They were taken outside her house a few weeks ago, probably when he went over to do some yard work for her."

Campbell nodded as the pieces came together in her mind. "He compared her to the older pictures of Katherine in those articles you found archived on his laptop."

"That's my theory." Keith's phone whirred and he pulled it

out. "Excuse me. Paducah P.D. calling. I asked them to pick up Lee Dorman."

He strode out into the hallway, and Campbell stared at her father.

"Did he say they're arresting Dorman, the researcher?"

Bill scratched his head. "He said they're picking him up, anyway."

They talked for a few more minutes. Several strangers came in and took seats at the other end of the room, talking quietly together. Campbell was about to suggest they go to the office for privacy when Keith returned, looking a bit harried.

Bill shot to his feet. "Keith, how does Dorman figure into all this?"

"We're not sure exactly, but Waverly says he asked Dorman to check in on Katherine and make sure she was okay after Tatton was killed. He says he just told him she was shook up because of her neighbor's murder. Well, guess what? He implicated Dorman in the first break-in at Katherine's house and also the snake incident."

"What?" Campbell cried. "That's crazy. Why would someone concerned about an old woman's health put a snake on her porch?"

"Exactly," Keith said. "I don't think Waverly's telling us everything. But the police in Paducah haven't found Dorman yet. He wasn't at his house. They're getting a warrant for his arrest and another so they can search his property. And there's one other thing—his sister works at the gift shop where the box Bill put the snake in came from."

Xina stood slowly. "So, Detective, what should I do now? Just go home to North Carolina?"

Keith's brow wrinkled. "No, not yet. I strongly suggest you contact both lawyers about those wills. The original will is valid, but the newer one isn't. Linda Braxton used it as a way to pass Katherine's estate to someone she had an attachment to—the Palmer family."

"Dwight Palmer saved her life," Bill said. "She cared more about him and his kids than she did about Katherine's nosy niece."

Xina actually laughed. "You're saying I will inherit the house after all."

"Yes," Keith said. "It will probably take a long time for the courts to sort through it all, but those two lawyers are both good attorneys. I'm sure they'll help you."

"Yeah, Barry McGann likely had no idea she was tricking him," Bill said. "He'll want to save face, and I'm guessing he'll bend over backward to help you through this mess."

"And you can ask them," Keith said, "but as far as I'm concerned, that house has been yours for the last five years. You ought to be able to stay in it and save the price of your hotel room until you decide to leave Murray."

"Oh, I'm not sure." Xina swallowed hard.

"Bad memories?" Campbell asked.

She nodded. "I will ask the lawyers, though. And, Campbell, if they tell me I can stay there, maybe you'd come over and help me make a few new memories there." Her faced sobered. "I should plan a memorial for Aunt Katherine. But ..."

"You'll figure it out," Campbell said. "There needs to be some sort of announcement or press release, for sure."

"Would you help me?" She turned to Bill. "You too, Mr. McBride?"

"Of course," Bill said.

Campbell patted her shoulder. "Would you like to have lunch with us at home? We can talk about it."

"That would be nice," Xina said. "I'll go to the hotel first, if you don't mind, and make a few calls."

"Keith?" Bill said. "Join us around noon?"

"I'm afraid I'll be busy, but thanks." Keith locked gazes with Campbell for a second and nodded. "I'll see you later."

THE NEXT DAY, Keith came to the True Blue office at nine in the morning. Campbell was surprised to see him so early.

"Where is everyone?" he asked, glancing first at Bill's empty workstation and then Nick's.

"Dad's at the courthouse this morning, and Nick's checking up on something for an insurance company."

"Oh. Well, I wondered if you'd like to take another ride with me today." Keith smiled down at her, looking very unbusinesslike.

"Where to this time?"

"Paducah again. The police up there didn't find Dorman at home yesterday, but I don't think they've posted anyone at his house. I thought I'd swing by there and see if he's around."

"What if he's on the run?" she asked. "He's got to know they're looking for him."

"Unless he was well prepared to skip town, I think he'll go home when he thinks things have cooled down."

"Surveillance, then?"

Keith chuckled. "You and your dad have a pretty good record using that method."

"Are you sure he's involved, or is it just Waverly's say-so?" Campbell reached for her purse.

"Linda Braxton told me this morning where she went the night she had her car accident."

Campbell stopped in her tracks to stare at him. "Where?"

"She arranged to meet Dorman."

Her jaw dropped. "Okay, details, Fuller."

"When you're safely ensconced in my vehicle."

"Let me leave Dad a note?"

"You can send him a text on the way."

She saw the logic of that. Her dad was becoming quite adept at texting.

"Okay." She buckled the seatbelt in Keith's SUV. "Why did she go to meet a researcher she supposedly hadn't used in years —not since she took over Katherine's identity?"

"Because Bruce Waverly told her to. He'd apparently had Dorman check up on Katherine-Linda after his first visit down here."

"You mean, when Ben Tatton was killed."

"Right. He didn't tell Dorman about the murder, but he wanted someone to keep an eye on Linda. He claims it was just to make sure she was all right—not sliding into dementia is the way he put it. He tried to think of someone they both knew, and he hit on Dorman."

"But Linda didn't know Dorman."

"Right." Keith frowned. "Maybe Waverly's still holding out on me. It's unclear whether he told Dorman she was an impostor or not. If not, then maybe Dorman still thought she was Katherine."

"Well, she fooled Xina, who'd known her all her life," Campbell said. "Dorman hadn't seen her for years, so far as we know."

"Right. Linda said her only communication with him was by phone. So she took her car—Katherine's car—out that Saturday night."

"She hated to drive at night," Campbell said.

"Yes, she did. But it was important. Waverly had given her a trash bag with something in it. He told her he had to catch a plane and couldn't take it with him. She was to hide it, and he'd get word to her what to do with it."

"The weapons," Campbell said slowly. "After they killed Tatton, he shoved the weapons off on her and told her to get rid of them."

"Basically, yeah."

"He could have taken them to Dorman himself, on the way to the airport."

"I don't think he wanted them in his rental car. If he got stopped, or if he couldn't find Dorman, he'd be stuck with them. And time may have been tight on his scheduled flight. He wanted to get back to Chicago asap."

"Put distance between himself and the crime."

"Definitely. He called her Saturday morning and told her he'd arranged for Dorman to take the 'package' and dispose of it. Then he told her where and when to meet Dorman."

Campbell stared at him. "She had the murder weapons at her house on Friday, while you and your officers were tearing Tatton's house apart, looking for them."

"That's what she claims. She hid the bag in her bedroom, so Rita wouldn't find it. It wasn't her day to clean the bedroom, Linda said."

"Of all the chutzpah! So she went out to meet Dorman with the evidence, and on her way home she almost hit a deer and wrecked her car and ruined her setup. I'm amazed she's talking about it."

"She didn't, until I laid out for her the evidence that she wasn't Katherine, and that she, Linda, had staged her own death and taken over Katherine's life. When the judge called me agreeing to sign an exhumation order for Linda Braxton's grave, she broke down. I think she's tired of living a lie."

"Wow. Is she in jail now?"

"The doctor said she should stay at the hospital a couple more days, but she's got a double guard around the clock."

"I'm surprised the P.D. would pay for that."

"There's no way the chief wants to lose this one," Keith said. "He's fielding calls from all the national news agencies. He loves it."

"But he won't keep a watch on Dorman's house."

"It's not in our county."

"Right."

"So, anyway," Keith said, "when the doctor thinks she's able, we'll transfer her to the county jail. No way she's going home."

"If she had a home," Campbell said. "That's not her house."

"You're right. If they grant bail, she'll have no place to go."

Campbell guided him to Dorman's house. When they pulled up at the curb, she touched his sleeve. "Look!"

The garage door was up.

"Hold on," Keith said. He quickly placed a call to the Paducah P.D., asking them to send a squad car to Dorman's house.

Campbell saw movement in the garage.

"Keith, he's packing the car. He'll be gone before they get here."

"All right, you stay back." He got out and strode toward the garage.

Campbell got out quickly and followed him, keeping well behind him.

As they neared the garage, the man turned with his hand on the raised rear door of the vehicle, and she recognized the researcher.

"Lee Dorman?" Keith said clearly.

Dorman scowled. "What do you want, man?"

"I'd like you to raise your hands above your head."

"You a cop?"

"Yes."

"What's this about?" Dorman's right hand rose to shoulder level, and his left stayed on the car.

"It's about Katherine Tyler and Bruce Waverly and your connection with them."

He eyed Keith warily, then his gaze darted to Campbell.

Too close. I should have stayed back by the SUV.

"So, the nosy broad is back."

As he spoke, Dorman reached into the back of the vehicle quicker than Campbell would have thought possible. He brought out a long stick and hurled it at the detective. Keith dodged it and pulled his gun.

"Hold it right there!"

But Dorman was already lunging past him.

Without conscious thought, Campbell stuck out her foot. Dorman tripped over it, and they both tumbled to the asphalt.

Her breath rushed out of her lungs. This was getting to be a routine.

"Are you all right?" Keith extended his left hand to her, keeping his weapon trained on Dorman's prone form.

"I'm fine," Campbell gasped. "I just need a minute. Tend to him."

Dorman let out a moan and pushed himself to his knees. Blood ran down the side of his face, and he cradled his right arm. He swore and glared at her. "She broke my arm. That's assault, you—"

"Take it easy," Keith said. "Ms. McBride, could you please call for an ambulance at this address?"

"I'd love to." Her hand rested only inches from the stick Dorman had thrown at Keith—a smooth ebony cane with a brass handle in the shape of a duck's head. Careful not to touch it, she clambered to her feet.

As she extricated her phone from her pocket, Campbell was cheered by the fact that she hadn't broken the screen in her hard fall. Even so, she thought, *Dad is going to read me the riot act for this escapade.*

———

A MONTH LATER, Keith leaned against his SUV in the parking lot of the Murray Bank's main branch. When Campbell and her father drove up in Bill's car, he strolled across the paved lot to meet them.

"Hi. Xina went inside a minute ago."

"Are we late?" Campbell asked.

"No. She said it may take a couple minutes to get ready."

"We heard from Steve," Bill said. "His friend Chris is off the hook."

"Yes, the professor declined to press charges." Keith opened the door to the bank and they filed inside.

Campbell took off her sunglasses and put them in her purse. Even in the artificial lighting, her green eyes were vivid.

"I suppose that's a big relief," she said, "but he was fired after it came out that he'd stolen the medal."

"That's too bad, but maybe he's learned a lesson." Keith hoped so, but he doubted the young man would find employment at another college anytime soon. "Oh, one more thing."

Campbell and Bill looked at him expectantly.

"We knew where the duck cane was—Dorman threw it at me the day he was arrested. Well, the Paducah police finally found the knife."

"Where was it?" Bill asked.

"Dorman had buried it in his back yard."

"Stupid," Bill said. "He should have thrown it in the river."

"Why didn't he bury the cane too?" Campbell asked.

Keith shrugged. "I think he like it too much. Wanted to keep it as a souvenir. But it's got minute traces of Tatton's blood on it."

In a glassed-in office to their left, Xina sat facing one of the bank officers. She rose and came out to greet them.

"I'm so glad you all could come," she said, a little breathless. "We finally get to know what is in that safe deposit box."

"It may have nothing to do with your aunt or her estate," Bill said soberly.

"I know. That's why I wanted Detective Fuller here. Linda Braxton opened her account here and rented the box after Aunt Katherine was dead. If there's any evidence against her in there, I want the police to have it right away."

Keith nodded. "We appreciate that."

The bank officer had waited for them, and Xina introduced her friends to Ms. Olson. She led them down a hallway and into an anteroom to the vault of deposit boxes.

"I'll have to ask the rest of you to wait out here while Ms.

Harrison and I open the box assigned to Katherine Tyler," she said.

"But I'd like Detective Fuller there at least." Xina turned troubled eyes on her.

"That's fine, after we've removed the box. I normally leave the customer alone in there anyway, for privacy. The detective can join you then."

"Go ahead," Keith told her. "I'll be right here."

Xina and the bank officer went into the room. Keith glimpsed several rows of lock boxes. The officer closed the door behind them.

After a moment's silence, Campbell said, "It could be empty."

"Or maybe it has a pack of bubble gum in it," her father said.

Keith laughed. "Most people wouldn't keep paying for the box rental to stash their bubble gum."

A moment later the door opened and Ms. Olson emerged. "You may go in, Detective Fuller. I'll wait just outside to replace the box when Ms. Harrison is done."

Keith stepped into the vault room. Xina stood at a table with a long metal box before her.

She gave him a wobbly smile. "It's unlocked now, but I haven't peeked."

"Whenever you're ready," Keith said.

Hauling in a deep breath, Xina lifted the lid.

"Cash. And this." She took out a nine-by-twelve manilla envelope. The outside was blank, so she carefully lifted the flap and pulled out a photograph of a handsome middle-aged man.

"Do you know who that is?" Keith asked.

Xina shook her head.

"I think it's Dwight Palmer, Janice Sandler's father."

"The man who rescued Linda from drowning." She looked into the envelope, frowned, and pulled out several sheets of paper. "It's a copy of the will."

"Which one?"

Xina quickly turned the pages. "The new one, listing Janice as her heir."

"She was honoring Mr. Palmer, all right."

"But no honor for my aunt, who gave her the lifestyle she wanted."

"Don't forget the money she stole."

She gazed down at the photo. "Odd that she didn't take a single photo of her real family with her when she left her old life, but she couldn't let go of this guy."

"I agree." Keith nodded toward the stack of bills in the box. "That cash may be from what she took from McCracken Finance."

"Or from the painting she sold last fall."

"True. She'd probably gone through all the money she embezzled before she sold that."

Xina picked up the money and held it out to him. "Would you mind counting it?"

"If you want me to."

"Please."

She watched, and Keith separated the bills by stacks of a thousand dollars each. When he'd finished, he looked up.

"Fifteen thousand even."

"Why?" Xina frowned. "Why would she keep so much cash this way?"

"People do it for lots of reasons. So that other people can't find out how much they have, for one. And she maybe didn't want large deposits showing up on her bank statements."

"I guess the royalties were tapering off and she needed more."

Neatly stacking the bills, Keith said, "Do you want to take this with you?"

"I'm not sure. She obtained this box fraudulently, in Aunt Katherine's name, and she may have stolen this money. Do I really have the right to take it? I had a conversation with my lawyer, and he felt anything in the box belonged to me, as part of the estate, but I don't exactly feel right about it."

"You could probably keep the box rental, and maybe you could have it transferred into your name."

She grimaced. "As much as I like my new friends in Kentucky, I don't want to keep driving over here from North Carolina. I'd like to close this out today."

"Then why not ask the bank to transfer it into your personal account?"

"I guess." She still looked ill at ease. "You take the envelope, okay?"

"Sure." Keith handed her the stack of bills. "Ready?"

She hesitated then said, "Yes."

As KEITH and Xina stepped into the anteroom. Campbell's gaze zeroed in on the stack of money Xina was carrying.

"Wow! That's a bundle!"

"It's fifteen thousand dollars," Xina said. "We also found a copy of her will and a picture of Mr. Palmer, the lifeguard. But no manuscripts or anything like that."

"So, what now?" Bill asked gently.

"I'm going to talk to Ms. Olson. Maybe the bank can give me a cashier's check or something. I don't want to carry this much cash around, but I want to close out the box. Still, I'm not sure I should have this money."

"Whose do you think it is, if not yours?" Bill asked.

"I'm not sure. Aunt Katherine's, or maybe Linda's former employers that she stole from."

Bill and Campbell exchanged a glance.

"I think it's most likely from that painting's sale," Keith said.

Bill nodded. "That's the most recent influx of cash that we know about. But she may have sold other things from the house that you're still unaware of."

"Yeah," Xina said. "Doris Conley was very helpful when I tried to create an inventory, but we'll never really know. There could be things missing that I never knew Aunt Katherine owned."

"Well, one thing's for certain," Keith said. "No court would ever give this money to Linda Braxton."

"She won't need it where she is now," Bill said.

Campbell slid her hand through the crook of his arm. "Careful, Dad. The trial's not for months yet. You don't know that she'll be found guilty."

Xina looked anxiously at Keith. "Should this cash be put in evidence?"

"We have nothing to connect it to Linda's crimes, other than her using Katherine's name fraudulently."

"The person she killed," Bill almost yelled.

"Allegedly," Keith said. "But even if a jury doubts she killed Ben Tatton, I still think they'll convict her on your aunt's death, not to mention the embezzlement, fraud, and several other crimes."

"She stole from *you*, Xina," Campbell said. "She lived on your aunt's money for years. That should have been yours."

Xina sighed, and her shoulders slumped. "I know. It's just—" She broke off and looked at Keith. "Can I give this money to McCracken Finance? They never recovered any of the fifty thousand she took from them. This is a lot less, but it's something."

"Are you sure you want to do that?" Keith asked.

"I think so. It feels wrong to use it, even if it's from the painting."

"I'm sure Mr. Trainor and the others at the company would appreciate it," Keith said.

"What about the house?" Bill asked. "You said you plan to sell it."

"I do. I'm happy where I am in Asheville, and I don't think I'd ever be comfortable in Aunt Katherine's house again. That sale will give me a little nest egg. I've also learned that Linda never dipped into the retirement account Aunt Katherine had with the financial planner here in Murray."

"She was probably afraid they'd recognize her if she went in there to sign the paperwork," Campbell said.

Bill nodded. "That's probably right, and it's a hefty retirement account. Go talk to the bank people, if that's what you want."

"We'll wait for you," Campbell said. "Then we'll all get some lunch."

"All right, but I'm buying," Xina said.

She left them, and the other three ambled out to the parking lot.

"I should get back to the station," Keith said.

Campbell was disappointed but not surprised. This seemed to be the norm in their relationship.

He smiled at her. "I'll call you tonight."

"Okay. What are you going to do with that flash drive?"

"That belongs to Xina now. It will be returned to her soon, since it wasn't stolen. There seems to be one complete book on it, with some partials and ideas. Waverly's not getting out of jail for a while, but I have a feeling that some upstanding agent could find a home for it, and Xina could get a nice fee for the unpublished novel."

"That will be a nice legacy from her aunt," Campbell said. "Better than a creaky old house that gives her nightmares."

"Oh, I kinda like that house," her dad said. "In fact, I was thinking about making an offer."

"Dad!" Campbell stared at him. "I thought you liked the house you're in now?"

He shrugged. "Feels kind of small, now that my daughter's living with me again."

"But that old house—"

"It has character," Bill insisted.

She sighed. "It does, in spades."

"We could do a little remodeling," he said. "And the snakes are optional."

She punched him lightly on the shoulder. "You are hopeless."

"Come on, admit it. You'd like to have your own suite, private bath, and a personal office or sitting room."

"Does Rita come with it?"

"I don't know if the budget runs that high."

Xina came out of the bank smiling. "Thank you all so much. I've got a check, and I'll hold it in my own bank account until I get some more legal advice on what to do with it."

"That sounds good." Campbell have her a little hug.

"I'm heading out," Keith said. "You all have a great lunch and a wonderful day."

"'Bye, Keith," Bill said. He looked expectantly at Xina. "Burgers, barbecue, Italian, or Chinese?"

She laughed. "I think we'd better hit the buffet at Sirloin Stockade. You can have whatever you want."

ABOUT THE AUTHOR

Susan Page Davis is the author of more than ninety Christian novels and novellas in the historical romance, mystery, and romantic suspense genres. Her work has won several awards, including the Carol Award, two Will Rogers Medallions, and two Faith, Hope, & Love Reader's Choice Awards. She has also been a finalist in the WILLA Literary Awards and a multi-time finalist in the Carol Awards. Three of her books were named Top Picks in *Romantic Times Book Reviews*. Several have appeared on the ECPA and Christian Book Distributors bestselling fiction lists. Her books have been featured in several book clubs, including the Literary Guild, Crossings Book Club, and Faithpoint Book Club.

A Maine native, Susan has lived in Oregon and now resides in western Kentucky with her husband Jim, a retired news editor. They are the parents of six and grandparents of eleven. Visit her website at: https://susanpagedavis.com.

ALSO BY SUSAN PAGE DAVIS

Blue Plate Special

by Award-winning Author Susan Page Davis

Book One of the True Blue Mysteries Series

Campbell McBride drives to her father's house in Murray, Kentucky, dreading telling him she's lost her job as an English professor. Her father, private investigator Bill McBride, isn't there or at his office in town. His brash young employee, Nick Emerson, says Bill hasn't come in this morning, but he did call the night before with news that he had a new case.

When her dad doesn't show up by late afternoon, Campbell and Nick decide to follow up on a phone number he'd jotted on a memo sheet. They learn who last spoke to her father, but they also find a dead body.

The next day, Campbell files a missing persons report. When Bill's car is found, locked and empty in a secluded spot, she and Nick must get past their differences and work together to find him.

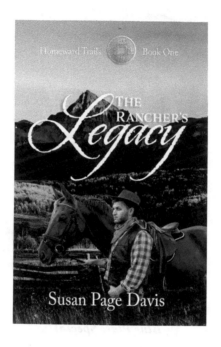

The Rancher's Legacy

Homeward Trails - Book One

Historical Romance

Matthew Anderson and his father try to help neighbor Bill Maxwell when his ranch is attacked. On the day his daughter Rachel is to return from school back East, outlaws target the Maxwell ranch. After Rachel's world is shattered, she won't even consider the plan her father and Matt's cooked up—to see their two children marry and combine the ranches.

Meanwhile in Maine, sea captain's widow Edith Rose hires a private investigator to locate her three missing grandchildren. The children were abandoned by their father nearly twenty years ago. They've been adopted into very different families, and they're scattered across the country. Can investigator Ryland Atkins find them all while the elderly woman still lives? His first attempt is to find the boy now called Matthew Anderson. Can Ryland survive his trip into the wild Colorado Territory and find Matt before the outlaws finish destroying a legacy?

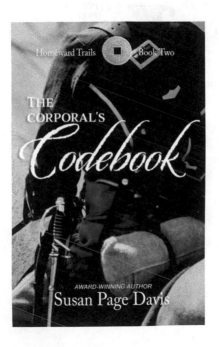

Watch for *The Corporal's Codebook*, **Homeward Trails Book Two,** coming from Susan Page Davis and Scrivenings Press in November 2021.

Jack Miller stumbles through the Civil War, winding up a telegrapher and cryptographer for the army. In the field with General Sherman in Georgia, he is captured along with his precious cipher key.

His captor, Hamilton Buckley, thinks he should have been president of the Confederacy, not Jefferson Davis. Jack doubts Buckley's sanity and longs to escape. Buckley's kindhearted niece, Marilla, might help him—but only if Jack helps her achieve her own goal.

Meanwhile, a private investigator, stymied by the difficulty of travel and communication in wartime, is trying his best to locate Jack for the grandmother he longs to see again but can barely remember.

Scrivenings
PRESS
Quench your thirst for story.
www.ScriveningsPress.com

Stay up-to-date on your favorite books and authors with our free e-newsletters.

ScriveningsPress.com

CPSIA information can be obtained
at www.ICGtesting.com
Printed in the USA
LVHW012248220921
698482LV00010B/415